I0598651

SHOWER OF LIES

DS Whitaker

This is a work of fiction. Names, characters, businesses, places, events, locales, and incidents are the products of the author's imagination or used in a fictitious and satirical manner. Any resemblance to actual persons, living or dead, or actual events is purely coincidental. Certain long-standing institutions, agencies, and public offices are mentioned, but the characters involved are wholly imaginary. The opinions expressed are those of the characters and should not be confused with the authors.

Copyright © 2020 by DS Whitaker

All rights reserved. No part of this publication may be reproduced or transmitted in any form or by any means, electronic or mechanical, including photography, recording, or any information storage and retrieval system, with permission in writing from the author.

ISBN: 978-1-7342595-5-1 (TP)
ISBN: 978-1-7342595-6-8 (EB)
Library of Congress Control Number: 2020922444

Back photo by Diana Lang
Cover Design by DS Whitaker
Cover Image from DepositPhotos.com, Free Attribution AllaSerebrina

To my coworker Jenna for inspiration

To Tim for his love and support

To my Beta Readers with much gratitude

Chapter 1

Jenna's phone rang, reverberating off the white builders-grade floor tile. Raven never called this early. She hit 'accept', wiping spittle from her face with a wad of tissue. "Rae, is everything all right?"

"You won't believe it!"

There was joy in Raven's voice. Yet Jenna froze. Her stomach churned with a pronounced gurgle. "Can you hold?" She shoved the phone away, twisted her body, and heaved into the toilet. Then inspected her work. Definite progress. Fewer chunks. *Still green.*

Rising from the floor, she picked up the phone and placed it on the toilet tank lid. "Hold on." She rinsed her mouth in the sink. In the mirror, she noticed the pock marks around her eyes. Like the time she and Rae did the Zombie Walk at the Jersey Shore. But now her normally olive complexion was paler, more convincing than Halloween makeup.

Jenna picked up the phone and sat on the closed toilet seat lid. "What happened?"

"I'm getting married! Jack proposed last night!"

Jenna searched her feelings. Just numbness, like the deep chill in her muscles. Maybe it was the lack of sleep. *Perhaps jealousy?* "That's great."

In a low, teasing voice, Rae said, "Jenna, it's crazy. Engagement sex is the best. I'm sore in places you wouldn't believe."

"That's nice." The chill in her bones made her shiver. Jenna wrapped a bath towel around her bare arms. *Were the hostilities over?* Could she attempt returning to the warmth of her bed?

"But that's not why I'm calling so early. I don't have much time. I need your help." Raven's voice was flat, serious.

"What do you mean?" She ran her fingers through her bangs; a clump of dried tomato broke off onto the floor.

"I've been awake for hours, excited, you know? I need you to plan my bridal shower for the fourth."

Then it dawned on her. Yesterday was Valentines. Which explained the mid-week proposal. Instead of being with Marcelo, Jenna went to her mom's for dinner. "You shouldn't be alone in your ratty apartment," Mom had said. Not that her 500-square-foot apartment was technically full of rats. But it wasn't Instagram-ready by any stretch of the imagination. In hindsight, she should have known better. But mom sounded so lucid on the phone, so happy. *Fooled again.*

Apparently, normal people, like Raven, had boyfriends in the same area code and got engaged on romantic holidays. And other people, with boyfriends living four hours away, received only a cute text.

Jenna shook her head. "Fourth of what?"

"March."

She worked out the math in her drowsy brain. *February had 28 days? Two and a half weeks?* "Wait, why so soon?"

There was a pause.

Jenna took a chance. "Rae, are you…pregnant?"

There was a bite in her tone. "No, I'm not pregnant." After a pause, Raven sighed. "Um, I don't want people to know. I'm having surgery soon. It's critically important it goes well. But I'm worried. Remember my cousin? She was close to my age when she died."

Jenna remembered. With early stage throat cancer, her cousin's prognosis was initially good, and the surgery was routine. *Did Raven have cancer?* When Raven was ten, her pediatrician diagnosed her with a heart murmur, saying she might need corrective surgery by her mid-twenties. At twenty-three, that would fit. But a few years later, another doctor told her she was fine. No murmur. Or did Rae tell a white lie so she wouldn't worry?

Jenna held her breath. "Rae, oh my God, do you have cancer? Is it your heart?" She wanted to reach through the phone and hug her.

"I'd rather not go into it. I'm trying to keep it private… only sharing with Jack and a couple of other people. You won't say anything, right?" Rae's voice quaked, sounding unlike her usually confident self.

Jenna understood people felt protective about their health information, but could Raven die? It would explain the urgency for the party and perhaps the engagement as well.

"Are you going to be all right? What can I do to help? Do you want me with you at the hospital?" Jenna let out a burp.

Her breath tasted like the rotten, left-over veggie casserole her mom pushed on her last night. The brown spot in the middle was a red flag. But mom, sloshed again, just scooped it out and said the rest was fine. Pushback would have led to arguing, and possibly an all-out battle. Yet, here she was, freezing, exhausted from hours of food poisoning. When would she ever learn?

Raven sighed. "Thanks, J-Bear. All I care about right now is having all my friends around me for an amazing bridal shower. It will put my mind at ease before the wedding. You would literally save my life by planning it. The doctor said I need to reduce my stress."

Jenna had no idea how to plan a bridal shower. But it was just a party. *Maybe a dozen or twenty people?* Eating cake and opening presents didn't seem that difficult. "Sure, whatever you need."

"Thanks, I knew I could count on you!"

"You just worry about getting better."

In a gleeful voice, Raven said, "I'll send you details. Chao, sweetie!"

Her phone beeped, signaling the end of the call.

Jenna flushed the toilet and steadied herself. Her gaze fixated on her bedroom visible through the crack in the door. A little sleep and she would be all right, she concluded. Any position outside of the bathroom floor would be a genuine victory.

Thumper was on her bed, stretched out like a king. She grabbed her cat around his bulbous middle and dumped him outside, shutting the door. The clock on her bedside table showed six-thirty. She texted Grant, her boss, saying she wouldn't be in. Hugging a pillow, she shut her lids tight, her thoughts chiding her to sleep.

She missed Marcelo. It had been two weeks since their last weekend together. Driving the eight-hour round-trip to Syracuse was wearing on her. Trying to ease her mind, she envisioned him beside her, stroking her hair, becoming lost in his eyes, and other blissful thoughts conducive to sleep. But wondered when he would ditch her for someone sexier, less nerdy, and more geographically available.

When sleep came, she dreamed Marcelo was with her; they were holding hands. Next, he was wearing a mailman uniform, and he yelled at her. Something about incorrect postage. He called Thumper a menace and insisted he be 'put down', his eyes seething with anger and disgust.

She woke, her heart racing.

3

A scratching noise at her door. Thumper was mewing and destroying her bedroom door again. *Yes, Thumper was a menace.* But she loved him anyway. The clock read seven. She placed a pillow over her head to muffle the sound. Her comforter felt so warm…

The psychotic thumping began. Her cat was repeatedly throwing its considerable weight against her door. Wham. Wham. Wham. Jenna threw off the covers and stomped over, yanking open the door. "Stop!" With a deep grunt, she succumbed to defeat. Her cat didn't understand the concept of 'stop' or 'no'. The torments would continue until he achieved his goal.

After feeding the cat, she took a shower. The water revived her somewhat; coffee would do the rest. She towel-dried her long hair absent-mindedly, wondering what kind of illness or cancer Raven could have. Raven's grandfather died from a bad heart, the same grandfather that left Raven a small fortune in a trust for when she turned twenty-four, about five months from now.

Raven was always cagey about the details of her inheritance. From hints Rae gave in past conversations, it had to be at least a million dollars. *Had the value of her trust fund increased past ten million?* Her inheritance was a hodgepodge of stocks. Raven stopped following the numbers years ago, acting like it didn't matter.

As Jenna pulled her legs into clean pajamas, her phone dinged. Raven sent a series of texts containing a long list of party requirements.

She scanned the list. "What?" she said aloud.

A hundred and twenty people. She shook her head. *No, that couldn't be right.* Surely, she meant just twenty. *Wait.* The party *had* to occur near Altoona, close to her alma mater, Penn State.

Jenna lived in Cherry Hill, New Jersey. Altoona was four hours away. A small town. *How many venues existed to host a party so large and with such short notice?*

The texts kept coming. Raven explained Jack's great aunt, Sister Mary Rose, a Maryknoll nun, was visiting from South America and wanted to give a benediction at the shower. Plus, the many food restrictions. Most of her friends were vegan and gluten-free.

Last, to Jenna's relief, Rae texted that Jack's mother, Blanche, would pay for everything. "Could you work directly with her?"

It was nice of her future mother-in-law to foot the bill. Jenna knew almost nothing about Jack's relatives. In fact, she'd only met Jack once. He had spoken little. She remembered he had thick, dark hair and a face like a young Brad Pitt. But there was something about him that irked her. *Maybe it was the way he glowered all the time? Like resting bitch-face, but sadder? The general aura of apathy he exuded?*

She called Raven. "Rae, why Altoona?"

"Do you remember the annual cancer Walk-a-Thon I organized for the sorority? It's happening this year on Sunday, the fifth. The girls begged me to come and walk with them. All seventy-seven of them plan to come to the shower, so it made sense to hold the party in Altoona because I'll be there anyway. With everything else going on, it's the only weekend I have free before my surgery on the 8th. It would be great if you could stay over and walk with us."

Jenna digested this information. It made sense. The Walk-a-Thon would be an activity close to Raven's heart if, in fact, she had cancer. Jenna knew the sorority was large. But the sheer number made her head swim.

The sorority had increased its membership several-fold during the years Raven attended, explaining why Raven's social calendar had been so full. After the first semester of freshman year, Jenna gave up asking Raven to come home to New Jersey to spend weekends together. And the one time she visited Raven at Penn State was educational; she learned quickly the sorority was not her kind of place. Too much drinking.

Jenna cleared her throat. "I suppose that *would be* more convenient, but why don't you ask someone in your sorority to plan the shower? They know the area."

"Oh, J-Bear, I love them, I really do, but organization is not their strong point. There's a reason I took over as event planner and treasurer. The first year of the cancer walk, the committee forgot to buy water and set up aid stations. It was a disaster. And they misprinted the t-shirts. I told Blanche, Jack's mom, you have systems for everything. You're the most organized person I know…other than myself."

Raven had a point. Growing up, Rae always teased her about her color-coded folders for homework.

Jenna said, "I appreciate the vote of confidence. I'll do my best. Um… can you send me the invite list?"

"Right away. Thanks, J-Bear. I've got to go. Love you."

"Love you, too."

Raven hung up.

A few minutes later, she got an email:

> "Get the list for Jack's side from his mom. She'll call you. Invite all our old girlfriends from the neighborhood, my coworkers and my sorority sisters."

This was not remotely close to a list. *Where were the names? Addresses?* Now she had to be a mind-reader? Surely, this was a sick joke. Where was the old Raven that created lists for everything?

Was this just another bad dream? She ate some dry toast and headed back to bed. Food poisoning was bad, but not as bad as cancer. *Why couldn't Rae tell her about her health issues?*

Raven had always been the brave one. In second grade, a bully named Mikey called Jenna names and stole her lunchbox. Rae pummeled Mikey during recess, behind the slide, until he apologized. But then she kept on him until he offered his own cupcake to make amends. No one messed with her or Rae for the rest of grade school.

But she looked out for Raven also. Raven's mom died of an aneurysm during Rae's freshman year. After the sudden loss, Rae clung to her. Jenna and Rae had a standing sleepover every weekend for a year, alternating between their homes. Rae's dad sought solitude to grieve alone, not helping the healing process. The first year was hard. But Rae came through her sorrow changed. Somehow stronger. Willing to live each moment to the fullest, without hesitation or concern for others' criticism.

It wouldn't be out of character for Rae to hide an illness or setback with outward confidence and a smile. Like when Joe stood her up at prom. Rae went anyway and was the life of the party, dancing with both boys and girls. Jenna knew the truth; it devastated Rae. She'd talked of nothing else for months and was crazy about Joe. But that was Rae, resilient and fearless.

Perhaps Rae would confide in her later, after a little time to emotionally process her diagnosis. She could be patient.

Jenna drifted to sleep, wondering what it would be like to have Rae's combination of beauty, self-assurance, and drive. But no, she realized, very few people were bestowed these gifts.

And she was not one of them.

* * *

The next morning, Jenna arrived at work at seven. The square brick building with its neon sign—Veloma Office Solutions—had a blandness that mirrored her work life. After graduating from college, she interviewed with Grant. He explained the company manufactured both commercial and home printers, copiers, modems and monitors, and that he led the Product Support Office of the Printer Division.

Despite her mechanical engineering degree, her position seemed administrative, entailing writing and revising product user manuals and generating monthly reports. Making matters worse, as a rite-of-passage, new hires had to work on the Customer Support Hotline two days a week for at least a year. Her days were Tuesdays and Thursdays.

Not challenging work, but looming student loans had forced her to be practical. Plus, the headquarters building was located close to home. Still, walking in the building, she wondered how life would be different, perhaps better, if she had moved to Syracuse instead to be with Marcelo.

As she hung her gray wool coat on the hook at her cube, Mindy bounced into view. Mindy was the Energizer Bunny of her division. In her mid-30's and still single, she had a hole in the side of her nose from an old piercing and short spiky ash blond hair. Mindy never conformed to normal office attire, but management looked the other way.

Today, Mindy resembled a Goth hippie pirate: a black bandana covered her hair, and she had one gold hoop earring. She wore canvas bellbottom pants, chunky black boots, and a body-hugging yellow turtleneck sweater.

Jenna was more conservative. Or maybe a better word was boring. Black dress pants, a white cotton button-down shirt, black ballet flats; no jewelry except for the small aquamarine ring Marcelo gave her, no makeup, with her hair in a low ponytail. They were a study in contrasts.

Mindy said, "Hey, Jenna, how are you feeling?"

"My stomach is better. But I found out my best friend is getting married."

Mindy leaned on the faded gray partition. "You don't sound happy."

"I'm supposed to plan her gigantic bridal shower." She scratched her head. "I've never been to one. What do people do at those?"

"I haven't been to one in a long time. Sorry. But I bet you could Google some activities. I remember folks making dresses out of toilet paper. Super lame."

Jenna gave Mindy the rest of the details.

Mindy burst out laughing. "Are you fricking kidding? Two weeks?

What kind of friend is this? It's impossible. Simply impossible. Just tell her you can't do it. Or postpone it for three months. Minimum."

"I already said I would. And she has a health issue. Raven wouldn't tell me the details. Something involving surgery. She sounded scared, like she might die."

"Jenna, sometimes I think you're too nice. If I were that sick, I'd just focus on my health. The last thing I'd worry about is a stupid party. I would have told her to fuck off." Mindy made an unveiled hand gesture, then turned serious. "Well, you said money isn't an issue, right?"

"Not sure. But I assume so."

Mindy cocked her head, tapping a finger across her cheek. "You need a wedding planner."

"A what?"

"Someone who plans weddings. A professional."

"But it's a bridal shower, not a wedding."

Mindy stared at her and shook her head. "They plan any kind of party, silly."

Her cheeks felt hot. *How was she supposed to know*? It was true she didn't know much about parties. But Mindy didn't need to rub it in.

"Do they cost a lot?"

"No idea. Probably. But with the parameters you laid out, you need an ace up your sleeve. Someone based near Altoona. They'll know all the good venues."

"Thanks, that's a great idea. But I have a meeting and then Customer Support duty all day. I'll find one later tonight."

"Okay, but the sooner the better. You should call on your lunch break." Mindy waved. "Good luck."

After Mindy left, Jenna looked at her wall calendar. Fifteen days left. No invite list. No venue. No food. No activities. *What could go wrong?*

Everything.

But she couldn't think about that now. She grabbed her notes and headed toward the large conference room. Her stomach grumbled. With only two slices of toast and an apple to eat yesterday and no breakfast this morning, she needed sustenance. The vending machine offered her a breakfast of champions: chocolate chip cookies and potato chips.

It was better than nothing.

Chapter 2

Jenna clutched the steering wheel as she drove home from work, realizing she hadn't called the party planner at lunch. *Did planners have office hours?* She made a mental list of party-related questions, preparing to call the minute she arrived.

Her phone rang, revealing a number she didn't recognize. Her 1996 Ford Fiesta—a car her own age—didn't have Bluetooth. Taking a call while driving was futile; the engine noise made it impossible to comprehend normal speech. Besides, it was probably a telemarketer. She hit 'decline' and motored on.

A few minutes later, she pulled into the parking lot. Her apartment building was constructed in the 1950s as a two-story roadside motel and later converted into small one-bedroom units. The worn red brick was repointed so many times it looked like a drunken mason built it, and the single-pane aluminum windows leaked air like sieves.

The upper units were connected by an exterior concrete walkway with iron railings. The metal staircase looked derelict, as if held together by its many layers of paint. But, in fact, it was solid. Attempts at landscaping by the owner, a phantom LLC, included some unkempt evergreen bushes and weedy patches of dirt supposed to be planting beds for seasonal flowers.

Her second-floor unit had choice views of a large antenna tower, a tree-less cemetery, and a highway overpass. It was the only place she could afford until she paid off her student loans. She had done the math over and over. With the low rent, she could pay off her loans in half the time, gaining her freedom seven years early. And it was hers. Which is all she really cared about. A quiet space she didn't have to share with her parents or another human.

Her phone rang again. *Raven.* She put it on speaker and yelled, "Hold on."

With the turn of the ignition, the rattling subsided. "Yes, I can hear now.

Hello?"

"Blanche just tried calling you. Why didn't you pick up?"

"I just got home." She sat in her car, staring up at her dark second-floor window.

"Well, she's driving me crazy. You have to talk to her. Now."

"Fine. Fine. What is she upset about?" She put on her gloves, opened the car door and began running for the exterior stairs, still holding the phone to her ear.

"She's not upset. Why would she be upset? Did you upset her?"

At the top of the stairs, Jenna slipped her key into the lock. Despite the cold, she stopped. "Um, no. I just want to know what she wants." She pushed open the door, took off her coat and placed it on a hook, when a blur of orange shot around her legs.

Shit. Thumper escaped.

"Well, she wants the party to be perfect—"

"Raven, I can't talk now. Dang cat." She hung up the phone, tossed it on a side table, and chased after him.

She saw Thumper on the edge of the walkway, three doors down, hunching his shoulders under the thin railing, like he would jump.

"Good kitty…" she whispered. "Come here." If Thumper jumped off the second-floor walkway, he would break his entire body.

Her front door slammed shut.

Thumper raced further down the walkway, but thankfully didn't jump. Instead, he began chewing on someone's dead potted plant.

Jenna inched toward her cat, whispering, "Good kitty," until she laid hands around his torso and scooped him up. *Crisis averted.*

She reached her own front door when the realization hit. Her keys were in her coat. And the door was locked.

It was near freezing and she had no coat, no keys, no phone, and had to maintain a death grip on her now ornery cat.

Headlights flashed below. A neighbor's car pulled up. She didn't recognize the man. He looked to be in his seventies or eighties. "Sir!"

The man looked around, but not up.

"Up here, sir." She braved holding the cat with one arm to wave with the other.

"Hello there," he called. He approached the staircase, but then continued walking straight past.

Jenna raced down the stairs, the cold air seeping through her clothes. She hugged the cat to her chest. Thumper hissed, perhaps affronted by the jostling. "Sir! Wait. I need help." She caught up to him and touched his shoulder.

"Missy, what are you doing out here without a coat? You'll catch your death. You walkin' your cat?"

The man was short with shocking white hair with a bald patch in the middle. In the dim light, she could still make out his dimples and thick brown eyebrows. He wore a canvas jacket with dark trousers and was carrying a small potted plant. It looked like a miniature rose bush.

"I got locked out of my apartment." She readjusted the cat's weight in her arms.

"What's your name, dear?"

"Jenna Mott."

"Well, Ms. Mott, I'm new around here. Name's Fred. Fred Blesky. Would you like to come to my place and we can work on your problem?"

She wasn't sure about going inside a stranger's apartment. But an old man carrying a plant didn't seem very dangerous. Thumper began kicking Jenna's arm with his hind claws. Despite the fabric of her long-sleeve shirt, the claws dug into her flesh; receiving the sort of scratches that puff up red and bleed. It was all she could not to drop him. "Can I bring him?"

"Well, I'm allergic, but I suppose in an emergency—"

"Thank you, Fred."

She followed behind him and he opened the door to 105B. It had the same floor plan as her apartment. Long and rectangular, with a large picture window at the front, an efficiency galley kitchen to the right behind a partition wall with little counter space. But his apartment's living room was sparsely furnished. A single recliner, a flimsy tray-table, a small dinette table next to the refrigerator with two folding chairs, a stack of books on the floor, empty off-white walls, no rug.

He closed the door behind her. "So, Ms. Mott, what's the plan?"

She placed Thumper on the ground and the cat raced out of the room into the kitchen.

"I guess I'll call the management company. Do you have the number?"

Fred placed the flower pot down, pulled out his phone from his shirt pocket and sat in his recliner. "I don't reckon. But their office closed at five. How about a locksmith?"

Jenna had never used a locksmith before. She figured they installed locks and made keys. "They can pick locks?"

Fred laughed and walked to the kitchen. "Let me go find a Yellow Pages." She followed.

Her cat bounded up to the top of the refrigerator, his eyes wild. *What has gotten into Thumper? How was she going to get the cat down without getting mauled?*

"Cat's got a temper, eh? He's had all his shots, I take it?" Fred thumbed through the thick book. "Here ya go. AAPlus Locksmith. Twenty-four-hour service. You want me to call?"

"Um, sure, if you don't mind. I'm in 201C."

Fred made the call sitting at a small dinette table. She approached the refrigerator, reaching up to pet Thumper on his head. The cat recoiled and stuffed itself further back under the oak cabinet.

"They'll be here in thirty minutes. Told them to come here first."

"Thanks. Um, Fred? I'm sorry, but I don't know how to get Thumper to come down." She let out a sigh.

He laughed. "I had a cat once. Actually, my son's. When he moved to college, it died soon after. Glad to be rid of it, to tell the truth. My eyes were swollen near daily." He opened an upper cabinet door and pulled out a can. "You hungry?"

Jenna looked at the label. *Tuna.* "No, I'll have a frozen dinner later."

He shook his head. He got out a can opener and placed the tuna on a plate on the floor. "It's for the cat…"

Thumper raced down to the counter and back to the floor in a seamless motion. He tore at the tuna with some grunting.

Fred chuckled. "See, cats are simple. Only care about food. Least that's my recollection. Can't coax a cat to do nothing. But bribery? Every time."

Jenna felt like an idiot. Nothing in her life was in her control. Least of all her cat. She changed the subject. "Fred, how long have you lived here?"

"About two months. Lived about a mile away for over fifty years. After my wife Ava moved to the nursing home, I downsized."

"Is she all right?" Jenna scanned the room for pictures, not finding any.

"She doesn't quite remember me most days. Ava's got the Alzheimer's and a bad hip. Been going downhill for some time. But they take good care of her."

"Sorry to hear that."

"Well, I just live one day at a time. I still got air in my lungs. Every day above ground and all that gobblety gook. That flower plant? It was hers. But the nurses said they didn't want to water it." He chuckled, "So now I have a roommate. I hear he tells great jokes. Come."

He took a folding chair from his hall closet. The kind that had multi-colored plastic webbing and opened it facing his recliner. "Sit." He sat down in his chair with a deep "Ooof. My back ain't what it used to be."

She sat. Behind Fred, she saw Thumper leave his tuna and wander into Fred's bedroom. "Um, sorry, my cat just went into your room. I'll go get him." She lifted her butt off the chair.

"Nah, let 'im go. Probably just curious. Talk with me for a spell. I don't get many visitors."

She sat her fanny back down. "You've lived in the area so long. Don't you have lots of friends?"

"Ha. When you get to be my age, everyone is dead, dying or moved to Florida. Ava and I thought about moving south, but it just never happened. Sometimes I go to the local VFW, but it ain't what it once was. Membership is down and I don't fancy drinking much."

"You were in the military?"

"Yep, Korean War. I was Navy enlisted. Did tours on submarines. Got trained in lots of stuff. But my favorite assignment was cooking on the sub, feeding five hundred sailors twice a day. Got first choice of the rations and I was everyone's friend. Besides, I was always more a lover than a fighter. That's what I used to tell Ava."

Jenna loved listening to him. He was equal parts crotchety and sweet at the same time. "How did you two meet?"

"Well, after I got discharged, I went to New York City with my buddies for the weekend. One of 'em, Terrence, had a girlfriend there. Funny story. They tried to fix us up with his girlfriend's friends. They were nice and all, but I only had eyes for one gal." A sly look crossed his eyes.

"Wait. You stole Terrence's girlfriend? Ava?"

He beamed and tapped his temple. "It ain't stealing if a girl chooses you. I told her all my best jokes. See, people think a girl wants a macho guy. But the good women? They want to laugh. I won her with my charms. She was a smart cookie. With freckles and a laugh that made my heart burst from my chest. I was a goner." Fred eyes were watery, but he beamed, his dimples grew deeper.

They talked some more and time seemed to fly. They talked about television shows and movies. Fred's favorite movie was Shane. Jenna's favorites were Aliens, Godzilla, and Jurassic Park; really, anything with excellent monsters.

When the locksmith knocked on the door, Thumper was happily sleeping on Fred's lap.

Fred gave Jenna his phone number. "Call anytime. And make a spare key."

Jenna picked up an annoyed Thumper and they said goodbye.

After the locksmith was done and wrote him a check, she collapsed on her sofa. The cable box showed the time: nine-thirty. Her phone showed five missed calls from the same mystery number, which she now surmised was Mrs. Forero. She turned off her phone, placed more food in Thumper's dish, laid out her clothes for the next work day, brushed her teeth, and headed to sleep.

Jack's mom would have to wait. It had been a long day. Once nestled in bed, her stomach grumbled. She'd forgotten dinner again. Touching the thin skin across her ribs, she wondered, *Am I getting too thin?*

No, she was too tired to eat.

During the night, Jenna dreamt about Raven's upcoming wedding. But oddly, Thumper was the groom; he tossed a hairball on the officiant. An earthquake. Walls trembled and collapsed. Guests ran for their lives. Raven, wearing a poofy wedding dress, screamed toward the collapsing ceiling. Jenna, a bystander, did nothing when Raven fell down into a dark gaping hole in the floor. Then the roof came down in chunks. She was about to die…

She woke, her eyes wide. It was only midnight.

What did it mean? It made no sense.

No, it was only a stupid dream.

Her brain struggled to recount all her questions for the event planner. She'd done more complex tasks before. Like the time she won the robotics contest at Drexel. Each task needed to be broken down into individual steps within a timeline.

She had to stop overthinking it.

It was just a party.

Chapter 3

Friday at lunchtime, Jenna dialed the only wedding planner based in Altoona, a woman named Candy Morris. Based on reviews on The Knot and other websites, reviewers labeled Candy "a Godsend" and "a consummate professional." Jenna hoped that "miracle worker" also applied.

After a few rings, a woman picked up. "Hello, Candy Morris Weddings." The voice was upbeat, pleasant, sing-song.

"Ms. Morris? My name is Jenna. I was wondering if you help with bridal showers?"

"Nice to meet you, Jenna. Congratulations on your engagement. Such an exciting time. Why, yes. I plan all types of events. I arranged ten showers last year. Do you need help with your wedding also?"

"Oh, I'm not getting married. It's for my friend, Raven. Her bridal shower needs to take place in two weeks."

"Dear, I'm not sure I heard that last part. How many weeks?"

"Two." Jenna held her breath.

"Do you have any more specifics? How many will attend? Do you have a venue?"

Jenna winced. "I don't have a venue. It will be in Altoona, so that's why I'm calling you. I'm supposed to plan for a hundred and twenty people."

"Wait. Hold on." Candy's voice seemed different. Lower, like a grumble. "Are you sure about that number? That seems very high for a bridal shower."

"The groom's family is large. All the female aunts and cousins are coming. And Raven's former sorority sisters."

"I don't know if I can help you." Candy's voice was now choppy and cold.

"Ms. Morris, you're my only hope. I live in New Jersey and work full time. I need your local expertise."

Candy sighed. "You seem like a sweet kid. But honestly, you should have contacted me weeks ago. With this kind of event, you can't wait until the last minute."

"I found out two days ago."

There was a pause on the phone. Jenna tried to imagine what Ms. Morris was thinking. Probably all the same questions and mental gymnastics she'd gone through.

After a few seconds, Jenna asked, "Are you still there?"

"What kind of budget do you have? I hate to say it, but this could be *quite* expensive."

"I don't know the budget exactly, but I was told her future mother-in-law will cover it. The groom's family is wealthy."

"Tell you what, send me an email with all the details and I'll send back a quote before the end of the day."

"Great. Thank you so much. You're saving my life."

"Let's not get ahead of ourselves, shall we?" The sing-song voice was back. "Email me right away. Every second counts. Have a nice day now."

"Um, you too—" Jenna realized Ms. Morris had hung up.

Jenna called Mrs. Forero next.

"Hi, Mrs. Forero. It's Jenna Mott, Raven's friend. Do you have time to talk about the shower?"

There was a pause. In an icy tone, "Jenna, what is wrong with you?"

"I'm sorry?"

"Do you *ever* answer your phone? My God. I left you so many messages last night. Are you this disrespectful to *everyone*?"

"Mrs. Forero, I'm sorry. I got locked out of my apartment last night. And I've been slammed at work. I wasn't trying to disrespect…"

"God, I hope Raven is right about you and your stellar planning skills. Because my plate is full and we have no time to waste. Fine. Whatever. Don't let it happen again."

"Um. Thanks for understanding, Mrs. Forero."

"Call me Blanche. Mrs. Forero was my mother-in-law and Lord knows I couldn't stand her when she was alive." She gave a nervous, tittering laugh at the end.

Jenna didn't know what to say to that. "Yes, Blanche."

"That's neither here nor there." Blanche huffed. "Look, Raven and I have our hands full planning her wedding at the end of June, so we're relying on you to do the heavy lifting with the shower. Understand?"

Jenna nodded. "Yes, I understand. But I have a question."

Another exacerbated sigh. "What?"

"Er, why does the party have to happen now? Why not after Raven's surgery? I mean, shouldn't she focus on her health right now?"

"She's fine."

"She seemed scared."

"Oh, she's just being silly. She's young, strong. I keep telling her it's nothing."

How could it be nothing? "Well, I still don't know why the party has to be now. I mean, even just another couple of weeks to plan would make a tremendous difference."

"Well, Jenna, I'm sorry this is such a huge inconvenience for you." Blanche stressed the word 'inconvenience' with pronounced sarcasm. "In fact, let's tell Raven to just reschedule her surgery and the wedding while we're at it. To accommodate your life."

This conversation was not going well. Jenna felt a lump in her throat and wanted to crawl under her desk and curl into a ball. Blanche was like a bitch in a steamroller. What kind of family was Raven marrying into?

"I didn't mean it like that," Jenna said.

"Oh? How did you mean it? You know, Raven insisted you were the best person to manage the party. I had my doubts and now you've confirmed them."

"Blanche, I'm sorry we got off on the wrong foot. Raven is my best friend. I'm just concerned about her health. But if you think I'm not the right person—"

"Hmmf, Fine. I'm willing to give you a chance for Raven's sake. I do love that girl. The party has to be perfection. Relatives are coming from around the globe to attend at substantial cost. You need to get your act together, Jenna."

"Raven said you'd be paying for the party. Is that correct? Do you have a budget? I'm getting a quote from an event planner in Altoona. She has excellent reviews. Ms. Candy Morris. I also need the invite list. Can you email it?"

"She can send all the bills to me. Don't worry about that. I have an invitation list for our side of the family, but Raven will have to provide hers. Oh, I have a final say on all the decorations, party favors, and menu."

Final say? This would complicate things, but Jenna didn't feel like she had any choices. At least money wouldn't be an issue.

"Sure, Blanche. Thanks again for all your support."

The phone line went dead.

Why was everyone so mad? She never hung up on people like that.

Jenna emailed the parameters to Ms. Morris and got back to work.

After two hours, her coworker Mindy came by. "How are things going with the party?"

"Good, I think? I talked with the wedding planner. She was a little upset about the lack of notice, but that's understandable."

"I still don't know why you don't tell your friend to plan her own damn party."

"You don't get it. Rae is like a sister. Actually, more than a sister." Jenna recalled in grade school they looked so much alike—with their skin tone, wide-spaced eyes, and long, straight black hair—their teachers thought they were twins. But after puberty, when they reached their full height of about five-foot-four, Rae had curves, and she kept her flat, cereal-box figure.

"Well, you need to learn to say no. Did you eat yet today? You don't look good."

"I'm fine. Had a sandwich. What about you?"

"A few of us went out for lunch. You should have come with. George and Russ got into an eating contest. It was hilarious. Russ won by eating thirty garlic knots. His breath stinks. I'd stay away from their aisle. George already crop-dusted our entire row."

"Ewww. I'm glad I missed that."

Mindy stared past her, toward the computer screen. "You got an email."

It was from Ms. Morris. "I'm afraid to open it." But she opened it anyway. Mindy read over her shoulder.

Jenna gasped and covered her mouth. "Thirty-K? That's like a brand-new car. A four-hour party costs that much?"

Mindy pointed to the bottom of the e-mail. "Look at the breakdown. The venue rent alone is twelve thousand for the weekend because it has a three-day minimum. The catering estimate is eleven."

Jenna read the next paragraph. "A 13,000-square-foot mansion? Is that really necessary?" She shook her head and stared at the ceiling.

Mindy read further. "The footnote says that none of the hotels in a twenty-mile radius have spaces that accommodate over 85 people. Except for one venue that is booked and not one that she would ever use. The mansion backs up to a woodland preserve. It has a 3,000-square-foot great room, a kitchen with professional grade appliances, a game room, seven bedrooms, a pool and tennis court."

Jenna wondered how this could be the only option. Surely, this was a non-starter. She considered taking another aspirin.

Mindy kept reading. "Wait, look here."

Jenna took a deep breath and read this part out loud. "Wedding favors include a two-ounce bottle of Chanel No. 5, rose gold plated compact mirror with engraving, a moonstone heart-shaped pendant, and imported Italian chocolate truffles... per 'your request'. Oh no."

"Did you request that?"

"No. Ugh. Blanche must have found Candy's info and contacted her. Why am I being put in the middle if Blanche will dictate everything? Makes no sense." She closed her eyes. "I guess I'll send this over to her and see what she says." She hit forward, sending it to Blanche.

"Good luck with that." Mindy smiled. "Hey, don't stress out. Maybe Raven and Blanche will realize how stupid this is and pull the plug. Then you'll be off the hook."

"Ha! I'm not that lucky."

"Let me know what happens. Got to run." Mindy was off.

Jenna hoped Mindy was right and her troubles would be over soon. How was she supposed to concentrate on work with all this nonsense? She reached into her drawer and doled out two aspirin.

Five minutes later, her phone rang. It was Raven. She braced herself.

"Blanche approved the quote."

"What? I figured you'd call the whole thing off. Or want to move it closer to Philadelphia."

"No, she loved the venue. Said it looked posh. She wants the four-course menu. But wants all the details before she signs the contract. Remember, vegan options and no gluten."

Jenna's head was spinning. Thirty-thousand dollars? Like it was nothing? Was this the reason Raven was marrying Jack? It couldn't be for his sullen demeanor. But Raven would be independently wealthy soon. Money meant nothing to her.

Jenna sighed. "I'll work with Candy to get the menu as soon as possible."

After several more calls, Jenna received the menu options and forwarded them to Blanche. The workday was wasted with calls and emails about the party. Why was she the go-between to describe all the ingredients in nearly every dish or pastry? Jenna wasn't sure if she could finish her monthly report on time if this kept up.

At the end of her workday—four o'clock—Jenna put on her coat and headed out of the office.

On the way to her car, Blanche called again.

"Yes, Blanche?"

"I need you to visit the house tomorrow. Make sure it's worth the money."

Tomorrow was Saturday. She had plans to drive up to see Marcelo. There was no way to do both. But Marcelo would understand, right?

Jenna knew the sooner they settled the venue, the sooner her life and sanity could resume. "Sure thing. If I can get in. I'll let you know." She continued walking to her car.

"And Jack will go with you. He knows how I like things."

She stopped. *Jack needs to go?* She barely knew him. "Um. Okay. But shouldn't Raven go instead? It's her party."

"Raven and I are shopping for her gown in Manhattan tomorrow. I pulled strings to get this appointment. Plus, some sight-seeing and a show. Jack will take pictures. It's fine. He'll pick you up at eight tomorrow so you can get there around noon."

These were commands, not questions. But they needed to lock down the venue. Everything else hinged on it. "No problem."

Blanche hung up without a goodbye.

Jenna reached her car and turned the key in the ignition. The death droning commenced. A belt was loose and screamed under her rusted hood. The other departing employees turned and gave her looks of concern. Perhaps it was best Jack would drive tomorrow. Her car might not make the long trip. She looked at the odometer. Nearly 240,000 miles.

And maybe, just maybe, she would get to know Jack better during the trip to Altoona and find he was a good person with a fun personality. Someone worthy of Raven. Or worthy of anyone. Yes, their trip was an opportunity to get to know him better and find his good traits.

She would try to keep an open mind.

* * *

As soon as Jenna got home from work, she called Marcelo. On a normal Friday late afternoon, she'd be packing an overnight bag. It was best to tell him sooner rather than later. She sat on the couch and pulled a throw blanket over her legs.

He picked up on the second ring. "Hey, babe."

Marcelo's tone sounded less enthusiastic lately. Like something distracted him. "Hey, I miss you. How was your day?"

"Fine. Are you still driving up tomorrow?"

It felt like a bad time to renege. Especially since they had missed Valentine's Day together. But what choice did she have? "No, I have to go check on things for Raven's party. But I can drive up the weekend after."

"But I got us tickets to see that band you like, remember?"

She remembered. It was a Tom Petty tribute band that was playing at the college. "Ugh. I'm sorry. Can you go without me?"

"Yeah, don't worry. I'll give the tickets to someone else in my building. I mean, the band is decent, but not worth going alone."

"Thanks for understanding. Raven's my best friend. It's important to her. Gosh, you wouldn't believe what goes into these things. I have to come up with a list of games to play. Plus, Raven keeps throwing out ideas like a karaoke setup and a make-up artist. And her soon-to-be Mother-In-Law is like a she-devil."

"Like I said, no problem. Hey, you remember the pancake house in Bar Harbor? They opened one just like it down the street. We should check it out."

Her heart sank. Pancake breakfasts with Marcelo were her favorite. "Sounds wonderful. Can't wait."

"Oh, hey babe, I have a game starting in five minutes. Call me tomorrow, okay?"

Marcelo loved gaming. She wasn't into it, but he had a whole posse of friends that played Fortnite, Outer Worlds, and other video games.

"Good night, my love." She wanted to reach through the phone and hug him. Look into his beautiful dark eyes. Run the tips of her fingers along his stubbled chin.

He gave a hurried, "Bye," and the call was over.

She stared at her phone. Was she making a mistake prioritizing Raven over Marcelo? She gazed at their framed photo on the console next to her television. Posing and smiling at the top of the Beehive Trail at Acadia National Park. She had been so sure Marcelo would propose to her at the summit. In hindsight, she had no real reason to think so. Just silly romantic hopes like those of a Hallmark movie heroine.

Thumper jumped up on the couch next to her, rolling his head upside down, inviting a chin scratch. She turned on the television and rubbed Thumpers face. But she couldn't get her mind off Marcelo.

Distance allegedly made the heart grow fonder.

But she was having serious doubts about that.

* * *

At eight-fifteen the next morning, her doorbell rang. She peered through the peephole, then opened the door.

"Jenna?" The guy in front of her was tall, dark, handsome. He wore a mid-length dark brown leather jacket, jeans and dark Timberlands. His hair was longer on top and shaved on the sides. In the gusty morning air, his bangs fell across his eyes. He brushed the hair away from his face.

His hazel eyes seemed a little spacey, as if focused on the wall beyond her.

"Hi, Jack. I'm ready." She buttoned her coat and followed him down the stairs toward his car, a gleaming blood-red metallic Audi. The A8 sedan model, a stunning car that oozed privilege.

Opening her door, the smell of new leather overtook her. But there was another smell. Was it new car odor? Possibly.

He slid into the driver's seat and revved the engine. Fastening his seat belt, he said, "I love this car. Dad gave it to me last week. Crashed my old car a couple weeks ago. A vintage black and gold '76 Firebird Trans Am with a V-8. Totally cherry. One just like in the Smokey and the Bandit movies."

"Was anyone hurt?" She fastened her seat belt, tugging on the strap to enhance the tension.

"Nah. Just the car. Slid on some ice and hit a telephone pole. The broken glass scratched my face a little. See?" He turned to face her, pointing to a small scab on his chin. With his stubble, she wouldn't have noticed it otherwise.

"I'm glad you're all right. Raven must have been so worried." Jenna wondered why Raven hadn't mentioned this before. A fiancé with a near-death experience would be something one might bring up.

"Raven wasn't worried. She says I lead a charmed life." He sped onto the two-lane road without looking for oncoming traffic.

Jenna felt every bump in the road because of the stiff sports suspension. But the car seemed to hug the road, quite unlike her Fiesta that swayed like a piñata in a hurricane if she didn't hold on to the wheel with all her strength. Did Jack appreciate the work of art he was driving? She would give nearly anything to have a car so nice.

"This is a beautiful car." She ran her hand over the leather-covered glove box. The gauges looked like Tiffany watches. "My car belongs in a junk yard."

"If you like this, you'd go crazy over my dad's car. He drives a Bentley."

"Wow." She didn't know what else to say.

Jack pulled onto the interstate.

After an awkwardly long silence, Jenna asked, "So, Jack, what are your hobbies?"

"I like to just chill. Watch TV. Go to parties." He reached across and opened the glove box. "You smoke?"

"No, never have."

Something crawled up Jack's side window. A small spider. Jenna shuddered and held her arms against her chest. "A spider! Kill it." She crammed her body against her door and clasped a hand over her eyes, viewing the arachnid warily through the gaps in her fingers.

"This little thing?" Jack pressed his thumb against the glass, killing the spider, leaving a black and red smudge.

She clenched her hands in her lap, squeezing her eyes shut. "Oh, no. How could you do that? Touch it like that? Ick. That's terrifying.

"Just a bug." Jack opened the plastic bag on his lap, pulled out a joint and placed it between his lips. After fishing a lighter out of his jacket pocket, he lit up and cracked the window a bit, blowing smoke sideways toward the outside.

Now Jenna understood the odd smell in his car. Weed. But she was still thinking about the spider, wondering if it had any friends waiting to pounce on her. She scanned the floor and the roof. *No spiders.* At least for now...none that were visible. Her shoulders remained tense as she kept a watchful eye on the situation.

Smoke wafted in front of her face. She coughed. Jack pressed a button and rolled down her window. It helped a little, but then the car sped up. Leaning over, she read the speedometer. The car had been at sixty since they reached the Interstate, but now read ninety.

"Don't you think we should slow down? We have lots of time. The planner is meeting us at noon."

"You need to chill." Jack puffed away; one arm draped over the top of the steering wheel.

Did Raven know Jack was a stoner? She recalled Raven telling her she'd tried pot at a sorority party once but hadn't enjoyed it. But was Raven being truthful? She had a way of giving half-truths. Like the time she said she didn't drink, but Jenna found a bottle of vodka under her bed. But that was in high school. Raven had to be a more responsible person now. She graduated at the top of her class with a dual degree.

A tickle on her spine *A spider?* She swatted at her neck. *Nothing there.* Maybe she was being paranoid. *Was the pot making her feel things that weren't there?* She'd never done drugs or been high.

She stared at her hands folded on her lap. The delicate ring from Marcelo looked so beautiful in the early morning light. When he gave it to her last Christmas, her heart leapt; for a split-second, she hoped he would propose. Although just a present, it made her feel connected to him, especially during times apart. Yet, something was off the last time she visited him. Like he was distracted or was more interested in playing his video games. And he was always so matter-of-fact on the phone; not one for long conversations.

Was he losing interest? Or was she being overly sensitive?

Jack finally finished his joint and now had two hands on the wheel. But he was still speeding. Jenna focused on the scenery. Pennsylvania was beautiful, despite the barren tree limbs. The rolling hills and old stone farm houses made her long for a home in the country, away from the congestion of Cherry Hill. Settling down with Marcelo in the countryside would be heaven.

She was in a blissful daydream when flashing lights rushed up behind them. She checked the side mirror. *A cop was pulling them over?* Jack wasn't smoking anymore, but the car smelled awful. *Would they be arrested? Driving under the influence?* The baggie of joints was still in the glove box.

She tugged on Jack's elbow. "Pull over!"

"What for?" He stared ahead, unflinching.

"The cop. You're being pulled over." *Could he not see or hear?*

Jack decelerated, and he steered the car onto the shoulder. Tractor trailers screamed by only a couple feet to their left. She hated sharing the highway with trucks.

He turned off the car, pulled out his wallet from his back pocket, and threw it on her lap. "Get my license out. The registration's in the glove box."

The same glove box full of pot? She opened it and found the registration. In the side mirror, she saw the cop still in his car, his head down, probably writing at ticket. She hid the baggie under her seat. Not to protect Jack. Only to prevent his arrest so they could keep their appointment with Candy. And there was no time to waste.

Jack smirked. "Don't worry. I have a prescription." From under his seat, he pulled a small spray bottle. He misted the air. It smelled like chemicals.

Jenna coughed, gagging on the toxic plume. She hit the down button for her side window. With the car off, it didn't move.

She yelled, "Jack, I can't breathe," slamming the window button repeatedly. It was no use.

"Give it a couple minutes. The deodorizing spray works best with the windows up."

She removed one of her gray wool gloves and pressed it to her nose like a face mask, while she resisted the urge to scream or call him an asshole. Her eyes glued to the side mirror, she watched the cop, wondering how this was all going to go down.

After an eternity, the police officer finally got out of his car and approached Jack's window.

Jenna saw a tiny spider, about the size of a head of a match, crawl along the center console. She should have panicked. But now the bug seemed inconsequential to the larger dismal picture. Biting her bottom lip, she braced herself for the cop's interrogation.

The car was registered to the car dealership. *Was it a lease?*

She prayed he wouldn't screw this up.

* * *

The officer was short, with a young, round face, and a thin brown mustache. He approached Jack's window.

Jack rested elbow on the window opening. "Hey, Officer."

"Sir, your license and registration?"

Jenna handed the cards to Jack, who transferred them to the officer.

The officer inspected them. "Do you know why I pulled you over?"

Jack said, "I was just following the flow of traffic, sir."

"I clocked you at a hundred and six."

Jack laughed. "It must be the car. It drives so smoothly, I guess I couldn't tell how fast I was going. Have you ever driven an Audi? This baby has over three-hundred and ninety horses. My family owns a dealership in New Jersey. I could get you a great discount if you're in the market for a new vehicle. There's a sweet blue Mustang with low miles I bet you would love."

Jenna stared at Jack. *Was this for real?* Was he honestly trying to sell a car to a police officer who stopped him for speeding?

The officer took a pen light from his jacket pocket and swept it across Jack's eyes. "Sir, are you under the influence of any illicit substances?"

"Nah, I had some prescribed medicinal marijuana earlier today. But I'm perfectly fine to drive."

"Sir, I need to ask you to get out of the vehicle." The officer glanced at Jenna. "Miss, stay in the car. Understand?"

She nodded.

Jack got out of the car indifferently, like he was off for a Sunday stroll.

Jenna loosened her seat belt, trying to view the action behind the car. Jack's head bobbed as he walked the twenty feet to the officer's car. Next, Jack spread his hands on the hood. The officer began patting him down.

The cop pulled a clear plastic bag from Jack's jean's pocket.

She needed to hear what was happening. Her window was closed; with the ignition off, it wouldn't operate. She crawled over the center console to the driver's seat, where she leaned her head through the open window.

The officer held the bag to the sky, jostling the round white pills. "Sir, what are these?"

Jack laughed. "Aspirin. I get headaches." He lifted his hands off the hood and stood upright.

"It looks like molly."

"Molly who?"

"Sir, I'm going to give you a drug test. I'll need you to sit in the back." He opened the rear door of the police cruiser.

"What if I refuse? I have rights."

The officer stared at him. He unhitched the cuffs from his belt. "Fine, we can do this the hard way."

Was Jack being arrested? They would never make it to the venue…

Jenna waved her arm out the window. "Officer," she called, "please." She opened the car door and placed her feet on the pavement, ready to pull herself upright.

The cop turned and yelled, "Miss! I said stay inside the vehicle." The cuffs fell to the ground; in a split-second, he trained his gun on her.

She froze. "Sir, I… I just wanted to talk."

He walked toward her sideways, aiming the gun at her torso. "Close the door. Are you trying to get yourself killed?" He pressed one hand against the driver's door.

She tucked her legs inside, and planted her hands on the steering wheel at ten and two, keeping her gaze straight ahead. Her heart pounded. "Sir, I just wanted to explain. Jack's fiancée—my best friend—has cancer. All she wants before her surgery is a wonderful bridal shower with her friends and family. That's where we're going today. To check the venue. There's so little time." The words flowed out of her like a stream of consciousness, her body bracing itself for impending doom. "God, she's only twenty-four. I mean, maybe it doesn't mean much to you, but Raven has always been there for me. When we were fourteen, I broke my wrist, and she carried all my school books for two months. I just want to give her a happy day before she goes to the hospital for weeks or months of treatment."

Jenna took a breath and then she fell apart. She wept. Her nose ran. Hiccups squeaked out between sobs. "Jack is sorry. We're both [hic] sorry. If you could [hic] let us go with a warning [hic], I'd be eternally grateful." She continued to sniffle, wiping her nose on her wool coat sleeve, leaving a trail of ooze like a slug. Her hand was coated with sticky snot; she dislodged it running her fingers through her hair. The definition of ugly crying.

The cop bared his teeth in disgust. "I'm sorry about your friend. My dad just died of cancer. A terrible thing." He checked his watch. "Look, I'll give you a break. On one condition. You drive the rest of the way. I'm still issuing a speeding ticket to Mr. Forero."

She sniffled. "Thank you. Thank you, officer." [hic]

The officer walked back to Jack, who was sitting on the hood of the police car, smiling.

"Sir, you can continue on, but if I catch you driving again today, I'll arrest you. Go sit in your car until I finish writing the ticket."

Jack sauntered back to the Audi, "Thank you for your service." He got in the passenger side and checked his hair in the visor mirror. He glanced at Jenna. "Raven said you were smart. Good one about the cancer thing." He reclined his seat and closed his eyes.

Cancer thing? Did he not know about Raven's surgery? Or was he just stoned beyond all recognition of reality? Stunned speechless, she rested her forehead on the steering wheel, trying to slow her breathing and stop her hiccups.

A couple minutes later, the cop walked back and handed the license, registration and ticket to Jenna. "Drive safe, miss."

She nodded. She started the engine and readjusted the seat and mirrors, double and triple checking the viewing angles. The cop pulled into traffic without hesitation. She waited patiently for a window of opportunity to merge back onto the road safely. After a minute of cars whipping past, she gave up waiting. She put her foot to the gas. The acceleration was so crisp, so forceful. She kept the car in the shoulder, amazed at the rate at which she quickly outpaced the SUV in the right lane, merging in front of it like the other car was standing still.

It didn't take long for her to realize Jack had made a solid point. This car made speeding nearly unnoticeable. She barely touched the accelerator and the car raced upwards of eighty miles per hour. But she backed off, finding her footing to keep the vehicle under seventy, the legal posted limit.

Five miles down the road, the scenery turned snow covered, with the roads clear from salt. Jack was snoring.

What kind of druggie idiot was Raven engaged to?

Apparently one that liked to taunt the police.

Her hopes of learning to like Jack evaporated.

And this was not a good sign of things to come.

Chapter 4

The clock on the Audi's dashboard read 11:58 when they pulled up to the large wrought-iron gate at the front of the driveway. A woman with long, wavy red hair and bright red lipstick—wearing a tiger-print spandex dress under a fluffy faux fur coat—stood on the other side of the gate. Candy was younger than Jenna had envisioned from their phone conversations. She guessed early thirties?

Jenna rolled down her window. "Hi, Candy?"

"Yes, hi, Jenna. Follow the driveway. I'll meet you by the garage." Candy pressed a button on a post and the gate slowly opened.

Jenna nodded and continued on. In the rear-view mirror, she watched Candy follow them, walking in four-inch heels, trying to navigate the patches of snow on the asphalt driveway.

Jack got out of the passenger's side and stretched his arms skyward, arching his back. He'd been asleep the last hour of their trip, to Jenna's relief.

Jenna marveled at the house. It was like a castle, but without turrets. She'd seen pictures online, but in person it was massive. Like a cruise ship made of stone. The hedges manicured to perfection. Despite the thin layer of snow, the grounds reminded her of pictures of Versailles, with topiary and statues.

Jack walked around the car to Candy. He extended his hand, "Hi, I'm Jack."

She shook his hand. "Ah, the handsome groom. Nice to meet you, Jack."

He looked Candy up and down, holding her hand a moment too long. Candy seemed embarrassed and gave a small laugh. Jack released her hand. "After you." He gestured to the house and gave a slight bow.

Why was Jack acting so weird? Like he was a chauvinist James Bond in a terrible 70s movie? Was this some of his 'salesman' charm? Not that it was charming. More like gross and fake.

Candy giggled and jangled a large key ring. "Follow me. You'll love it. Everyone does."

There was a plain-looking side door closest to the parking area. She expected Candy to head directly for it. But she kept walking past it, toward the front of the house.

Jenna stopped. "Ms. Morris? Why don't we go in here?" She pointed to the plain door with a grid of windows on the top half.

"Honey," Candy said short laugh, "that door goes to the kitchen. But I want you to get the full experience. Come."

They followed her to a massive mahogany double door with more wrought iron and beveled glass. Candy unlocked the door. A soaring twenty-foot high foyer came into view, with a crystal chandelier, marble floors and gold flocked wallpaper. It reminded her of a salon in a Paris estate. Everything gilded. Not that she'd ever been to Paris. But she'd seen pictures and movies.

Candy's heels clacked against the marble, echoing in the half-circle shaped hall. A curved stairway to the right, made of more marble and brass, showcased large contemporary oil paintings on the walls.

The stillness of the house made Jenna wonder whether if it was okay to intrude. She recalled the movie "The Shining." *Would they find "redrum" on the mirrors?*

"Let's go see the kitchen first. By the way, if you want to rent it for March fourth, I'll need the deposit today. I take all major credit cards. Five thousand." Candy locked eyes with her. "The rest is due in a week."

Jenna looked away and continued toward the kitchen. The kitchen was as large as her entire apartment. Perhaps larger. Two islands, covered in marble with waterfall edges, with leather-covered bar chairs. An eight-burner blue enamel range with an ornate brass hood. A sixty-inch wide white stainless-steel counter-depth refrigerator. Antiqued wood cabinets. A round rustic table in an adjacent area seated eight; light flooded in from skylights. Everything looked brand new, as if no one had ever used it. Not a stray crumb in sight. It took her breath away.

Jack remained mute but took some pictures on his phone.

"Spectacular, right?" Candy said, leaning on the first island. She took off her fur and draped it across the back of a counter seat.

"Beautiful," Jenna said, staring at the range, running her hand along the front.

Jack—out of Jenna's view—said, "Yeah, gorgeous."

Jenna turned to ask Jack a question. Out of the corner of her eye, she saw Jack run his palm over Candy's derriere. Candy gave Jack a side look, but framed in a smirk. *Did Candy just lick her lips? Were they both flirting?*

"Um, Jack, did you get a picture of the entrance?"

He nodded. "Yes."

Candy stepped away from Jack, smoothing her skirt. In a business-like voice, she said, "Let's go to the ballroom. It will be the primary room for the party."

They followed her to the other side of the house. Another immense room. About seventy feet long, ceiling at least sixteen feet high, gleaming white-ash herringbone wood floors, walls covered in arabesque patterned wallpaper, gold and crystal sconces and three massive crystal chandeliers spaced down the center. Jenna walked the perimeter of the space. You could play football in this space, she thought. Or at least three regulation volleyball games.

With such a large room span, the builder must have used steel I-beams. The ballroom was empty except for a black lacquer grand piano, a sandstone fireplace, and some tufted benches. French doors leading to a bluestone patio lined the rear wall, with large windows above, flooding the room with light. The room had two entrances. One near the kitchen, the one they had just gone through, and one connected to the front hall through a formal living room.

Jenna continued walking the room's perimeter. Passing a sconce, something caught her eye. She stared at it. "Candy? Is that what I think it is?" From far away, the sconces looked like three cherubs playing. Up close, there were worse things happening between the chubby figures.

Candy laughed. "Yes. I suppose the sconces are the only decoration remaining from the old days."

"Old days?"

"The house has quite a history. Two decades ago, a beer magnate and his wife built the house and threw lavish masquerade balls. Some folks called them swinger parties. Very scandalous."

Jack said, "Hmm. Could be my kind of party. With the right lady…."

Candy turned red. She hugged her folder. "Some people think this place is haunted…that it turns them into nymphomaniacs. But that's plain silly."

31

Jack walked over to Candy. "I don't know. I'm starting to feel something."

Jenna kept walking. *Could it seat 120 people for a meal?* Probably. Jenna did some math in her head, counting on her fingers.

As if reading her mind, Candy walked towards her and showed her a glossy 8x10 photo from her folder. "This is what it looks like dressed for a party. We can seat a hundred with round tables. For larger parties, it's best to use longer, rectangular tables. But we could accommodate up to a hundred and seventy-five, if we don't need a dancefloor."

Jenna studied the picture. Yes, it was more than feasible. "And will you arrange table set-up?"

Candy said, "Of course. I work with a rental company. I assume you want the comfortable chairs?"

From the direction of the kitchen, a woman's voice shouted, "Hello? Candy?"

"Oh, that's the caterer. Her name's Tanya." Candy spun on her heels and they followed her back to the kitchen.

"There you are. Goodness, it's so easy to lose people in this place." Tanya came over and shook Jenna's hand. "Candy's told me all about your party. Congratulations on your wedding."

"No, not my wedding. My friend Raven's. This is her fiancé, Jack."

Tanya shook hands with Jack. "Well, we don't have a minute to spare. I brought all my menus with pictures. Come sit." She motioned to a chair at the island. "Let me show you."

Jack and Candy were discussing something on the other side of the room. From his body language, Jenna could tell Jack had no interest in the menu or the party.

For twenty minutes or more, Jenna and Tanya discussed the main dishes, hor d'oeuvre's, beverage packages, food restrictions, and prices.

When they came to a discussion of the cake, Jenna couldn't remember what kind Raven liked most. In middle school, Rae loved angel cake with strawberry filling and vanilla frosting. For Valentines in 7th grade, Raven brought in handmade strawberry cupcakes for her homeroom. But Rae was grown now. Tastes change.

She called out, "Jack? Do you know…" Looking over, Jack was gone. Candy too. Vanished into thin air.

Tanya said, "I think I heard them talking about the home theater in the basement. Maybe she went to show it to him."

Jenna called out louder. "Jack! Hello?" No response. She closed her eyes. *Would Jack really...?* No, she couldn't think about it. Guys could be harmless flirts. *He wouldn't. Would he?*

She resolved to focus on the task at hand. "Um. Let's go with the vanilla cake with pink strawberry frosting. Raven has a pink theme. It should look nice. You said it can be gluten-free?"

"We can do anything you need." Tanya jotted some notes. "Got it. I think we're all set. I'll need the deposit now. Twenty-five percent." She got out her phone and calculated the number. She added it to the bottom of a receipt and handed it to her.

"Thirteen-hundred dollars?" Jenna pressed her hands across her forehead. She let out a long breath. "Let me go get Jack."

Jenna hopped off her seat and headed toward the front hallway. *Where was the basement door?* She began opening doors randomly. *A coat closet. A bathroom. A utility room.* She wandered further. Her heart beat faster. The sums of money spent on the deposits today alone would pay for her apartment for half a year. Giving up on finding the basement entrance, she checked the ballroom again, then tried upstairs.

After a few minutes, she returned to the kitchen, ready to admit defeat, but Jack and Candy were there, talking with the caterer. Jack's hair was disheveled. Candy had a run in her black stockings along her knee. It confirmed what she had feared. Jack was a lying snake. A low-life. A cheater. *Man-whore.*

She didn't want to cause a scene in front of the caterer. "Jack, could you work out the deposits? I'm going to step outside for some air."

Jack grunted a "yeah" and Jenna raced to the front door. She pulled out her cell phone from her cross-body bag and called Raven.

Pick up, pick up! She paced the walkway, brushing the snow off the hedge with her free hand. The cold seeped through her skin, but she kept scooping snow, wanting to feel something other than the knots in her stomach. On the sixth ring, Raven said, "Hey, Jenna. Can you hold?"

"No!"

"Wait, I can't hear you. We just drove into the tunnel. I'll call you back."

The line went dead. It was close to one o'clock now. She paced some more, shaking her numb hand to put back feeling. Gusts of freezing air overwhelmed her without her coat. She walked over to Jack's car and tried the passenger door. *Locked.* She tried the others. All locked.

She leaned against the side. The metal felt warm where it met the sun's rays. *"Come on...come on..."* she willed the phone as she shivered, bouncing on her heels. When her phone rang, Jenna accepted the call, teeth chattering. "Raven. I need to tell you something."

"Oh, my God. Is the mansion just like the pictures? I bet it's dreamy."

"Yes. No. Listen to me."

"What?" In the background on the other end, car horns honked relentlessly.

"Jack. I think he's...cheating on you."

"Sorry, the traffic is loud. What about Jack? He's chewing something?"

"No! Listen. I'm pretty sure Jack had sex with the Candy. You know, the wedding planner."

There was a pause. It wasn't like Rae to be quiet.

"Are you there?" Jenna paced in circles, bouncing up and down on her heels to stay warm.

"I'm here. Jenna, I love you and I know you're trying to help, but I don't want to hear about it. It's okay. Complicated, but fine. Don't worry about me. Just arrange the bridal shower. I have to go."

The call disconnected.

It's okay? What did she mean by complicated? Did they have an open relationship? This was not the Raven she grew up with. Younger Raven would have been supremely angry. Even vengeful.

What the hell was going on?

None of this seemed remotely correct or plausible. Her body seethed with hate for Jack; she wanted to smash his smug face in. Not that her tiny wrists could inflict the desired force.

Her mind raced. Hitting him would be satisfying, but it wouldn't solve the situation. She could simply confront Jack. They had a long drive back to talk. But with such a long drive, perhaps it was safer to play dumb for now. Just get through the rest of the day. Thankfully, Jack wasn't the talkative type. They could drive back in silence, which might be awkward, but better than the alternative of hearing whatever lies he might spew forth.

She decided her best move would be to talk with Rae. Preferably in person, away from Jack the snake. Face-to-face, Raven would have to open up to her, right?

They had been so close before college. But living hours away from each other for the last four years took a bit of a toll. Every time she saw Raven in recent times, there was always a perceptible difference. Like they were growing apart, having different interests. That was to be expected, she thought. People grow up. But deep down, at their core, they understood each other, loved each other. That could never change.

Jenna needed to understand Raven's love for Jack. How was he possibly worthy of her? And why was she choosing to get married so quickly? None of it made sense. Unless Raven was dying. That could explain everything. But that theory must be wrong. Had to be wrong. She couldn't imagine her life without Raven and wasn't going to start now.

No, there was something else going on. Something sinister, perhaps?

And she would find out, come hell or high water.

Chapter 5

Sunday morning, Jenna woke with Thumper's tail against her cheek. She wiped a wad of fur from her lips and coughed, then reached for her phone. Raven had finally texted her back. They'd meet at noon at Rae's apartment, when Jack wouldn't be around.

Perfect.

She had stayed up late last night writing out a script of the questions she would ask. They all made sense at midnight. Now, in the bright morning light, they were the ravings of a crazed, hostile person. Not the questions of a best friend.

Jenna crumpled up her list and threw it across the room. Thumper leapt up to chase it, running over her legs, his tiny paws hammering her shins with his dense weight.

"Ow."

How could she ease the conversation to the subject of Jack's infidelity? She watched a few YouTube videos on the subtle art of interrogation. Yet she felt like the criminal in this scenario. Tricking Raven into opening up wasn't her goal. She just needed honesty. They had always been painfully honest with each other their entire lives. But now things seemed different. Raven seemed different. And she needed different tactics.

At noon, she rang Rae's doorbell. Raven lived in a two-room apartment on the ground floor of a beautiful Victorian house in Medford. It was only a fourteen-mile trip but with traffic, could sometimes take forty-minutes. Was this the reason they drifted apart over the last year? Or maybe with their new careers and boyfriends, they didn't have the energy.

The last time she spent meaningful time with Rae was six months ago, when she accompanied her shopping for new work outfits. Pre-Jack. Pre-'the current wedding insanity'. *Possibly pre-cancer?*

Rae answered the door, a wide smile, wearing black leggings and an oversized black cashmere sweater. Her black hair was in a long, thick wavy ponytail. She had false eyelashes, heavy rouge defining her cheeks, and pink lip gloss. She looked like Raven, but far more glamorous. Was this the same girl that made dirt forts with her when they were eight?

Raven embraced her, crushing her bones beneath her dense wool coat. "EEEE! I'm so happy to see you. I have so much to tell you."

Jenna forced a smile. "I'm glad to see you, too."

Raven released her and ushered her inside. "Can I get you some hot chocolate? I have mini-marshmallows, your favorite." Rae headed to the kitchenette and grabbed a couple mugs.

Jenna took off her coat and looked around the apartment. She'd been there before, but only briefly. It looked like a magazine. Tall ceilings with plaster molding, white walls with white trim. Potted plants by the bay window, a blush pink velvet sofa faced an antique boarded-up fireplace. White faux-fur covered arm chairs. Black and white photos on a sideboard of Jack and Rae in silly poses, smiling and holding hands at the Jersey shore. A small, faded picture of her and Rae when they were six, playing in a sandbox in Rae's parent's backyard, both smiling, each with front teeth missing. Those simpler days seemed so long ago.

She turned her attention to the glass coffee table: a stack of bridal magazines dotted with small pink post-it placeholders, an open box of chocolate covered strawberries that looked sumptuous.

Rae poured their cocoa. "The strawberries are Jack's valentines present. He knows me so well. Have some. I can't eat them all. Watching my weight for the wedding."

Jenna recoiled from the box. No, she wanted nothing associated with Jack the Rat. But she took the mention of Jack to launch into her reason for coming. "I guess Jack really loves you."

Rae came over and set the steaming mugs on the coffee table. She curled up on the sofa, drawing a thick chunky knit blanket over her legs. "Sit. I'll tell you all about it."

Jenna sat on the other end of the sofa, clutching a throw pillow to her torso. She attempted a smile. "I want to hear everything."

"Remember me telling you how we met?" Rae picked up a strawberry, but kept her thickly lashed eyes on Jenna. Raven bit into the strawberry, but Jenna noticed a flash of metal. Did Raven have a stud in her tongue? She cringed. The Raven she knew didn't get weird piercings.

"Wait, is that a stud?" She pointed at Raven's mouth.

Raven finished chewing and stuck out her tongue. "It's new. Jack thinks it's sexy. Of course, I don't wear it all the time. So," she shook her head, "the story of how I met Jack."

Mesmerized by this new information, Jenna tried not to stare. Was Raven throwing caution to the wind because of her illness? She closed her eyes, trying to focus on their conversation. "Yes, when you got your new car?"

"Uh-huh. I leased a car from Jack's family's dealership in Hamilton. After I finished the paperwork, I was wandering around the showroom, waiting for the car to be pulled around. You know, they wash it and put on the temporary plates. But whatever. Anyway, Jack was showing a car to a young couple."

"Jack's a salesman?"

"Not usually. But he pitches in all over. Most of the time he manages the service department. Well, he isn't the best salesperson. The couple hemmed and hawed. Then I walked over. Mind you, I had come from work and was wearing my pin-striped suit. I started selling the car for Jack. It wasn't long before I had the couple right where I wanted them and closed the deal."

"Why?"

"Why not? I was bored, and it was fun. Jack grinned the whole time. I could tell I impressed him."

Jenna couldn't imagine Jack being impressed with anything. His stoner expression was so blank. So lifeless.

"And he asked you out?" Jenna asked.

"He asked if he could buy me coffee. I told him to pick me up for a steak dinner later that night. Least he could do, right? I probably got him a two-grand commission."

"Rae, if I'm honest, I've got to tell you I'm concerned. You've had only three boyfriends. How do you know Jack's the one?"

"Well, he's a total hottie. And his family has money. I don't have to worry he's after my inheritance." Raven gave a coy look and sipped her cocoa.

Jenna grabbed a corner of the throw pillow and rapped Raven's knee with it. "Come on. For real."

Rae grabbed the pillow away and hit her back, laughing. "Fine. Look,

Jack isn't perfect, but he respects me. Let's me do what I want. And he's so sweet. Sends me little love notes all the time. We just click. From the first time we met…I can't describe it. And the sex is amazing."

"But why get married so quickly? Why not have a longer engagement?" Jenna felt like she was pushing now, going against her recent 'training' in subtle questioning techniques. She grabbed a different throw pillow and hugged it to her stomach.

"I just want to be settled. He makes me happy." She stared at her hands and grimaced. "I don't want to be in my late thirties wondering if I'll ever have a family."

Jenna saw something in Rae's eyes. A hint of the sorrow from the days after Rae's mom died. *Did Raven want to get married to fill a void?* Jenna couldn't really understand Rae's grief and how it affected her decisions. Perhaps the loss explained Rae's impulsive behavior, particularly where men were concerned. *And who was she to judge?*

"If he makes you happy, then I'm happy for you. But…"

Raven crossed her arms and raised an eyebrow. "But what?"

Jenna braced herself, squinting as the words came out. "Jack's cheating on you."

Rae shook her head. "No. Not really."

Where was the anger? The outrage? The hurt and questioning? How could Raven look so complacent?

"What? I'm confused. I saw them. They clearly…"

"We have hall passes until the wedding."

"Wha—"

"A hall pass. We can sleep with anyone we want. Only rule is we don't tell each other, unless the other asks, and we have to use protection."

Jenna shook her head and closed her eyes. "That's crazy."

"It was *my* idea." Raven's face was serious.

Jenna was at a loss for words. *How was this a good idea?*

Rae said, "I want us to be sure. Get everything out of our systems. Like you said, we're young. I've only been with three men. I love Jack, but I told him it's a condition for me accepting his proposal. He understands."

"So, you're, what? Sleeping around with random men?"

"No, not yet, but I might." Raven arched her eyebrow. She seemed to be teasing, but her words were serious. "We're both adults. And Jack and I love each other deeply. That won't change."

Jenna closed her eyes to sort this out. *Jack had permission*. But a decent guy wouldn't have a quickie with a woman he just met. Especially a woman planning the bride's shower. If Jack really loved Raven, wouldn't he stay true? There was no way to win this argument now. She had to move on. There was one other burning question. It was a sensitive topic, but she got the words out. "Does getting married have anything to do with your surgery?"

"No. Don't be stupid." Rae's voice was harsh. But then her eyes softened. "I'm sure I'll be fine."

"Sorry. I just worry. I want to be there for you. If something happened…you know you can tell me anything." Jenna reached out her hand.

Rae took her hand. "I know, J-Bear. Really, everything is great. Really great."

Jenna turned her eyes away. Usually when Raven called her J-Bear, it recalled a happier time when Raven's mom was still alive. Raven's mom nicknamed her Rae-Bear. On a hot summer evening, when they were seven, Raven's mom called the girls to come inside for dinner. "*Come Rae-Bear, come Jenna*." Raven refused to come inside until her mom renamed Jenna as 'J-Bear' so their names would match. Since then, the name recalled solidarity and affection. A sisterhood.

The moment felt awkward. Perhaps she had to accept Rae's decisions. She reached for a strawberry and bit into it. The chocolate was creamy, not too sweet. Probably expensive. "Yep, these are good."

Rae beamed and twisted her fingers through her ponytail. "Do you want to see which dresses I'm considering?" With a bounce, she picked up a tabbed magazine.

Jenna nodded, devouring the rest of the strawberry.

They spent a good hour looking over dresses in magazines and critiquing each. It felt like old times, when they used to flip through Teen Vogue examining every detail of celebrity fashion and hair styles. Rae with her preference for the latest trends and sleek silhouettes, while Jenna opted for traditional and romantic.

Despite the reverie of rekindled girlhood chatter, Jenna wondered if Rae was truly all right. She showed no signs of illness, given the glow of her skin and hair and overall energy. If Rae was having surgery to remove cancer, she'd likely follow-up with rounds of chemotherapy. Her hair might fall out. She tried to envision Raven bald. There would be no shame in that, but it was understandable if Raven wanted to have her bridal shower while she still had her hair. Raven always called her hair her best feature. Which was funny to Jenna, because Raven had perfect bone structure and facial symmetry, and a cute nose. Really, there were no unattractive features. Which probably explained why Raven had always been more popular.

Still, the nagging doubts in her brain couldn't be drowned out by glossy, stunning images of gangly airbrushed women draped in taffeta and lace. Something felt very off. Perhaps even rotten.

Rottener than her mom's veggie casserole.

Over the coming days, she hoped she could pinpoint the source of her unease.

* * *

Six-thirty Monday morning, Jenna walked out to her car ready to head to work. A thick sheet of ice covered her windshield. Given the weak heating system in her wreck of a car, she would need to turn the defroster on full blast for fifteen minutes and scrape the outside with extreme prejudice.

The unmistakable sound of sobs echoed through the darkness. Across the parking lot, twenty yards behind her, a man wearing a thick coat and knit hat, his back to her, was leaning over his car, crying into his scarf. It was unusual to see a neighbor so early in the morning. Unsure of what to do, she began scraping her windshield.

The man turned to open his door. It was Fred.

Dropping the scraper, she strode towards him. "Fred? Are you all right?"

He shook, as if startled. Wiping his eyes with his gloved hand, he said, "Jenna…I'm…I…I really don't know. But don't let me trouble you. I'll be fine. I've got to get going." He shooed her away.

"You're crying. You aren't fine." She placed her hand on his shoulder.

Fred exhaled. There was a terror in his eyes. His voice quaked. "She passed. Just now. The home called."

"Your wife? I'm so sorry."

"I've been expecting it…deep down, I knew." He stared at the pavement. "She looked so weak. I don't know. She's probably in a better place..."

Jenna knew what she ought to do. Using another vacation day was a tough decision, especially with no notice. But Fred was clearly in need.

"Does your son live nearby?"

"He's in Minnesota. I called, but he can't come out until next weekend. But I said, hold off, 'cause I may hold the funeral later. Ava wanted to be cremated. We can have the service anytime." Another tear rolled down his face; he wiped it with the end of his coat sleeve.

She couldn't leave him like this. "Do you have anyone else that can be with you today?"

"No, but like I said, I'll be fine. Everything's prearranged. Just got to do some paperwork."

She read his face. He wasn't fooling her. His eyes were red, the skin below puffy. Fred turned his head and cleared his throat.

Then he straightened his back. "You go on now. I'm sure you have things to do." He tucked himself in the front seat and pulled the door.

Jenna held onto the door frame. "No, I'm coming with you."

He pulled harder. With a raised voice, he said, "Stop that now. You're making me late."

She felt foolish for playing tug-of-war with him. If their neighbors saw this, they'd assume she was harassing him or assaulting him. She looked around and noticed her car. It was still running, unattended. "Wait here. I've got to turn off my car and get my handbag."

She strode back across the lot, turned off her car and was reaching for her bag when the slam of a car door echoed off the icy pavement. Fred gunned the engine and drove away; his exhaust left a cloud of white water-vapor in a line through the parking lot.

His car turned left onto the main road. *Could she catch up?*

Examining her windshield, the answer was a clear, 'no'. *Stupid frost.* With her best effort, Fred would have a ten-minute lead. She continued scraping. Even her hand scraper was crap, taking off only thin streaks with each pass. When she got off all she could, she waited for the defroster to finish the job. Or at least provide a narrow sliver of visibility she could work with.

A notification 'ding' from her phone. She received a message from Blanche about party favors and transportation.

"I have a great idea for party favors. I need you to pick up 130 pink gift bags with custom lettering. Raven wants you to arrange for two buses for the sorority sisters to get to the party and back. Also, look into renting champagne fountains."

Were the fountains for the buses or the party? Either way, it was idiotic and shallow. Right now, a good person—a sweet old man—was going through a level of heartbreak she couldn't conceive of. A fifty-year marriage gone in an early morning phone call. No one by his side.

She recalled Raven's grief when her mother died. How she held Rae's hand during the funeral and burial. Is this what Fred was going through? Did he have anyone's hand to hold?

Jenna turned off her phone and ran the windshield wipers. Enough of the window area was exposed to allow semi-safe driving. It would have to do.

She drove out of the lot and made the same left turn. There was an assisted living facility off Route 70 about five miles away. It was a gamble. She sprayed wiper fluid on the front window repeatedly to speed up the ice removal. But it only froze again, setting her back. With the wiper blades moving and cranking the heat of the defroster, a clear portal to view the road eventually appeared.

The car radio played some news and then a Journey song. She began singing along, finding her eyes moist at a stop light. What was wrong with her? She turned off the radio and took deep breaths. If she managed to find Fred, she needed to be his rock. Not teary-eyed and weak.

Pulling into the facility, an ambulance sat parked near the covered walkway by the front door. The vehicle's lights were off and back doors were ajar. She didn't see Fred's car. The parking lot was nearly full. She drove around to the side to the first open space and walked to the main entrance.

At the front desk, she told the receptionist she was looking for Fred Blesky.

"Are you a relative?" the woman asked.

"No. I'm just a friend of Mr. Blesky's." She gave a smile.

The woman, young and short, behind the desk huffed. "Wait here." She whispered with an older, larger woman in the back office.

The larger woman with curly brown hair and a brown polyester suit walked up to the desk. "Miss, I'm sorry. The family requested privacy. I have to ask you to leave."

A wave of embarrassment brought heat to her face. "Oh. I see. Well, if you see Mr. Blesky, please tell him Jenna will check on him later today."

The large woman gave a "Hmmm mmm" and walked away.

Jenna walked out, trying to sneak a look inside the ambulance. *Nothing.* She let out a deep sigh. If Fred didn't want her around, then she had to respect that. Her watch showed seven o'clock. She'd be late to work by a few minutes.

A realization struck. Her first meeting of the day was starting at eight. She jogged to her car and started the engine. It sputtered and died.

She waited a ten count. *1, 2, 3...*

Another turn of the key and the engine hesitated but came to life.

Thank goodness.

She gently gave the engine more gas. Not too much. Not too little. What she wouldn't give for a more reliable vehicle. She recalled Jack's Audi. Driving it last Saturday was supremely blissful, even if it was only for a few hours. The wheels tracked straight. The interior was quiet. Acceleration was immediate and forceful. And it didn't smell like unburned gasoline or smelly gym socks.

Why did cheating stoner assholes get the good cars?

It seemed impossible for Rae and Jack to have the strong, loving marriage that Fred and Ava had. *Could Fred could talk some sense into Rae?*

No, Fred had more important things to deal with. Including his own loss, emotional health, and funeral arrangements.

Jenna put the radio back on to distract herself from the traffic and the growing list of things she had to do for work and for the party. Plus, she had to make time to travel up to see Marcelo next weekend and check in on Fred tonight. Prioritizing made her head spin.

She needed a Gantt chart.

Another but different Journey song came on.

This time her eyes watered. Sad over Fred's loss. Sad from lack of sleep. Sad that Marcello hadn't called her on Valentines. Sad about her car. Sad about the loss of her friend Raven.

The last realization startled her. But it was true. Rae didn't seem like the same person. The girl who rode dirt bikes with her through the woods was replaced with a glam-azon who only cared about expensive parties, dresses and an awful fiancé with six-pack abs.

People often grow apart.

She hoped Rae would come to her senses soon.

Chapter 6

It was ten o'clock. Jenna got back to her desk and checked her phone. More emails from Blanche, each with a different subject line.

The first subject was "More invitations." Her heart almost stopped. She had just dropped the invitations at the post office, affixing specifically requested heart-themed stamps on each one, taking twenty minutes out of her half-hour lunch break. Blanche added fifty more people.

Fifty.

She held her breath and opened the attachment. There they were. Another slew of addresses. They needed the final count for the caterer in five days. Even with a rush job to have more invitations printed at Kinko's, these new ones wouldn't arrive for another three days. How were they supposed to RSVP in time?

She called Blanche.

"Hi, it's Jenna."

"You got my messages? I sent them over two hours ago. Where have you been?"

There was an annoyance in Blanche's tone that she didn't appreciate. "You didn't know about these extra people earlier? The caterer will kill me."

"Oh, I should have mentioned this. We don't expect these people to show up. Look at the addresses. Mostly California and Wisconsin. My step-mom's family and some distant cousins. I'm just trying to get more presents for the happy couple. Their registry is fairly extensive."

Jenna hadn't even looked at the registry. In fact, she hadn't considered giving Rae a gift at all. But whatever she gave, it would not be from a registry. Possibly something homemade. Just putting the party together should be gift enough. She scribbled a note to herself to look up the list, out of curiosity.

"Wait. So, I don't have to worry about these people showing up. Like, at all? Whew." She exhaled.

"Well, I can't promise that. But they likely won't."

"Right. Um. I don't know if I can get them sent before Saturday. Is that all right?"

"Sure, honey. I know you have so much on your plate. Rae and I really appreciate all your efforts."

Jenna wasn't buying into this newly found sincerity. Blanche had been nothing but difficult and strident in her continual requests. But it was nice *not* being yelled at in this precise moment.

"Well, Rae is like a sister. Our moms used to call us twins. When we were little…."

"Raven is so beautiful and smart. I'm lucky my boy found her. We are so excited to call her our daughter."

Jenna didn't know how to reply. Jack didn't deserve Rae. But she had to say something. "I'm sure they'll be very happy."

Blanche replied gruffly, "They had better be." She followed it with a nervous laugh. "Well now, I'll let you get back to party planning. Toodles."

Jenna said goodbye and ended the call. *What did she mean, "they better be?"* And the line, *"get back to party planning"* made her chuckle. Didn't anyone realize she had a full-time job with real responsibilities and deadlines? Blanche was delusional.

She worked on the monthly report, but something was nagging at her. Something the wedding planner said about building capacity at the venue. *If any of these extra people came and they crossed the threshold...*

Jenna had to confirm the parameters for her peace of mind. She opened her folder and read the contract. The type was so small. She found the passage.

Parties over 130 would require written approval of the Altoona Fire Marshall and may incur Fire Watch fees. Plans must be submitted at least two weeks prior.

She didn't have two weeks. The party was in ten days.

What was a fire watch?

From her Google search, the primary result read: *"One or more qualified persons keeping watch for fires, ensuring means of egress, being prepared to contact the fire department, ready to extinguish fires with portable extinguishers and warning occupants of any need to evacuate.*"

How much extra would that cost? Still, Blanche said these fifty extra people wouldn't be coming. She debated whether to tell Mrs. Morris. But no, it would only upset her. Besides, they didn't have RSVPs back.

No, until she had a final head count, no need to tell the planner…or the caterer.

Jenna's brain was lost in internal debate when she Mindy called, "Hey, Jenna." Startled, she held her hands to her chest. "Don't sneak up on me like that."

"Sorry. Do you have the quarterly warranty repair report ready? Grant said he needs to brief it in an hour."

The air left Jenna's lungs. She hadn't even started it. Well, she had the raw data, but hadn't crunched the numbers or completed the graphs.

"Um, I'm almost done. I'll have it to him soon."

Mindy crossed her arms. "You didn't start it, right?"

Did she read my mind?

Her shoulders sank. "No. I've been dealing with party stuff. Twelve emails in the last two hours. I'm trying to work, but you wouldn't believe the crap Blanche is sending me."

Mindy chuckled. "No, I can imagine. My neighbor got married last year, remember? Look, let me help. Send me the files and we can split it up. You crunch the numbers for November and December, I'll do January."

"Really?"

"Yes," Mindy waved. "Now go. Wait, give me your phone. No more distractions. Come on, let's get after this." Mindy grabbed the phone and disappeared down the cubical passageway.

In a blur, Jenna emailed files and started her spreadsheets. She had automated much of it, but transcription errors were still possible. Like the time in her first month on the job, she missed a couple decimal points, and the mistake made it appear their division was a million dollars over budget. Grant had been very cross over that kerfuffle.

But why was she doing financial reports anyway? As a recent graduate, they gave her the mundane tasks that no one else wanted.

She focused on the numbers in front of her. It felt good to get lost in something that made sense. Math had rules and order. Numbers didn't lie or cheat or demand pink personalized napkins with hearts and the happy couple's initials.

With only five minutes to spare, Mindy returned. "I'm done. Sent the file back. Do you need help merging?"

Jenna kept typing. "I'm almost done. Wait." She hit a few more keystrokes "Done."

Her boss Grant appeared behind Mindy. "Jenna, I need the report. Now."

"I, um, it's mostly ready. Just have to merge a couple files. Can you give me another four minutes? I'll email it."

"There's no time for that. I'm walking over to my meeting now. Just read me the bottom line."

"Sure, ah…" Jenna opened Mindy's file. "It, ah, says here, wait. This isn't right."

Mindy peered over Jenna's shoulder. "No, it's right."

She realized her mistake, wincing. She had given Mindy last year's data by mistake. In her rush to send the file, she had just noticed the word "January" and not the year. She mumbled, "I, um, gave you the wrong file."

Grant let out a long "humpf" and glared at her over his glasses. "This is unacceptable."

Jenna felt like crawling under a rock, or hiding under her desk. "Grant, I'm sorry. I really messed up. I need another half hour." She wouldn't blame Grant for firing her right on the spot.

"Fuck." He checked his watch. "Jenna, get up. Get your coat and your laptop. Follow me."

Her worst fear. Losing her job. How was she going to pay her rent? She'd probably have to move home. When dad was home, he and mom fought all the time. Plus, the nights of drunken hugs or screams. Never knowing which to expect. Being unemployed, she'd be the target of mom's daily anger, disappointment, and name-calling.

The air left her lungs, envisioning the terrors that would come. Still, she gulped for breath, pulling her shoulders back. She followed Grant down the hallway, then through a courtyard. She focused on the back of his head. *Had he given himself a haircut again?* It looked a little wonky. Then she noticed they weren't heading toward HR.

"Where are we going?"

"To my meeting in building two. You'll sit in the back and work. If we're lucky, they'll call on me to present the quarterly numbers near the end and you'll be ready to feed me the data. The *correct* data. Forget the graphs for now."

She stopped cold. *I'm not being fired?*

"Come on. Stop dallying." Grant waved her forward, continuing his stride.

She rushed up behind him. Her heart was beating so fast. Fast from their walking pace. Fast from the exhilaration of keeping her job. At least for now.

How much longer could she keep all these balls in the air? She was failing. Failing hard. Last night she forgot to call Marcelo at their regular time. But he hadn't called her to find out why. *Did he forget too?* Or was he mad at her?

She would call him tonight. After she checked on Fred. She should probably bring Fred some dinner. That's what you do when someone passes, right? *Bring over a covered dish?* Her cooking was terrible. Pizza was always a good option. Did he like pizza? *Do old people even like toppings?*

They arrived at the meeting room.

Grant looked at her. "Are you all right? You seem a million miles away."

She bit her lip. "I'm fine." Quickly scanning the room, she dashed to the back row of seats furthest from the projection screen.

Opening her laptop, she began entering data. As the division managers arrived, they gave her odd looks. She nodded a shy greeting but quickly returned to typing.

Now every manager in the company is wondering what kind of screw-up I am. Her cheeks felt hot. The center of the conference table held an assortment of cookies, donuts and bottles of spring water. She longed for one of the water bottles to sooth her throat. *Were they meant for everyone? Even someone as lowly and uninvited as she was?*

Division heads kept arriving. She glanced at Grant, who was chatting with the woman next to him at the main table.

Jenna made her move, flowing in between those arriving to snatch a bottle of water, then returning to her seat. *Just in time.*

The owner of the company walked in. Everyone stood and sat down again. She tried not to listen to the meeting, needing to concentrate on her task. Her fingers clacking on the keyboard caused managers to give her odd looks. Jenna's cheeks burned but she kept her head down.

After twenty minutes, she finished the report in record time, celebrating by opening her water bottle and taking a sip. But somehow, in her nervous state, she dribbled water all down the front of her blouse. A few of the managers noticed and snickered. Others at the table noticed the others gaze and looked over.

She had nothing to dry herself with. Grant pushed back his chair, picked up some napkins from the table. He handed them to her and whispered, "E-mail them now and go."

She nodded and he returned to the main table. She transmitted the numbers and gathered her laptop. *But now what?* Should she say "excuse me?" Or should she just stand up and go while people were speaking? *What's the protocol?*

She stood, looking to Grant for instruction. He shook his head and put a finger to his lips, indicating silence. Clasping the laptop to her chest, she strode to the glass door. Several people looked at her. She held her breath, easing the door closed, inch by inch, to minimize sound. Grant staring at her through the glass.

It was a grim look.

She was toast.

And her hopes of keeping her job appeared shaky at best.

* * *

Grant hadn't spoken to her the rest of the work day. She wasn't sure if that was a bad sign or if this meant everything was good. To avoid future disasters, she set up a series of scheduled tasks in her Outlook calendar to ensure she got future reports in at least three days early.

After work, she picked up a large pepperoni pizza. The smell of it on the passenger seat, steamy, cheesy, made her stomach ache with longing. With the debacle at work earlier, she worked through lunch to catch up. The nervous knots in her stomach, waiting for Grant to come back from the morning meeting, had suppressed her appetite. In hindsight, skipping lunch was a bad idea.

She lifted a corner of the box. Perhaps she could steal a small portion of crust. *Would Fred notice? Just a tiny crumb…*

No, she couldn't defile a grieving widower's dinner. That would be a new low. She resolved to do better in life.

It was close to six when she got home. The sun was setting. She marched the pizza up to Fred's door and rang his doorbell. His apartment window was dark.

The door opened. Fred said, "Oh, you." He was wearing a robe and slippers, his hair disheveled. *Had he been sleeping? Great, waking a heart-broken old man.*

"How are you doing? I tried to track you down this morning. But…ah. I…um…brought you dinner." She presented the box to Fred.

He cocked his head to the side and scowled. "What kind?"

"Pepperoni."

Fred scratched his chin. "Extra cheese?"

"No. I didn't…"

"Fine." He pulled the box out of her hands and closed the door in her face.

She turned around on his doorstep and scanned the area. She rubbed her forehead. *Was he serious?* Grieving or not, that was very rude.

Jenna turned back and knocked. "Mr. Blesky?"

He opened the door, still holding the box. "What?"

"I'm worried about you."

"Oh, like you can help. Well, ya can't. What do you know about any of this? Not one damn thing. You're just a teenager. Go play a video game or post something on Facebook or…whatever foolish thing your generation does. Leave me alone."

He closed the door, but Jenna pushed back against it. He was surprisingly strong despite using only one arm.

"Fred, stop."

He stopped pushing and Jenna fell into his apartment, breaking her fall with her hands and knees onto the cold vinyl floor. "Ow."

Fred walked away, toward his kitchen, carrying the flat box.

She got up and inspected her hands. Scrapes on her palms with traces of blood peeking through.

"What the hell's wrong with you?" Jenna shouted, following him. She flipped the switch by the door and an overhead dome light came on. The light seemed blinding compared to the previous blackness. "Shoot. Sorry. I didn't mean that. Look, I just want to know how you're doing and what I can do to help. You need people around you now. Why are you being such a butthole to me?"

He placed the pizza on the counter. "Jenna, you seem like a sweet kid.

Don't waste your time with the likes of me. I'm not a good man. I left…I left Ava all alone in that rotten place…for years. I wasn't with…." Fred placed his hands over his eyes. A blast of sound emanated from him like that of a cow but deeper. *Perhaps a distressed buffalo?* Then recognizable human sobs, drops running down the side of his nose. He smeared them around his wrinkled face. "Just go." He grabbed a nearby dishtowel, blew his nose into it and threw it on the floor, kicking it to the side.

Now she understood. He was angry. Angry at himself. She needed to diffuse the situation. The best tool was distraction. Like when her mom got angry in the evenings, Jenna would turn on a sitcom and mom would forget to be upset.

"I'm starving. Let's eat." She took off her coat and placed it on the counter, opened a kitchen cabinet and took down two plates.

Fred's arms dropped to his sides. He stared at the pizza box, then wiped his nose again, but this time with a paper napkin. "Okay."

She put a couple slices on each plate and handed him one. "I'm just going to be here for you and listen. We don't have to talk if you don't want to. But I intend to eat first."

"Yeah, you're looking a little thin." He folded his slice and bit into the pointed end.

She inspected herself. Wearing her usual outfit of black trousers and a button-down white shirt, she didn't discern any weight change. "It's the stupid party. But I don't want to bore you with that." Because she was chewing and talking with her mouth open, this sounded like "Ba ah dunt wan ta bah yuh wit tha."

He took his plate and sat at the dinette table. "It would get my mind off things. I've been trying to write her obituary. Well, she wrote it herself years ago, but it needs updating. The funeral home needs it in the morning."

She joined him at the table and finished chewing. "I was the editor of my high school newspaper senior year. I can work with you on it if you'd like."

He opened a leather folder on the table. He rifled through and took out a piece of paper. "Here ya go. I started a markup, but having another set of eyes…"

"Absolutely." Jenna slid her plate to the side. Studying the page, Ava's life was fascinating. "She was a math teacher? That's wonderful. I love math and science."

"Yeah, she was the brains of the operation. Until…you know."

Jenna couldn't imagine what it was like to have a relative with Alzheimer's. Particularly a spouse that no longer remembered you. She asked about Ava's earlier life. "Did she teach locally?"

"No, back in Brooklyn, before we got married and had kids. I always wonder if she would have been happier working. But those days, that's just how it was. She never complained."

"Looks like she did lots of volunteer work."

"It's not in there, but she was an advocate. Raised money locally and through our Congressman to have the new library built. Well, new like decades ago. If you ask me, they should have named it after her."

"That's amazing. You must be so proud of her."

"Yep. After our son left home, she held workshops at the library every Saturday, reading stories to kindergartners. Wait, I think I have a clipping." He walked out of the room.

Jenna used the opportunity to grab a third slice, stuffing it into her mouth indelicately. Looking down, orange oil had dripped onto her white shirt. Why was she so clumsy lately? She dabbed at the spot, only to spread the stain further.

When he returned, he held a large cardboard box, the top open, filled with books, photo albums, and miscellaneous greeting cards. "This is her box of goodies. That's what she called it. All the sentimental stuff she had with her at the home. I haven't seen most of this in years."

Jenna recalled Rae going through her mom's belongings, specifically her jewelry box. That had been a tough time. With every touch of a ring or necklace, more memories, emotions, and hugs in between. Some boxes Rae didn't open for weeks or months, knowing what lay inside. Like her mom's baby bracelet or the locket Rae gave her for Christmas the previous year.

Now Fred had a box full of what were probably similar sentimental items. To Jenna, it might as well have been filled with hand grenades. But emotional ones, where if you looked at them too long, they'd rip your heart out of your chest.

"Hey, if it becomes too much, you don't have to show me."

He took out a news clipping. "See, she wore her favorite dress to the fundraising dinner. God, she loved that dress. The perfect shade of red, she called it. I nicknamed it the devil dress. Cause she was red hot and smokin'. Ha. Really more like an angel, in truth. I still keep it in my closet."

The picture was black and white and the paper faded to a dusty yellow, but she could see his wife was an elegant woman. "She looks beautiful."

He scratched his chin. "I bet that dress would fit you."

"What? No. Wouldn't someone else in your family want it?"

"I only had a son, Gabriel. He's married, but it wouldn't fit his wife Patricia anyways. Plus, I think Ava would have wanted someone to love her dress the way she did. I'll get it."

Before she could protest, he bounced up and was off again. She followed him to his bedroom and stood in the doorway. He located the dress easily. There were only two women's items hung inside of the wide, shallow closet.

"Here ya go." He took out the dress, covered in a thin plastic garment bag, thick dust on the shoulders. Holding it up towards her, he said, "Yep, thought so. The red looks good with your complexion."

"No, Fred. I couldn't." With her track record, she'd ruin it in no time. The new stain on her blouse was evidence.

He shoved the dress at her. "You want to make an old man happy? Shut up and take it. You're doing me a favor."

How was this a favor? She didn't understand. But he seemed almost angry again. She played along. "Thank you, Fred. I'll take good care of it." The fabric looked like satin and the label read 'Prada'. It must have been expensive.

"Now, enough said about that." He dusted off his hands on his brown cardigan and headed back to the kitchen table.

They spent about an hour going through Ava's box of treasures and revising the obituary. When Jenna looked up at the clock on Fred's stove, she gasped. "I've got to go. I need to feed Thumper and call Marcelo. God, they're both going to kill me."

Fred chuckled, "Thumper's the cat, right? Yeah, sounds about right. But who's Marcelo?"

She looked through her handbag for her phone, wondering if he'd tried to call her. "He's my boyfriend. Lives near Syracuse." *Where was it?* Her hand fished through the bottom of her bag. *Did it slide under the torn lining again?* "Oh, my God."

"What's wrong?"

The realization sunk in. "Mindy still has my phone. She took it this morning. In all the chaos, I forgot."

"Well, this Marcelo guy will have to get over it. Did I tell you that one time I was called up for the Navy Reserves for an entire month and didn't talk with Ava for weeks? That's how it was. No need to talk frivolously every single day. Heck, everyone is so tied to phones now. It's good to take a break."

"Still, I should still go." She put on her coat and picked up the dress hung from a hook by the door.

He opened the door for her.

"Can I come by tomorrow?" she asked.

"Suit yourself."

She draped the dress carefully across her arm and found a piece of paper in her bag and wrote her phone number. "I'll pick up dinner again. Text me what you want. Something takeout."

He took her number. "Okey-dokey."

"Have a good night, Fred." As soon as the words left her, she realized how stupid it sounded. His wife died less than sixteen hours ago. How was he going to have a good *anything*?

She winced. "Um, you know what I mean. Sorry." She hugged the garment bag and walked out.

The door shut behind her and the frigid night air stung her face.

Jenna was sure that Thumper would forgive her delay. He was easily persuaded with food and an extended tummy rub. *But Marcelo?*

Climbing the stairs, she remembered the time she couldn't visit Marcelo on his birthday. How he pouted for a couple days. And then it blew over. Marcelo could run hot and cold. But Rae had been the same way. And her own mom. Temperamental. Borderline bipolar. Some people were like that. She tried not to let it bother her.

Although she wondered why she was always the stable one in all these relationships. Did she let people take advantage of her good nature? Still, it felt nice being needed, relied on. She liked to imagine if she were in trouble, the people in her life would rise to the occasion and support her.

Hopefully that day would never come.

Chapter 7

The next morning, Jenna pulled into the Veloma parking lot, earlier than usual; only a handful of cars present. It was still pitch-black outside. When she entered the office, her quadrant of the building was dark. She walked to the bank of switches and turned on all the overhead lights.

Without her phone, anxiety and uncertainty clouded every waking thought. She desperately hoped Mindy realized the mistake and left the phone in her cube. She'd been able to catch up on emails with her laptop last night; messaging Marcelo but didn't get a reply. Perhaps he'd tried to call her and went to bed early?

As she approached her row, she noticed an odd explosion of colorful paper atop someone's cube. Something wasn't right. The office was normally gray. Gray carpet. Gray file cabinets. Light gray fabric partitions. Surrounded by dull, off-white walls.

She reached her cube and gasped. Pink and purple crepe paper streamers crisscrossed the top of her space. Red construction paper hearts taped to her walls. A wastepaper basket sat upside down on her chair, decorated with more paper to look like a wedding cake, with a cardboard cutout topper of a man and woman that read, "Mr. & Mrs. Jack Ass."

A mock wedding invitation was taped to her monitor. In large lettering it read:

Please join us for a Beastly Shower
In horror of Ms. Raven West
@ The eighth circle of hell, Altoona PA
RSVP by 2 weeks ago (time travel optional)
Registry: Central NJ Suppository Outlet

Who had done this? Mindy? Was this an attempt to be funny? Because it was anything but. She didn't need this aggravation.

She looked around. At least no one was in yet to see this debacle.

With a scowl, she ripped down the streamers and began putting her workspace back together. Crumpling the colored paper and forcing it into her foot-high metal trash can. After she finished, the overflowing bin looked like she'd just mutilated a Powerpuff Girls themed birthday party. She took the trash to the dumpster outside, bent on destroying all trace of her humiliation. On her way down the hall, she didn't see any other employees. Perhaps she was out of the woods.

Back at her cube, she opened all her drawers and overhead storage shelves. No sign of her phone. She turned on her computer. No emails from Mindy. Based on the time, Mindy would arrive in thirty minutes.

She spied the 'economy size' bottle of aspirin in her top drawer. Rattling it, there were a handful left compared to the five hundred it once contained. Perhaps it was time to slow down on the aspirin. She reclined in her chair and stared at the ceiling, breathing in and out slowly, trying to calm her nerves. It wasn't working. Frozen with anxiety, she heard a voice. *Grant.*

"Good morning," he sang out, hurrying past her cube toward his office. She could only see the back of his head above the partition.

Did Grant know about the prank? He was a 'cool' boss. At least that's how he described himself with his self-deprecating humor. Not much older than most of the folks in his division. A screenshot of the movie Office Space hung on his wall, where the principal characters were beating a printer with a baseball bat; the words, "Die, Motherf**ker" scrawled in black marker across it.

The staff often played pranks on him, and he took it very well. Even taking part himself. Like the time one of the guys chained an old rusty bucket to his chair. He had reciprocated by surreptitiously smearing petroleum jelly over the offender's monitor. But with the fear of escalation, Grant sent out an email warning that pranks would not be tolerated.

She followed behind him. As he unlocked his office door, she asked, "Do you know what time Mindy is coming in?"

"The usual, I suppose. Why?" He entered his room and dropped his laptop bag on his desk. He wore a light blue dress shirt with a green striped tie and pleated khaki trousers.

She leaned against his doorway. "Um, she has my phone." She avoided eye contact and picked at her cuticles. "Hey, Grant?"

He appeared preoccupied, inserting his laptop into the docking station. Without looking up he said, "Yes?"

Digging her hands into her pockets, she said, "Are we okay? I'm sorry about yesterday."

Grant took off his coat and hung it on his coat tree. He smoothed his tie. "You're fine. Just don't do that to me again." He looked at her over his rimless bifocals, his eyes stern.

She nodded. "Absolutely. You can count on me."

"Good." He extended his arm, pointing to the doorframe. His usual signal for "dismissed."

She returned to her desk. A few minutes later, Mindy stopped by, grinning, still wearing her coat.

"You cleaned that up fast," Mindy said. She took Jenna's phone out of her purse and handed it to her.

Jenna swiveled in her chair with her arms crossed. "Yeah, you got me. Ha, ha."

"Oh, don't be mad. A few of us went out for drinks after work. When I mentioned I had your phone, Russ and George swiped it from me. They figured out the pass code. Not difficult." She pointed to her Groot bobble-head toy on her shelf. "But they got carried away reading your emails."

She recalled she once joked to Mindy and George her passwords were 'Thumper', 'Marcelo', or 'Groot'. In hindsight, that was a stupid thing to do. She couldn't even remember the context of how the subject of passwords came up before. But that was no excuse for what they did. "Why didn't you stop them?"

"Oh, Jenna, you had to be there. It was epic. They acted out the emails and texts from Blanche and Raven. Using the worst impersonations. The entire bar was in stitches. Well, drinking all those shots didn't help…wait, I think I drank most of the shots. Russ only drinks diet soda. Anyway, Russ and George suggested we come back to the office to customize your decor. It was a riot. They cleaned out the break room of all the leftover party decorations. We thought it would cheer you up."

"Cheer me up? You're lucky I got here early enough to take it down before Grant arrived. He already thinks I'm a screw-up." She swiveled faster, holding her forehead in both hands, fixated on the dirty commercial carpet tiles. "Honestly, I know you were just having fun, but please, I can't take much more."

"Oh, honey. I'm sorry. That Raven chick is a nightmare. She texted you last night. Said you need to instruct all the guests to wear white. For some group photos. Like you're supposed to email over a hundred people listing the fashion rules. Why are you letting her do this to you?"

An excellent question. But the answer was simple. Because Raven was her best friend and the person she'd relied on to survive her childhood.

As she tried to formulate an answer that didn't seem irrational or sad, Mindy continued, "Hey, let me make it up to you. Take you to lunch? Anywhere you want to go."

Eating food away from her desk sounded awesome. But she mapped out every minute of her day with tasks. "I can't. I have to send out the next batch of invitations. I barely have enough time to get to the post office and back." Did she even have time to add the 'wear white' note?

Mindy frowned. "The post office? That's insane. Why not send out riders on fucking ponies? They would get there faster. With your timeframe, why wouldn't all the invitations be electronic? Just use e-mail."

Jenna sighed. "Blanche insists that mailed paper invitations are the *classy* way to go. She's paying for everything. I can't win."

"Fine. Tell you what. I'll go with you to the post office and I bet Russ would go out and bring us back lunch. What do you say?"

"Sure." Jenna should have smiled back but still felt only defeat. Some caffeine would help. "I'm going to get some coffee."

"I could use some too. Let me drop off my coat."

Mindy scampered away. Jenna checked her phone. The power was down to ten percent. She plugged it in and checked her texts. As described, there were several from Blanche, Raven, and Candy, the party planner.

When Mindy returned, Jenna saw a text from Marcelo. "Give me one second."

The text came in at two a.m. last night. *What could he be texting at that late hour?* She opened it. It read, "T, U up?" with a bare-chested picture of himself standing in front of his gigantic television. From the military-clad figures on the screen, he'd been playing the game Call of Duty. But the focus of the picture seemed to be on his pecs and not the game.

Who was 'T'?

Her breathing stopped. Marcelo had a cute neighbor named Teresa. There were a couple times she noticed his gaze linger on Teresa's cleavage as she walked down the hall of his apartment building. He had laughed about it, saying he didn't like women with such enormous bosoms…that he found them grotesque. But Teresa looked like a Kardashian. Hardly grotesque to most men.

Although, Terrence was the name of Marcelo's college roommate. Sometimes Marcelo played video games through the night. Was he asking Terrence to join him?

Mindy rapped her knuckles on the metal frame of her cube wall, snatching her out of her stupor. "What is it? Are you all right?"

No, she was not okay. Not close at all.

Marcelo had been growing distant for weeks. She thought it was her imagination. Or something that would be remedied by the next long weekend together. With the party coming up, she wouldn't be able to confront him in person for another two weeks. Should she break it off now? Save the trip? Or give him a chance to explain.

"Jenn, coffee?" Mindy tapped on the wall.

"Um, sure." She plugged in her phone to charge it and got up to follow Mindy to the break room.

She couldn't think about Marcelo right now. Today was a Customer Support day. Fielding calls from ten to four from little old ladies trying to un-jam their printers. Yes, she needed coffee right now more than anything. Before the onslaught. Before the endless attacks on her patience.

No, Marcelo could wait.

Perhaps forever? *Possibly.*

Something had to give.

And it could easily be her health or sanity.

* * *

It was the twentieth call of the day. Her phone headset was digging into the side of her head. She rubbed the area and adjusted the plastic head band.

Customer service was a tiered system. As a last resort, genuine humans fielded calls from users unsatisfied with the AI customer service rep. Unfortunately, it was Tuesday, and she was one of those humans. Customers were spun up and frustrated by the time they reached her.

Sometimes she spent more time placating customers than solving their problems. It was best for her to follow the 'script' and she knew it by heart.

"Hello, thank you for calling Veloma Office Solutions. My name is Jenna. What is the nature of your issue?"

"I've been on hold for a half hour. Are you a fucking actual person?"

"Yes, sir. My name is Jenna. What can I help you with today?"

"My printer won't work."

"I'm sorry to hear that. What model is it?"

"The Velo-2003."

"And when did it stop working?"

"It was fine until I got my new laptop."

"Is your new computer running Windows 10 or higher?"

"I don't know."

"What version of Windows did your previous laptop use?"

"I don't know."

Jenna sighed. She knew the likely cause of the problem, even without the answers to these questions. *Was it worth walking him through the process?* Probably not. But it was her job.

Over the next ten minutes, they went back and forth. She described what icons to hit, what menus to select. Finally, her original suspicion was confirmed.

She took a deep breath. "Sir, unfortunately your printer's drivers are incompatible with your new operating system."

"What does that mean? Can you send me a new driver?"

"Sir, your printer is twenty years old. We don't have software available that works with modern operating systems."

"Great, you're telling me my printer is junk? That you don't stand behind your products when it gets inconvenient? Motherfu…"

"Sir, I understand your frustration. I can send you a coupon code for our new Velo-2020. It prints forty pages a minute and uses eco-ink, that will save you money in the long term."

"I paid $600 for my printer."

"You'll see our newest printers cost a fraction of that. Would you like me to send a discount code for ten percent off? What's your email address?"

"What? So you can put me on some goddamned mailing lists, clog up my inbox, and sell my personal data to the Russians? No, thank you. You fucking corporations. Always pushing folks to spend money. Hard earned money on your crap pieces of shit."

"Is there anything else I can do for you today?"

There was no response. Just a dead line.

She had another three hours of calls to take. It was amazing how unsatisfied users were with the support hotline system. The script didn't help. It honestly made her seem like a robot. Or more like a tin can to be kicked and despised. She imagined Blanche calling in. That would be funny. Could she resist the urge to tell her directions that would wipe her entire computer clean? Irretrievable. Brick-like.

The next call arrived. She adjusted the headset again and hit the flashing button.

"Hello, thank you for calling Veloma Office Solutions. My name is Jenna. What is the nature of your issue?"

"My printer is jammed."

Jams were the worst. Often people broke the little plastic tabs on the roller when trying to dislodge crinkled paper making the problem far worse. Why did the company make the most crucial components out of the flimsiest stuff? How much money did the company save in production compared to sending out warranty replacement parts? On her own home printer, she fashioned her own parts out of aluminum and epoxy at her small workbench. If only she could design the next printer. The folks in development had no interest in the maintenance or repair side of the company.

She kept a running list of the things she would change or redesign for each printer model. Some were simple software diagnostics tweaks. Others involved simple redesigns of basic parts. Often the issues came from sources of supply that didn't meet any kind of reliability standard. Circuit boards that easily fried or springs that lost elasticity. Stupid stuff like that.

From the call center report, there were at least a hundred calls a week that all boiled down to a bad tension spring. A spring they spent two dollars in mailing and another twenty dollars in call-center labor. For a two-cent part. It made no sense.

After a few more calls, her lunch break arrived. Surely, Grant would want to know about this spring nonsense.

She knocked on his doorframe. He turned. From his screen, he appeared to be approving timesheets. "Yes, Jenna?"

"I've been on call center duty today."

"Everyone's favorite."

"I guess. Um, I wanted to talk to you about something. Is this a good time?"

"Sure, what's on your mind?"

She showed him the data she'd collected on the number of calls, price data for parts, the whole lot.

"By my calculations, the company could save ten thousand dollars a year by changing vendors of the tension springs."

"Do you know how much design changes cost? Renegotiating contracts? Supply chain issues? Might not be worth it."

"Design changes? It's an interchangeable part. Same dimensions. Same everything. Except better quality."

"The last time we had a production change, it took six months."

"What? Why so long?"

"Not sure. I can look into it."

"I have a list of small things we could change to improve quality and save money long-term."

"And I'm glad to hear them. Tell you what, generate a white paper for me, with cost analysis. I'll bring it to the design team lead during our standing meeting this time next week."

"Next week?"

"Yep. Get it to me first thing Friday so I have time to look it over."

"But I have call center on Thursday."

"Well, you had best use your time wisely then, right?"

She wanted the opportunity to show her worth to Grant, but two days to research and write a coherent analysis? She couldn't say no. Not after yesterday's screw up. "Um, sure."

"You should go get a sandwich. You're looking pale." He turned away from her, focusing back on his screen. She took it as a signal to leave.

Shit. One more thing on her plate.

A bad realization came. She needed to be at the post office. She wasted half of her thirty-minute lunch break. Could she make it now? Would Mindy could go for her? She could hear Mindy's jeering now. It was commonplace for employees to go out to lunch and take a full hour. Management often looked the other way, as long as staff didn't abuse the privilege. But Jenna still felt like a newbie. Someone still on probation. She didn't want to operate outside the official lunch time.

But this batch of shower invitations were for folks who wouldn't be coming to the party, right? She could send them out tomorrow. Would anyone know the difference?

Walking back to her cube, she mentally tallied the recent turmoil to her life.

> ➢ Food poisoning

> ➢ A best friend with a mystery illness
> ➢ Planning a party from hell
> ➢ A sweet elderly neighbor losing his wife
> ➢ Nearly getting fired
> ➢ Becoming the laughingstock of the office
> ➢ Possibly a cheating boyfriend
> ➢ Self-inflicting herself with a ridiculous project deadline

And to make matters worse, she had a nearly dead car and kept forgetting to eat. What else could go wrong?

One day at a time. That was all she could handle. Perhaps one hour at a time. She reached for more aspirin. The bottle was almost empty. She popped the last two in her mouth and checked the clock.

Time was running out.

In so many ways.

She reclined in her office chair and closed her eyes. Despite the ambient noise of voices, phones and metal file drawers closing around her, she relaxed, dozed off, began to dream.

Thumper was sitting in Grant's office, human-sized, wearing Grant's suit, asking her for the recipe for fried cod. Russ came by, but instead of his usual body, Russ had the body of a kangaroo, with short arms and a pouch containing M&Ms, asking if Grant had a three-hole punch. The two asked her to help them look for it, going row by row through the office on a scavenger hunt. Thumper called out, "Huzzah!" when he found a dead mouse instead. She felt repulsed when Thumper—with no hesitation—cut it in two, giving the back end to Russ, each eating their half with packets of hot sauce applied liberally.

She woke to the sound of her phone ringing; a white paper bag placed on her desk. A post-it from Mindy said it contained fish tacos, her favorite. She felt her face. A bit of drool on her cheek. What a sight she must have been.

Jenna reached for the phone and began her script. As the customer relayed the problem, she nibbled on the tacos, thankful Mindy came to her aid.

At least someone wanted to help. But would that be enough?

Something had to change. She just needed to get through March 4th. Only two more weeks.

Yes, should could do it. Even if it killed her.

Chapter 8

It was the end of the day. Eighty calls. Not a record, but still a top five day. She knew other folks dallied with each call, to reduce their stress and avoid burnout. Only she couldn't help but want to assist these people who spent all that time waiting on-hold, listening to the most awful elevator music. Actually, the music was worse than awful. It was a scratchy melody interrupted by a robo-voice every two minutes telling them to find their solution through the website.

That made her laugh. Their website was a joke. The only useful part was the user forum, where end users posted their complaints and bush-fixes. Despite working on the new user manual for the next printer model, she learned so much from the workarounds and suggestions on the forum. One time she posted an anonymous 'fix' herself. The responses were positively glowing for her secret posting.

At work, she routinely edited updates to user manuals, trying to add genuinely helpful information, but her suggestions were rejected. Apparently, the stuff she wanted to add would be an admission by the company that they had a 'flawed product', which obviously wasn't the case in management's eyes.

Jenna didn't consider herself the subversive type. When a system wasn't working, it was best to fix it properly instead of tinkering around the edges. But it was very tempting to post more secret 'hacks' to the user forum.

As she gathered her coat and bag to leave for the day, Russ came by.

"Hey, Jenna." Russ had a long face. He leaned his six-foot one body against the corner of her partition. His sandy brown hair was a kind of cow-licked mop, like in Good Will Hunting. Despite being a few years older than her, his face was boyish, with a couple pimples on his forehead.

What did he want? He had a lot of nerve… "Hey," she said, not making eye contact, instead focusing on the buttons of her coat.

"I wanted to say sorry. We got a little carried away. Mindy said you were sore. I just thought it would give you a laugh."

She gave a half-smile. "I know you didn't intend to be mean…"

"Absolutely not. When I saw those emails? My heart went out to you. That lady Blanche is a nightmare. The groom's mom? Right?"

She noticed a button missing on Russ's shirt collar; the collar point curled oddly, jutting out.

What could she say? She agreed? That wouldn't really help. No, it was better to carry on and not dwell on Blanche. "Russ, I need to get going. A friend's wife just died. My boyfriend might be cheating on me… I just…I'm tired and want to get home."

"Sure. Just wanted to apologize. And if your boyfriend is cheating on you, he must be a real idiot. You're the nicest person in this rat's nest."

"Thanks." She recalled her dream earlier where Thumper and Russ shared the mouse. Maybe it was a rat's nest. She squinted at him. "Hey, you're a guy."

He looked at her blankly, then arched one eyebrow in mock suspicion. "I'd like to think so?"

"Can you keep this to yourself? If I show you something?"

"Yes, no problem." He raised a hand. "Scout's honor."

She showed him the early a.m. text from Marcelo and explained about the sexy neighbor and gaming friend. "What do you make of this?"

"Hmmm. Ah." Russ frowned. "Well, you know him best." He dug his hands in his pockets and looked at the ground.

"That bad?"

Russ whistled through his teeth. "I'm not saying a thing. Ugh. Yikes. Well… I think you have reason for concern. Dudes don't send shirtless pictures to each other. Generally. I mean, I don't know. You know? Forget I said anything. Really." Russ rocked on his heels. "But now I'm kind of dying to know what he says when you ask him."

So, she wasn't paranoid. Yet Russ's validation brought no relief. "Thanks, Russ. It helps to have an objective opinion." She picked up her handbag and brushed past him. "Have a good night."

She didn't look back but heard him say, "Hey, I'm heading out, too. Wait a sec."

She turned to watch him jog to his cubical, his head bobbing above the partitions. He strode back towards her with his coat and keys in hand. "I'll walk out with you."

They walked out to the parking lot in silence. Her car was in the front row. He waved, "See you tomorrow," as he continued on to his car a row further back.

It was a reasonably mild February evening. A rare occurrence. She wondered if Russ was being nicer to her now that she might be unattached soon. He was a little older. About seven years. But acted like a teenager with his juvenile sense of humor. No, she couldn't date a coworker. Too many instances of office romances had gone badly at Veloma. Despite outward professionalism, hostilities between certain individuals seemed to boil under the surface for years. Jenna had been on the job for only eight months but had learned a decade's worth of scandalous corporate history overhearing water-cooler gossip.

She turned the key in the ignition. Nothing. Not even a whine or rumble. She pulling the key out and reinserted it firmly. Turned it again, no dice.

With a heavy sigh, she got out and opened the hood. Her engine was a sooty mess. Nothing was detached as far as she could tell. The battery was connected. The serpentine belt was still holding on. It had to be electrical.

Jenna heard a car roll up slowly, and a man's voice, "What's the problem?"

She glanced around the hood to identify the driver. It was Russ.

"Car won't start."

Russ leaned over his center console, to make eye contact. "Want me to try?"

"I turn the key and nothing happens. But the battery is less than three months old."

He parked his car in place. He opened his door and faced her over the roof of his car. "Probably the alternator. That's a costly job. How old is your car?"

"Ancient. Like, he has a cassette player, old." She wasn't sure why the car was suddenly a 'he', but it seemed appropriate.

He laughed. "You should really get a new car. Does it even have airbags?"

Russ had a point. Her car was a death trap. "Nope. It hardly has a rear fender." She pointed to the back, where the bumper sloped downward, held on with a roll's worth of duct tape on the right side.

She considered calling a tow truck, but how long would that take? "Um, you live south of here, right?"

He waved her over. "I can drive you home. Hop in."

She closed the hood of her car, locked the driver's door, and got into Russ's car. "Thanks. I live between Route 38 and 70."

Russ drove a dark-colored Honda Accord. Not a brand-new model, but not a beater either. A respectively bland and reliable vehicle. A tinge of envy washed over her. What would it be like to get in a car and just drive…the thought of breaking down not even crossing your mind? That would be a real measurement of success in life.

She gave him her address, and he used a navigation app.

"That's not too far from my place. I'm a couple miles southeast." Russ drove off. He didn't talk too much for the first few minutes. Her fears of him coming on to her melted away. Not that Russ was a creep. But it was best to keep one's guard up in these situations.

When he began talking, he asked her about her day. She told him of her project, summarizing all her low-cost design solutions. He asked her a few questions about it, but mostly she yammered on about a few of the more idiotic customer support questions. A few of them were funny. Like the time last November, a customer put ketchup in the magenta ink cartridge. When George heard about that, he left ketchup packets on her desk every day for a week.

Russ said, "Hey, did I ever tell you about the radio contest?"

The way he said it, she was almost afraid to ask. "No…what contest?"

"Well, when I was an intern, a bunch of us were working late. Must have been seven years ago. Someone dared me to take a photocopy of my butt on the new DEXPRINT-200. It's that massive office printer model. You know it?"

"Yeah, I've heard of it."

"They offered me fifty bucks. So, not one to back down from the challenge, I hopped on up, bare cheeks and all. BOOM! Glass breaks. I'm now stuck *inside* the copier, glass shards all around my sensitive areas. The guys lost it."

She cringed. "Ouch."

"Ouch all right. They had to pull me out. But first they tortured me by running the copier a couple times and man, I tell you, that thing is hot."

"That's awful."

"Well, in hindsight, it was funny. I got out mostly unscathed. But that's only part of the story."

"Huh? There's more?"

"There was a radio contest a couple months later. Call the radio station with the funniest true story and listeners would later vote for the best. I got through and told the story on the air. Wouldn't you know it, the people voted, and I won a free trip to Disney World." Russ grinned ear to ear.

Her apartment complex came into view.

"I'm glad it worked out."

"Hey," he slowed down the car and looked her in the eyes, "management doesn't know how the copier broke. Keep it between us, okay? I mean, it was years ago, but still." He parked in front of her place.

"Yeah, no problem. Thanks again for the ride."

"Have a nice night. See ya on the flip side."

She got out quickly and watched him drive away. He was such a screwball. She managed a small laugh, but as his car disappeared, she quickly wondered with alarm how she would get to work the next day.

Mass transit was nearly non-existent in this part of New Jersey. Ride sharing apps might work, but for how long? Her mom always told her ride-shares were unsafe and cited news stories about women being held up at knife point or worse. Not the safest option for a petite young woman. Not that she was scared. Not exactly. Not always.

No, she needed a car. It didn't need to be extravagant, but new. New-ish. New-adjacent, at least. Less than fifty thousand miles. From a non-smoker. No history of accidents. Well maintained.

After she fed Thumper, she called Raven. She didn't want to. But what choice did she have? It was the best option she could think of. If it saved her considerable money, she could deal with the devil.

When Raven answered, Jenna exhaled. "Hey, remember that offer?" She pulled her hands into fists and tensed her jaw as she uttered, "I need to take you up on it."

* * *

Asking Rae for help was difficult; but not as difficult as the next call she needed to make that evening.

Marcelo.

Should she check on her neighbor Fred first? Would Fred have good advice about how to confront Marcelo over his late-night text? She hadn't known Fred long, but could imagine him saying something like, "Just ask him, straight up. Grow some balls. No hedging."

Asking Rae for advice would be her usual move, but that would come with a different humiliation. And there was no way to talk to her mom about this. Her mom thought Marcelo was too good for her. She'd only said that openly once, when plastered. Alcohol was mom's truth serum sometimes. But other times, caused her to rant and spew hate that amounted to nonsense words. Even if she could catch mom on a sober night, she didn't trust her advice, nor could she trust her mom not to throw this back in her face at a later time.

It would be easier for everyone for her to end it. Over the last couple of months, Marcelo rarely talked about their future and she couldn't commute to see him forever. Two weekends ago, she asked whether he'd consider moving to New Jersey after he got his graduate degree; he seemed noncommittal. Breaking up was the logical choice. If Marcelo was tempted by other women, perhaps their ending was an eventuality.

She sat on the edge of her bed, Thumper at her side, when she dialed his number.

He picked up on the sixth ring. Not that she was counting. She took a deep breath.

"Hey, Jenna. You're calling early. I missed you last night." There was a smile in his voice.

"Hey. Missed you too. I've been having an awful couple of days. My car just died."

"Well, I'm not surprised. What are you going to do?"

What was she going to do? "Buy a new one. If I can afford it. It doesn't make sense to keep repairing."

"Do you think you'll be able to come up this weekend?"

Her head began spinning. Did she have the time? Probably not. Asking him about the text in person might be better. Or it could be far worse. "Sorry. I don't think I can." She paused, swallowing air. "I need to ask you something."

Marcelo said, "I would come down to you, but I have an early meeting with my thesis advisor on Monday."

"No. I mean, that's not what I wanted to ask."

"Do you need help with a down payment for your car? I could lend you a few hundred."

This was getting more difficult. She would have to blurt it out. "I saw your text to Theresa last night."

There was a long pause. "What?"

"You sent it to me by mistake."

Another long pause. "I don't know what you're talking about."

It was her time to pause. "Look. I know a long-distance relationship is hard. I love you. Just be honest with me. I won't be mad. I promise."

"Shit." Another long pause. "I'm...I can't believe you. Um. Okay, I've...got to go." Marcelo hung up.

She stared at her phone for a minute. Did he just break up with her? Without saying goodbye?

Her throat closed up, and she gasped for air. Tears welled and her nose ran. She reached for Thumper to give him a hug and he leapt away from her with a "grrr". Instead, she reached for a pillow and placed it on her chest, weeping into it. Did she do the right thing? Had she accused him of something he didn't do? Or was this the validation of her initial instinct?

After a few minutes of sobbing, her phone buzzed. A new text from Marcelo. It said, "I can't anymore. Please don't hate me."

Part of her *hated* him in that moment. The other part in a sea of confusion. She threw the phone on the floor. Then an odd crunching sound. Thumper was chewing the corner of the plastic case.

She wiped her eyes with the back of her hand and bent down to retrieve her phone. "Stupid cat." She opened her bedside table drawer and pulled out a ping-pong ball, and threw it out her bedroom door to the hallway. Thumper scampered after it.

A part of her was relieved. The other part devastated. Would anyone ever love her again? Should she have taken a job closer to Marcelo in the first place? Was it her own fault?

She wanted to drive to Raven's and curl up on her sofa. Talk through the whole situation. Raven was a great listener. Or had been. They hadn't had an actual heart to heart in ages.

It seemed like everyone was changing in front of her eyes. Was this part of growing up? If so, why wasn't she changing?

Ice cream for dinner was the logical choice. Not that she was hungry. After filling a bowl, she sat on the sofa and opened her laptop. She needed to research vehicles and interest rates on loans for her outing tomorrow morning. Solve one problem at a time.

Not that she considered Marcelo to be a problem. A person couldn't be a problem, right? And what if the distance was the problem? People just do the best they can in a situation.

Her mind raced. Would he take her back if she moved to Syracuse? She began searching online for jobs near Marcelo. There were some mechanical engineering jobs, but none of them seemed like a great fit. Not that her current job was incredibly satisfying.

It was close to eleven when she noticed the time. Why had she spent hours looking for a new job to be closer to a guy that didn't want her anymore? She regarded the pale blue ring on her left hand. Why was she still wearing it? Pathetic. Her mission was researching cars. Which ones had the best ratings. Which had good gas mileage, lowest cost of ownership, best warranties. And she should have been creating a spreadsheet of monthly payments based on bank rates to know the upper end of her budget.

She couldn't remain awake open any longer. Between crying and all the screen time, her eyes felt scratchy and raw. Sleep was the only cure.

Tomorrow was another day.

Another day to tackle problems.

And hopefully a day that didn't add new ones.

Chapter 9

Jenna took a taxi to the car dealership in Hamilton. It wasn't cheap, but there weren't other options. Dad was out of town and she obviously couldn't count on mom.

The Forero Automart had a vast lot of cars of all makes and models. The dealership building itself was a two-story gleaming white boxy structure with tall glass windows. Jaguars, Porsches and Land Rovers surrounded the entrance, punctuating the air of prestige. To the right of the tall principal building was a low structure providing a connection to a service center with four garage bays.

Rae was confident Jack would give her the wholesale price of any car she wanted. Not that she could even afford wholesale on a new car. She really didn't want to work a second job to pay for it. But Jack's family sold pre-owned cars as well. Rae assured her that there would be options in her budget.

Scanning the vehicles in the lot, there didn't appear to be anything remotely affordable. Her budget was ten grand to up to fifteen, assuming her fledgling credit score was good enough for decent financing. She wondered if there would be haggling. She despised haggling.

Leasing a car made no sense. There were too many stories of people penalized for going over annual mileage limits or for minor dents. Buying and keeping a low-cost car over a long-term was the most practical option.

Walking into the showroom, she felt exposed, vulnerable. Like a snow-shoe rabbit locked in a den of wolverines. As the bell jingled above the door, a half-dozen salespeople glanced over at her. Then they looked away, signaling they didn't take her seriously as a potential client. As much as she didn't want salespeople to assault her, not being worthy of their attention made her feel worse.

The main showroom was a tall structure with an open floor, cars down the middle and sales desks along the sides. Along the back wall, three glassed-in second floor offices looked down over the operation, like sentries.

She scanned each of the desk placards for Jack's.

But she couldn't help but glance at some sticker prices on the showroom floor. Gorgeous vehicles, mostly SUVs, with price tags over seventy-five thousand. What had she gotten herself into? This was not a dealership for someone like her. Someone that buys the lowest grade toilet paper to save a dollar on a twelve-roll. Still, she had made an appointment with Jack and needed to find him.

She took a deep breath and walked up a salesperson sitting at their desk, one of the many ignoring her. His nametag read, "Milton".

"Hello? My name's Jenna Mott. I'm looking for Jack Forero."

The obese, balding man in the pink button-down shirt and cheap suit stopped typing. "Is he expecting you?"

"Yes. I think so. He said to come at ten-thirty."

"Well, miss, I'll page him for you. You can get yourself a cup of coffee in the meantime. The guest lounge is around the corner, in the back to the right."

"Um, got it." She turned to look where he had pointed. It wasn't clear exactly where he meant, but when she looked back, Milton was on the phone, so she walked to the back and right, hoping a path would become clear.

As she passed by a red sports car, she read the sticker. *A hundred thousand dollars.* She was well out of her league here. Looking down at her faded blue canvas sneakers, the caked dirt on them made her look homeless. Her wool coat was missing a button and one of the outside patch pockets had a small tear. No, she didn't belong in the same world as these vehicles.

She walked further, finding a white box hallway that led to the right, toward the auto repair end of the building. The maze-like hall made hard ninety-degree turns in either direction for a bit and eventually landed her in a lounge area right outside the door for the service center. Three coffee makers, with sets of single-serving flavor pods, sat on a counter on the far wall. A news program and talk show played on separate flat-screen televisions mounted on the longest wall, with closed captioning instead of sound. Two rows of black leather rectangular arm chairs were arranged in the center. The room was sterile and modern, but the seats looked comfortable.

A man in a black suit, sitting alone, said, "Good morning." He didn't look up from his phone, and continued scrolling. He was thin, his hair was slightly longer than a crew cut. A black, hard-shell briefcase sat on the floor next to his feet.

She sat down across from him.

Without looking up, he casually asked, "Are you having your car serviced or looking to buy today?"

Jenna unbuttoned her coat at the neck and hide her sneakers under the seat. "I need to get a new car. My old one died yesterday. But I don't know if anything will be in my price range. How about you?"

The man in the black suit put his phone away and leaned forward. "I'm here on business. I'm meeting with Mr. Forero soon. What kind of car are you looking for?"

The choppiness of his voice made her feel like she was being interrogated, but his eyes were soft with genuine concern.

"Something that can get me to work and back. That won't stall out or explode. Really basic."

He chuckled. "*Not explode.* I like that. You're funny." He relaxed in his chair. "I own a Volvo myself. It's fifteen years old and still runs like a Swiss watch. Of course, it's all in the maintenance. I've never wanted a flashy car. In my line of work, I'm on the road all the time. Reliability beats speed any day."

"You can say that again. I'm Jenna."

His eyes widened momentarily. He smiled. "I'm Benjamin. Call me Ben. Have you bought cars here before?"

"No. I'm a friend of a friend of Jack Forero. He's going to help me get a good deal. But I have to admit, the cars here seem to be out of reach. Even pre-owned."

"Well, I hear they deal in all kinds of things." He crossed his arms, and the smile left his face. "Don't go buying a red Audi, though. I hear they're bad luck. You know, I'd be interested to hear how this turns out." He reached for his inside jacket pocket and took out a business card. He wrote something on the back and handed it to her. "That's my personal cell. Text me if you find a used car here today. Give me the model, year, mileage and price. I can tell you if you're getting a good deal."

She took the card. It simply read "Benjamin Radcliffe, Forensic Accounting" with his cell number hand-written on the back. No company name. No address. No email. Despite the card's mysterious nature and her having no clue what forensic accounting meant, she liked the idea of having an ally in her car-buying process. "Thanks. To be honest, I feel like I should have prepared more. It's like I'm going into a knife fight holding a wooden spoon." She tucked the business card into her coat pocket.

Ben said, "Ha! Yes, car buying can be quite daunting the first time. Like negotiating a volume discount with a hit man."

Jenna hadn't heard that particular analogy before, plus it didn't seem like a good fit to her situation. But Ben smiled like it was a joke, so she smiled back. "Hmm. Good one, Ben."

Jack strode into the lounge. He wore a suit, his hair slicked back. Nothing like her previous image of him in jeans, smoking weed. "Jenna, come with me." He said this rather stone-faced, a hint of contempt in his voice.

She got up and waved goodbye to Ben. He waved back.

Jack stalked out of the room and she followed. After silently walking back through the hallway maze, they arrived at the showroom and he continued on to his desk. He spun around.

"What did that man say to you?" He glared at her, his hands on his hips.

Why was he attacking her? "We talked about cars. He owns a Volvo. Why?"

Jack's eyes narrowed. "That's all? I need to know everything."

Why was he being so aggressive? "He said he had a meeting with your father."

"Did he say what the meeting was about?"

"No. What's going on?"

"Nothing. Forget it." Jack put his stupid grin, switching into a different, more friendly person before her eyes. "Hey, let's find you a car. Rae said you don't want to spend much. What monthly payment were you thinking of?"

Not the monthly payment nonsense. She knew little about buying cars, but she knew about this sales tactic. Inflate the price of the car, but distribute it in smaller monthly payments over a longer-term loan. Dealers made insane amounts on the extra interest payments. No, she needed to redirect the discussion to focus on the actual *purchase* price. With no undercoating or long-term maintenance contracts.

"What cars do you have under ten thousand?" She hid her hands in her coat pockets.

He flashed a smile, then stroked his chin. "We have a few. There's a green one you might like. Let me grab some keys and we'll walk the lot. Do you have your drivers license with you? I need to make a photocopy."

Confused by this, she reached into her wallet and handed over her license. Jack took it and handed it to a colleague. "Great, now let's find you a car." He clasped his hands together, then gestured to the exit.

What did they need her license for? She felt trapped without it. Like they took a piece of her identity away. She walked to the exit, and pushed the door open slowly, glancing back to see what the other salesman was doing with her license. She couldn't tell from that vantage point and continued outside.

They walked the lot and looked at ten different cars. All were in the twenty-thousand range except for a ten-year-old VW bug in lime green and faded cloth seats. The odometer read seventy-two thousand miles. Far fewer miles than her current car. In her world, nearly new. The bug was only eleven thousand dollars. Probably the only real option open to her.

She examined the sticker. "What's the wholesale on this?"

"We could let it go for eighty-five hundred."

"Can I test drive it?"

"Sure. Let's go back to the office and get your license."

As they walked back toward the showroom, she noticed Benjamin across the parking lot, holding a clipboard, apparently reading off some VIN numbers on the dashboard of a fancy white four-door sedan. It seemed curious, but she kept following Jack.

Back at his desk, Jack said, "Wait here. I'll be right back."

He walked away, toward a staircase to some upper offices. Probably where the more senior management resided. She used the time to check her phone. No messages from Marcelo.

So far, she'd been there almost two hours and hadn't even test driven a single car. She assumed this was why people hated car dealerships. Exhausted, she wondered if she'd made a mistake. She couldn't afford to waste another day car shopping. Right now, she had little to show for her time.

The air was so dry and stuffy in the showroom. She reached into her coat pocket—the one without the hole—for her Chapstick. Ben's business card was still there. Should she text him about the VW Bug option? She waited for Jack another couple minutes, her eyes wandering around the showroom floor, listening in on the conversation in the next cube where Milton was giving a hard sell on a Dodge Charger to a thirty-something, bearded guy wearing a bolo tie.

Bored, yet anxious, she texted Ben the VW info. A minute later, he texted back,

"I see it. I'll run the VIN. BRB."

Apparently, Ben was still in the parking lot doing whatever he was doing. Was he an employee of the dealership? Based on the way Jack reacted, she suspected a more adversarial relationship. And despite only talking with Ben for a couple minutes, she intrinsically trusted him far more than Jack.

She continued to wait. Her bladder registered the need to pee soon. What could take Jack so long?

There was a loud crash from the upper office area. Through the tinted glass, she saw three figures talking. She couldn't make out faces but inferred it was Jack with his parents, because the nameplate next to the doorframe read "Mr. John Forero, Owner." *Did they drop something?*

The office door flew open and Jack walked out, closing the door quickly behind him. He jogged down the stairs and came up to her. "Here's your license. Sorry. Impromptu family meeting." He practically tossed the license at her as he changed direction to head outside. She followed him to the VW, now parked on the curb outside the showroom. The keys were in it, with the engine running, and the driver's side door ajar.

The test drive was uneventful. She drove it on a loop on the highway for about five minutes. Jack played with the radio, putting it on a hard rock station. The acceleration of the vehicle was far from outstanding, but it seemed solid. Despite hating the color, the car was peppy and easy to park.

"It seems fine." She said as she pulled back into the car lot.

"We have a hundred-point inspection process for used cars. The warranty covers the first six months, fender-to-fender."

"You said eighty-five hundred?"

"Yep, best we can do. The friends and family discount."

She turned off the car, and they got out. "I could use the rest room."

"It's off the customer lounge. Meet me at my desk when you're ready. We can discuss financing."

She headed toward the lounge. When she entered, an older couple were whispering to each other, huddled next to the coffee maker.

"I don't care if he has a warrant," said the tall woman with big hair, long purple fingernails, with several diamond rings.

The sixty-ish, short, unnaturally dark-haired man, wearing a striped tie with a gold tie-tack, whispered, "Be cool. Don't do anything. He'll be gone soon."

"I want to smash his arrogant face in. He can't walk around our lot scaring customers off."

"Nobody knows he's here." The man rubbed the woman's upper arms and kissed her forehead. "Why don't you go home and take a hot bath. We'll get through this."

Jenna realized she stood frozen near the lounge entrance, because the man turned his eyes to her. "Can I help you with something, miss?"

She shrugged. "Ladies' room?"

The woman scowled and pointed further down the hall. "That way, on your left. By the water fountain."

Jenna nodded and hurried away, feeling their glaring eyes on her back.

That was Blanche. The voice was unmistakable. Jenna cringed inside, wondering whether she should have introduced herself. Because, eventually, Blanche would know it was her. She wanted to crawl under a rock and never come out. Could she hire a taxi to take her home and forget this day ever happened? Tempting.

But she couldn't take another day off from work to shop for a car. Half her day was down the drain. She had to stick it out.

After using the bathroom and washing her hands, she checked her phone. Ben had replied by text.

"Call me. Urgent."

She dialed him. "Hi Ben. Did you look up the car?"

"Yes. Sorry it took so long. I wanted to confirm. Did the salesman tell you the car was in a flood?"

"What?"

"I guess that would be a 'no'. Hmm. I looked up the VIN. The car sold at auction for parts about six months ago. Hold on. Yep, then it went through a private seller where the Forero dealership bought it for fifteen hundred."

"Oh, no."

"It's possible they rewired the car and repaired any damage, but I would steer clear of it if I were you."

Would Jack really sell her a defective car? And lie about the cost? As a mechanical engineer, Jenna knew floodwater was a death knell to a gasoline engine and all its complicated electronics and wiring. She didn't know much about car-buying but this she understood.

She let out a sigh. "Thanks, Ben. I guess I'll start over."

"Probably the best choice. You might try a different dealership. I've heard good things about Auto City in Plainsboro. A friend of mine bought a car there and said it was a good experience. Good luck to you, Jenna."

"Thanks, I'll need it." She hung up the phone and opened her notes app, typing in the dealership name and city.

Leaving the ladies' room, she went back to the lounge—now deserted—and called a taxi. The dispatcher said a driver would be there in fifteen minutes. She contemplated another cup of coffee. All her energy was drained, both physically and mentally.

Jack entered the room. "Jenna, I can walk you through the financing. Ready?"

"Um, I've changed my mind about the VW."

"Really? How about any of the other cars we looked at? That Sonata wasn't too far outside your budget."

Jenna almost laughed. The Sonata was five thousand above her budget. Not that she would even entertain the notion. For all she knew, every car on the lot could be defective; death traps held together only by Bondo putty. "I appreciate all your time. I…"

What could she say? Tell him she knew about the flood damage? No, he would just deny it or make up a lie about it being fixed. Sure, there was a chance the dealership repaired it fully, but there was no way to know for sure. She just wanted out. "I think I need a day or two to think things over. My dad always says never to buy the first thing you see."

"Well, if you change your mind, just call me. Do you need a ride home?"

"I arranged a taxi. I'll just wait here until it arrives, if you don't mind."

"Sure." Jack walked off without a goodbye.

Was he mad? Did she care? She didn't owe him anything.

She slumped down with her head against the low back of the leather chair and stared at the ceiling tiles for a minute. Her best friend planned to marry that goon. And what did Mr. Forero mean by *we'll get through this*? Another customer walked into the lounge, waking her from her troubled thoughts. She sat up and played Sudoku on her phone. After she finished the puzzle, she fiddled in her coat pocket for her key ring. It was gone.

Oh, no.

It must have fallen out of the hole in her pocket. She checked the ladies' room. Nothing. She needed to check the showroom; thinking maybe her keys fell out by Jack's desk.

Heading back through the winding hall and arriving at the showroom entrance, she heard overly loud voices coming from the offices directly above her. Blanche was yelling at Jack. Jenna tucked herself under the overhang to listen out of view.

"That was Jenna?" Blanche hissed.

"Yeah, what's the big deal?" Jack said.

"She heard us talking about the IRS audit. Where is she now?"

"Don't worry. She's in the lounge. And Jenna's a timid loser. She wouldn't tell Raven."

"She'd better not. This wedding has to go as planned or we are done. Done! You understand me, Jack?"

"Ma, I got this. The wedding is set. Raven loves me. But if you want me to talk to Jenna and smooth things over, just give me a green light."

"No. Let's hope you're right. We'll just wait. If she says something, we have our cover story about the expansion."

Jack said, "Got it."

Heavy footsteps descended the stairs.

She raced back to her spot in the lounge. Out of breath, her heart pounding, she found her keys lying on the seat cushion she'd previously occupied. *Thank goodness.* She tucked them into her jeans pocket for safe keeping.

When she looked up, Jack was striding toward her.

"Still here, huh? I can give you a ride, no problem." He gave her a big smile. A salesperson's smile. Like before, but somehow more unsettling and skeevier.

Jenna's phone dinged. A message from the driver saying he was out front. The taxi arrived with perfect timing. "See, it's here. Thanks again,

Jack." She didn't wait for a reply and quickly headed to the closest exit, next to the rest rooms, by the auto shop.

She felt like Indiana Jones narrowly escaping a huge rolling boulder. Only she escaped further deceit from Jack and his thieving, two-faced family.

She directed the driver to the dealership in Plainsboro; the one Ben recommended.

Should she call Rae right away and tell her what she heard? But then, she wasn't exactly sure what it meant. She suspected the Forero's were after Rae's inheritance to bail them out of some financial trouble. Or even legal trouble. Or both. But she didn't have any hard proof. Just wild conjecture based on overhearing a partial conversation.

One thing at a time, she told herself. First, she needed reliable transportation. Second, she needed lunch or dinner or whatever sustenance opportunity presented itself first. Last, she needed to go home and take a nap. These were her priorities.

Raven's complicated future in-law situation had to take a back seat.

At least for now.

As she sat in the taxi, she reviewed used cars on the Plainsboro dealership's website. They had lots of inventory under fifteen-K. Even a cute 2008 special edition Icy Blue Miata with low mileage and saddle brown cloth interior.

She imagined driving with the top down when the weather got warmer. Bathing in sunlight, the wind tossing her hair. She could buy a gorgeous vintage headscarf at the thrift store and wear it like Audrey Hepburn. Making the voyage up to Syracuse in a snappy blue dream car would be amazing. Not that her relationship with Marcelo was salvageable. But she didn't want to think about that now.

It would feel weird not calling Marcelo tonight. Perhaps after a few nights to think, he would call her, plead for forgiveness, and describe their shared future. She knew that wasn't likely. Was it sad that an ember of hope still smoldered within her? Probably.

Perhaps after she got a new car, the planets would align and everything would go right for her for a change.

Although, how could anything go right when she didn't have the guts to confront Jack and his family about, well, everything? Didn't karma favor the bold?

Or maybe that was something she'd read from a fortune cookie.

She thought about all her interactions with mom, with friends, with coworkers. There was one common thread; avoiding conflict and confrontation at every turn. In those moments, her goal was to preserve peace and harmony. Long term, perhaps that came at a greater cost.

Jack called her a timid loser.

Maybe he was right, and no one respected her. And, in fact, perhaps she didn't actually respect herself.

That thought stopped her cold.

After a few minutes, she realized she *had* self-respect. It manifested itself in a more controlled and rational manner. She could stick up for herself when the stakes were high enough. When she chose to.

Deciding not to yell or scream or confront was an adult choice. Usually the right choice.

That sounded right.

And maybe, just maybe, the problem was everyone else.

Chapter 10

The next morning, Jenna decided that driving was her new favorite activity. Her new car started with the first press of a button. The engine purred. The windows defrosted quickly. The steering was true. And she could see her reflection in the paint. She decided to name her new best friend, Mia.

Mia the Miata.

Not the most inventive name, but it seemed to fit. Although, she hadn't named her old hunk of junk. But if she did, it would have been Damian. Or Lucifer. Or Todd.

There were no good Todds in the world. Like her second cousin Todd that went to prison, or Todd the incompetent graduate student who lost all their midterm tests. In third grade, a Todd kept pulling down his pants in front of the girls.

No, she never met a good Todd.

Jenna pulled into the empty office lot and parked Mia next to Todd. The contrast was striking. Mia with her curves and low, sleek profile. Her old Fiesta was a rusty, dented box of turds.

It took little time to remove her personal possessions from her old car and remove the license plates. The wrecker's flatbed was arriving in a few minutes. She contemplated a eulogy for the car. It was her first, after all. Looking back, there were very few good times in this excuse of a vehicle. She'd only driven it because it was a free hand-me-down from her parent's next-door neighbor. It didn't deserve a special goodbye.

In fact, in that precise moment, she wanted a sledge hammer above all else. Smashing it was the correct and rightful tribute to mark the end of her driving misery. Could she could bash it with the lug wrench? She opened the trunk but quickly saw she'd have to remove the spare tire to access it. Not worth the effort. She closed the trunk and looked around. Then she saw it, a large decorative rock, the size of a bowling ball, next to the shrubs by the office door. The rock used to prop open said door when needed. The rock needed a name like Stevie.

She questioned her sanity. Why the urge to name everything this morning?

Did she dare?

She walked to the planting bed and picked up Stevie. It was red and jagged. A rock heavy enough to make a good impact, but still light enough to carry back to Todd. Red dust transferred to her gray coat.

Jenna tossed her hair back and cradled the rock in the crook of both arms, straining to hold it a few inches from her body to minimize soiling the front of her coat. Scanning the area for potential onlookers, she scurried forth.

Headlights appeared, coming toward her. A SUV pulled into the parking lot. *Mindy's.*

Foiled. Jenna dropped the rock with a thud and dusted off her sleeves.

Mindy got out of her car and waved. She pointed to Mia. "Hey, is this yours?"

"Yes." She walked toward Mindy. "Isn't she beautiful? And she runs." Jenna grinned.

"Nice. So, what's happening to that POS?"

It took Jenna a second.

"Piece of shit," Mindy explained. "Your old car?"

"Yeah, um, a tow-truck should be here soon."

"What were you doing with the rock?"

Dang. Mindy missed *nothing.* "I was going to smash Todd, but I probably shouldn't."

"Todd, eh? Yeah, good name. But why not smash? He's going to the scrap yard, right?"

"I think so. I guess."

"It's a fuckin' fantastic idea. Go for it."

"But what if Grant or anyone else saw me? They'd think I was a lunatic."

Mindy put her hands on her hips. "Jenna, you need to cut loose sometimes, you know?"

Cutting loose at the office didn't seem appropriate now that there was an eyewitness. "I don't want to make a mess. What if the glass breaks? The truck driver will call me when he gets here. I'm…I'm going inside. See you later." Jenna dug her hands into her pockets and headed back toward the office. Behind the building, the sun was coming up in a blaze of orange.

A couple seconds later, a crash of stone on metal startled her. Jenna turned.

Mindy was standing on Todd's hood, reaching for Stevie, now nestled on the newly dented car roof. She picked it up, aiming to drop it again.

"Mindy! What are you doing?"

"Come on. Join me. You can hurl it next." Mindy got down from the hood, still holding the rock. "It feels amazing."

"No, I'm fine. Just be careful. Don't break the glass." She turned and hugged her coat close to her chest. Mindy was certainly crazy. But she seemed to enjoy herself.

Mindy ran up behind her. "Wait. Come on." Mindy tugged her coat sleeve and pulled her to a stop. "I have something for you. Nothing involving broken glass. Promise. Follow me."

Jenna sighed. She followed Mindy.

Mindy popped the hatch of her purple Toyota RAV 4, revealing a cardboard box holding a dozen cans of spray paint, most with their caps missing and nozzles peppered by dry colorful drips. Mindy picked out a bright magenta can.

She handed the can to Jenna. "Do it."

"Do what?"

"Sheez." Mindy grabbed the can back and walked to the opposite side of Todd, ducking out of sight. The rattling of a spray can pierced the quiet morning air, followed by the unmistakable swishing noise between strokes.

Jenna wasn't sure if she should stick around. *Was it considered vandalism to spray paint your own car?* Her curiosity overcame her reluctance, and she walked around to the other side of Todd to witness Mindy's handiwork.

After a few seconds, the message was clear: 'Todd Must Die!' plastered in tall pink letters down the full side of the car, with skull and crossbones added for emphasis. Somehow, the words looked like they had always been there, blending almost seamlessly with the faded black paint, dented blue replacement quarter-panels and patches of rust.

"Whatayathink?" Mindy said.

"It's…It's freaking awesome." Jenna felt her eyes water. Not from the cold. The finality of the moment overtook her. Todd was dead and never coming back. Feelings of freedom and loss surged through her brain. The combination was euphoric.

Mindy put her arm around Jenna's shoulder, admiring her work. "Yeah, it's bitchin'. Happy to help. You sure you don't want a crack at 'er?" She offered Jenna the can.

Jenna wiped her eyes with her fingers. "No, it's a masterpiece. I'd just ruin it."

"Well, enough fun and games." Mindy went back to her car to put away the spray can.

Jenna waited for Mindy and looked around. The tow truck was coming down the street toward them. She said to Mindy, "Just in time."

"You know, they should give you a couple hundred for the scrap metal." Mindy closed her hatch.

"Really?

"Absolutely. Want me to talk to them?"

"Um, no, I got this."

"Okay, send me a picture before he loads it up." Mindy waved and walked away.

Jenna got out her phone and took pictures of Mindy's artwork. The truck driver approached and rolled down his window.

"Hey, is this the car?" He pointed to Todd.

"Yes." Did she have the guts to ask the driver for money? Negotiation wasn't her thing. Perhaps she should have taken Mindy's offer? No, she decided. She was simply grateful to have it taken off her hands for free.

She wondered why Mindy had all that spray paint. *What was that about?*

Mindy was an enigma. Kind of scary, too. *Who smashes someone else's car without even asking?* Not that she minded, but still.

She glanced at the time. Another jam-packed day at work, plus she still hadn't emailed the party guests about wearing white. Customer Support calls would begin in an hour and she needed to work on that PowerPoint for her special project.

The truck driver began affixing a wire rope to the underside of the car. She approached him. "Here are the keys. Do you need anything else from me?"

"Nope. Have a nice day." He waved.

She waved back. "You too." She mumbled to Todd, "Goodbye,

forever," and ambled into the building.

* * *

Jenna was still going through morning emails when Russ came over.

"Mindy said you got a new car."

"I did. I love it." Her heart surged with joy at this declaration.

"Congrats. By the way, yesterday Grant told me about your project. Do you want some help? I'm a master of PowerPoint."

Jenna squinted at him. *Why was he being so nice?* "Um, sure. I'd appreciate that. I feel like I can't concentrate lately. You know, now that you ask, I really need the financials for the last five years of warranty claims. But I don't know who to talk to."

Russ chuckled. "I know a person. Craig in accounting could run a report. But he's difficult. Fortunately, I know his weakness. I'll bring him some M&Ms. That always softens him up."

Jenna's weird dream about Thumper and Russ flooded back. The image of Russ's kangaroo pouch filled with candy was unforgettable. Should she tell him about it? No, he'd think she was off her rocker. "Thanks. It would be an immense help."

Russ crossed his arms. "No problem. Hey, what happened with text boy?"

"Text...?"

"Your boyfriend. Did you find out who 'T' was?"

Heat rose to her face. She didn't want to talk about Marcelo. Not to Russ. Not to anyone, really. It was too humiliating. The shock of their breakup hadn't really sunk in. Likely because they were apart so often. "I'd rather not talk about him."

Russ let out a whistle. "Ooh. Sorry. But you know, it's his loss. You're smart, pretty. A nice person. If you ever want to talk, I'm a good listener." His face became more somber and his voice softer. "I had a bad breakup last year. Didn't see it coming. Probably for the best, but at the time? It was like 'whammo'. She told me she fell in love with a guy she met on a bus. Honestly, who does that? But I'm over it. Just took a couple of months. Try to stay busy." He shook his head slightly. "Wait, I guess you have that covered. But also stay away from donuts." He patted his belly and smiled. "They're a killer."

She wasn't sure how to react. Here he was being nice, and she still wanted to crawl into a hole and die. Luckily, her phone rang. "I've got to take this." The barrage of calls from disappointed consumers had resumed.

Russ said, "Sure. Hey, congrats again on the car." He walked away.

She picked up the receiver and began her speech, her mind still on their conversation. Why was she so defensive talking to him? He was harmless. She didn't want to give him the wrong impression. Sometimes just talking with a guy led to him believing there was a romantic possibility. But Russ wasn't the smooth type. Perhaps he was just being sociable. When he called her pretty, there was no icky inflection. It sounded like a quick statement of fact.

She got her head back in the game, dispatching the first few calls without issue. In fact, one person actually thanked her for her time. That was cool. She hoped the day would go quickly, with no drama or heated remarks. When customers lodged complaints, a detailed report was sent to Grant and other company officials.

It only happened once so far to her, and it wasn't her fault. But it still stung her pride, reading the criticism and having to explain herself. The customer in question said Jenna didn't care about her problem. Of course, she cared about fixing the problem. The customer's dog chewed on the printer's electrical cord and got shocked. And yes, she didn't ask about how Fluffernutter was doing. Nor did she offer to pay for the vet bill. But the customer manual didn't have a script or policy for injured pets. She simply recommended a new cord. How was that cold and inappropriate?

During lunch, she checked her personal email. Fred asked if she wanted to have dinner. She replied he should come over at six and she would make hot dogs with mac and cheese; maybe watch a sitcom afterward. He replied with a curt, "Yep."

She smiled. It felt good knowing Fred could lean on her a bit. Despite her inability to cook grown-up food.

Before her return to the reign of terror, she needed to visit the vending machine and get a soda. Something with sugar and caffeine to stay alert. At the bank of machines, she sorted through her change. Did she have enough for a soda and pretzels? Sometimes she squirreled away stray nickels and dimes in her desk drawer. She might go back for pretzels later.

She selected her soda, and it appeared below the plastic guard.

"Hey, Jenna."

Russ. He was holding a thick three-ring binder. She hadn't noticed before how wrinkled his dress shirt was. *Did he own an iron?*

"Hey, Russ. How's your day going?"

He rocked on his heels. "I should ask you that. Customer Support Hotline is the worst. Luckily, I don't have to do that anymore. Hey, I talked with my contact in accounting. He'll send you a slug of data by close of business. In the meantime, I'd be happy to look over what you have so far."

She bent down to retrieve her soda. "That's great. About the accounting data. I have to admit, all I have are random scribbles and bullet points so far. Since I'm on call duty, I can give you the folder now. Maybe you can give me some ideas on how best to present it."

"Sounds like a plan. I'll stop by to grab it. Right now, I have my sights set on some Fritos." He took out his credit card and started the transaction on the reader of the snack machine. "I swear, I think the vending guy should re-label this slot to just read 'Russ'. I clear it out every week. Do you want anything? On me."

"No, I don't want to impose."

"Okay. Well, see you later."

She returned to her desk. There were three buttons flashing, calls waiting on her. She answered the first one, while gathering up all her special project notes and stuffing them in one folder. When Russ came by, she handed it to him, while trying to follow what the customer was saying. Something about downloading 'eco-font' software. She had to defer that one, promising to look into it and call the customer back later.

After taking two more calls, she noticed something on the top of her shelf. A bag of Fritos with a post-it note reading, "Machine dropped an extra. Enjoy." She couldn't help but smile. *Was Russ flirting with her?* Could salty snacks win over her heart? Possibly. More so, he was genuinely helping her with a crucial assignment. She wouldn't have figured out how to get the finance data without him.

Russ had nice eyes, a sweet temperament, when he wasn't being gross or trashing her cube. He was like a big goofy kid, with a bad haircut and a few extra pounds. But he wasn't ugly. With a little tidying, he might be sort of handsome. Like an old house, covered in vines, that just needed some pruning and a paint job. Not that handsome mattered. Marcelo was gorgeous, and obviously that hadn't worked out.

They could be friends, she decided. She'd never had a guy friend. There were guys in High School she had hung out with in Math League, but that friendship seemed slightly different. They only talked about math and gaming. Nothing real. Nothing resembling genuine life issues. And the Math League guys never helped or listened. Only talked about their own problem-solving conquests and overall greatness.

She wondered if her attraction to Marcelo had been his dispassion. Their conversations had always been superficial; and that had been okay, because after dealing with mom's tirades and insults, Marcelo was her reprieve.

Maybe that was her mistake. Choosing calm over real connection.

Somehow, this made her feel worse.

All her choices led her here. Alone again.

And she didn't know what to do next.

Chapter 11

Fred came over precisely at six. She knew this because she set a timer on her phone and it went off the same time her doorbell rang. Had he been standing outside waiting, staring at his watch? She wouldn't put it past him.

She turned off the stove and let him in. "Right on time. Dinner is almost ready. But let me warn you, I'm not a great cook. This is about as good as I can do."

Fred looked around her living room. "Nice place." He took off his coat and hung it on the open hook by the door.

Nice? It was a place, certainly. But Fred was being overly polite. While Fred's place was sparse, hers looked like a landfill threw up in a thrift store. She had gotten a reduction in rent in exchange for the landlord not repainting the walls. Her living room had crazy neon colored paint, each wall a different wavelength of the rainbow, with odd stripes, like a groovy seventies tour bus.

Her sofa was a hand-me-down from her grandmother that had been sitting in her parent's basement for the last ten years; it had a synthetic fabric resembling burlap in color and texture. Her previously white rug originated from her college dorm room and Thumper had scratched it and thrown up on it so many times, the geometric pattern was unrecognizable. And her lighting was the most laughable. Or lack thereof. There was a small overhead dome light and a lamp that had a SpongeBob shade, a remnant from her childhood. Crack dens had more style and panache. Except her place was cleaner; not littered with used needles.

Her prized possession comprised the only art in the space, a vintage 1965 framed movie poster of Gamera tearing apart a Japanese train. Dad got it for her at a comic book convention on her ninth birthday. One of her fondest childhood memories when dad spent time with her. Before mom's drinking and before his continual excuses to leave town on business trips.

"Thanks. Come sit at the table. What can I get you to drink? I have…" What *did* she have? She looked in the fridge. "I have water and iced tea. And one can of ginger ale."

Fred took a seat at her dining table. It wasn't really a dining table. Actually, an old drafting table tilted flat with two mismatched chairs. She had placed a freshly washed green dishtowel down the center like a runner in an attempt at decoration. "I'll have the ginger ale."

She handed him the can. "How many dogs would you like?"

Her phone rang. It was her mom. She answered, "Mom, I have company. Can I call you later?"

"Jenn, I need you. Ta go get me a bottle. Your father's nah hum." Her words were slurred. Obviously very drunk.

"No. I'm not getting you booze. Just go to sleep, okay?"

"Fine. I'll go drive myself. But if anything happens, it's your damn fault."

"Do *not* drive. You've had enough."

"It will only take you fifteen minutes. Why are you being such a brat? Well, go fuck you. I'm gonna…"

Jenna heard a loud crash and then some crying.

"Mom, are you okay?"

All she heard were soft moans.

"Shoot." She considered her next move, while a sense of paralysis washed over her.

Fred said, "What's going on?"

"I don't know." She said into the phone, "Mom, are you there?"

No answer.

"Mom might have passed out."

Fred asked, "Does she live close by? Should you call an ambulance?"

"Not too far. I should probably check on her. We've had too many false alarms with the EMS company."

"Good. I'll go with you." He got up and picked up his coat by the door.

It was going to be embarrassing for Fred to meet her messed up mother. But after everything that had happened lately, she accepted his support. "Thanks, Fred. I'll drive."

She should have felt more urgency, rushing to get her coat and keys. But awful thoughts crossed her mind. Like, perhaps if she took her time, her mom would be 'gone' when she arrived. One less worry in her life. But

Fred was standing there, holding the door open. She couldn't dawdle. She grabbed her things, scanned the kitchen to ensure all the appliances were off, and dashed to the door.

On the short drive, she gripped the steering wheel like she was in a death match with a boa constrictor. Fred said nothing. Did he notice the anger in her breathing? When they arrived at her childhood subdivision, she felt a wave of shame. Ashamed of all the times during her childhood the neighbors called the police after hearing mom's screams. Her stomach hurt.

The colonial-style house, surrounded by mature oak trees, was dark except for a small light in an upstairs bedroom. Jenna dialed her mom again. Still no answer.

Jenna got out of the car and Fred followed her. At the front door, she used her old key, pushing the door open slowly, and flipped on the hall light. She turned to Fred, "Let me check on her first. Stay here."

Her mom was prone at the bottom of the center stairs, her nightgown disheveled revealing her boobs, mascara splotches under her eyes, her medium-length silver curly hair matted to her skull with a patch of red ooze. She looked like death. Except for her lungs expanding and contracting, punctuated by intermittent snorts. No, her mom was sleeping. *How she could sleep in this fashion, on a cold slate floor?*

Jenna took her pulse. It seemed strong. She quickly straightened her mom's gown and fastened the upper buttons to make her presentable. Fred poked his head through the door. "Is it all right if I come in now? It's freezing."

"Yeah. It's not a pretty sight. But she's alive."

"I got some medic training in the Navy. I'll check for broken bones. Not as good as an x-ray, mind you."

Jenna stood back and watched Fred inspect mom's limbs and the gash on her head. She noticed a patch of broken drywall, mid-way up the stairs. It must have been quite a fall to bust the wall like that.

She held her breath as Fred continued. Her mind ran through their options. If she had to call an ambulance, she'd also need to call Dad. And he would have to cut short his business trip, blaming her. Well, not precisely *blaming* her, but certainly resenting her for the *inconvenience*.

Fred stood up and arched his back. "Well, she'll have some bruises, but nothing's broken. She's got a quarter inch gash on her head. Heads bleed a lot, so it looks worse than it is. If she complains of headaches later, she should see a doctor."

Jenna sighed with relief. The last time mom fell, six years back, she twisted her ankle badly and chipped a tooth. Jenna didn't feel up to inspect mom's teeth tonight. "We can't leave her here. But I don't think we can carry her."

"I'll try waking her up." Fred bent down and patted her hand. "What's her name?"

"Helen."

"Helen? Helen, you need to wake up, dear." He pulled her into a sitting position and said, "Jenna, could you get me a washcloth with cold water?"

Jenna nodded and jogged to the kitchen. She ran a dishtowel under the faucet. She scanned the calendar on the refrigerator. Dad was in Tucson at a conference. That would be a long trip back.

She jogged back and handed him the towel.

Her mom mumbled something. Then her eyes went wide, and she shrieked. "Jenna, who is this strange man? Why is he in our house?"

"Mom, this is Fred." Jenna enunciated her words as if she were talking to a toddler. "He's my friend and he's here to help you."

Fred said, "Helen, we need you to stand. Can you do that?"

Helen nodded.

They each took an armpit to hoist her up.

"Let's bring her into the den. She can sleep on the sofa." The trio shuffled down the short hall to the den. It was dark, but the light from the hall let them avoid walking into furniture. They sat her down on the sofa.

"Mom, here's a pillow. Why don't you get some sleep and I'll call you in the morning?"

Helen began weeping. "I'm so sorry, baby." She grabbed Jenna's arm, pulling her with substantial force onto the sofa next to her. Jenna lost her footing; she braced herself, holding the back of the sofa to prevent her face from being bashed. "Let me give you a hug." Her mom wrapped her arms clumsily around Jenna's shoulders, nearly choking her. She came in for a kiss on Jenna's cheek; it was more like a head-butt, mom's cheek bones slamming into hers. Mom tried to stroke her head, but her fingers got caught and now she was pulling Jenna's hair. All these motions occurred almost simultaneously, with Jenna tensing all her muscles to ward off the flailing assault.

"Ow. Mom. Let me go." Jenna wiggled and pushed back against Helen's shoulders.

After extricating herself, Jenna backed away, out of the range of mom's incongruously strong orangutan arms. Helen closed her eyes and flopped sideways; she appeared to be sleeping again. It was an odd pose, with mom's feet still on the floor and the rest of her body lying flat, but Jenna didn't want to risk waking her again to rearrange her legs.

Fred said, "I think she's out again."

Jenna nodded and walked into the kitchen, turning on the light over the stove. "Fred, I'm making a sandwich, leaving it in the fridge for mom when she wakes up. I'm having one too. Can I make you one? Ham and cheese or turkey?"

He inspected the stack of cold cuts. "Turkey, with mustard if ya have it."

Jenna made Fred's sandwich first. With each pass of the knife, slathering mustard on the rye bread, the embarrassment, sorrow, fear, and anger coalesced, constricting her throat further. She handed him the sandwich without making eye contact, then paused. A tear rolled down her cheek, the first crack in the dam.

"I...I can't do this anymore." She slid down to the floor, holding her head.

"Oh, dear. Stop that now. You're stronger than this." Fred bit into his sandwich and chewed.

"No, I'm not. Everything in my life is shit. Did I tell you Marcelo broke up with me? Just like that. Like I didn't matter to him at all." Her chest heaved with sobs.

"Jenna, get off the floor. That's an order, young lady." Fred extended his hand.

An order? That startled her brain. She woke from her pity trance. The old guy was effective. She waved off his hand and worked herself upright on her own.

"That's better." He put his hand on her shoulder. "You need to face life head up. None of this self-pity nonsense. Life is shit. For everyone. Get over it. You think *my* parents were like the Cleavers? My dad beat me with a leather belt. He was a nasty piece of work. But it made me strong." Fred flexed both arms. "Ha, well I used to be strong. I'm an old geezer now. He taught me an excellent lesson. On how *not* to act. Sometimes that's just as good a lesson. And you are nothing like Helen. You know that, right?"

She wiped her eyes with her hand, then ripped a section of paper towel off the roll and dried the rest of her face with it. "Yeah. I guess. I've just had a bad week."

"You need to eat something." He handed her the other half of his sandwich.

She let out a sad chuckle and took the offering. "I *am* a bit hungry."

"Of course, you are. Got to keep up your blood sugar. Come, let's eat and talk about your problems. Do you have any milk?"

From across the room, a loud snort pierced the silence. Mom was snoring like a wildebeest. Or how Jenna imagined one would snore. The tension broke. Jenna laughed.

Over some much-needed sustenance with chocolate milk, Jenna told Fred about her encounter with Jack and his parents at the dealership. And the odd presence of Ben, the forensic accountant. Fred listened with a few clarifying questions and "a huh's" sprinkled in, but he didn't say much until she finished the story.

"Your friend picked a real winner, eh?"

Jenna sighed. "I can't think of one redeeming quality Jack has. Except Raven says he's a sex god, and he's good at killing spiders."

"Jack doesn't have sex while killing spiders, right?" He picked up their empty milk glasses and rinsed them in the kitchen sink.

Jenna snorted. Fred had such a cornball sense of humor. Oddly, it reminded her of Russ's jokes.

She checked the time on her phone. "We should probably get home. I'll go look in on her before we go."

Jenna tiptoed into the den, just a few feet away, and saw that Helen was now curled up in a normal sleeping position. A throw pillow under her head. Not snoring, but a slight whistle when she inhaled through her nose. Jenna picked up a sweater that was on the floor and held her breath as she draped it over mom's legs. Thankfully, her mom remained still. Her mom's face was calm, almost cherubic; the normally deep lines between her eyebrows were soft. A good time to leave.

Fred stood at the front door, his coat on, holding her coat out to her.

She said in a whisper, "I'm glad you came with me tonight." Her eyes misted.

He patted her shoulder. "There, there. Now, let's fly this coop."

On the drive home, they didn't talk. Fred tried the radio, but the presets were all heavy metal stations apparently set by the mechanics at the dealership. Jenna hadn't looked at the owner's manual yet to determine how to change them. So, they drove in silence.

As she said goodnight and walked up the stairs to her apartment, she felt oddly calm. She should have been sad or upset or embarrassed. But Fred had a way of making things all seem okay. Even normal.

That was a good feeling.

To feel normal.

It occurred to her she didn't even ask him about the visitation service coming up Sunday. But perhaps he didn't want to talk about that either. The chaotic evening probably gave him a distraction from his own troubles.

When she opened the door, Thumper tried to make a dash for it. But she was ready for him, scooping him up in a way he hadn't counted on. "Huzzah! I got you."

She nuzzled his coat and carried him to the kitchen where she gave him dinner.

She texted her dad about mom's fall. After ten minutes, he hadn't responded. Which didn't come as a surprise. He often became impossible to contact during his work trips. Not for any discernible, good reason like bad cell service or time zone issues. No, Dad used his trips to hide from his home life. Part of her understood his need for escape; the other blamed him for allowing problems to fester.

It was time to sleep. Tomorrow was a busy day. The last day to pull together the information she promised Grant. But for now, she had to concentrate on relaxing. To think about Marcelo or mom or Raven would mean more crying, and she was too worn down for that.

A couple hours later, in the dark, she woke briefly when Thumper flopped down next to her. She had been in the middle of a dream. A dream where Jack was now poor and driving her disgusting Ford Fiesta to a new job selling vacuums door-to-door. He wore an ill-fitting black suit and a bolo-tie made of beef jerky. Then, as Jack stepped onto someone's porch to ring the doorbell, a wild pack of dogs attacked him, ripping flesh from his legs.

It was a delightful dream. A wonderfully grotesque and righteous dream.

Not that she really wanted Jack torn to bloody bits.

No, she thought with a yawn, that would be too much to hope for.

* * *

Her alarm rang at five. Jenna got ready for work, barely taking time to dry her hair fully, and dashed out the door at 5:20. She drove straight to mom's. The front door squeaked, and she winced, hoping her mom was still asleep.

She took off her shoes and padded to the den, peering around the corner to view the sofa. Mom was still there. Her head to the side facing into the room, the sweater that once adorned her legs was in a heap on the floor. No snoring. No sound at all.

Even in the dark, she could sense Mom was eerily still. *Was she breathing?* Holding her own breath, Jenna placed one foot in front of the other, taking her time like a Ninja. Avoiding the coffee table, she knelt next to her mom's face and placed a finger an inch from her nose. Mom's breathing was slight but steady. Crisis averted.

She eased up and retraced her steps when she heard a stir. She did not want to talk with mom. Who knew what would happen? No, she needed to avoid any confrontations and get to work on time. She dashed around the wall and peeked back. Mom settled back down into slumber. *Whew.*

Half of her felt she should leave a note. The other half just needed to get out.

Jenna put her shoes back on in slow motion, then incrementally shut the front door behind her. One problem solved. Well, not really solved, but resolved perhaps. The next phase of her day would be to condense all the financial data from warranty claims before ten o'clock. On the drive to work, she wondered if she should bring Russ a thank you present. Like a box of donuts. Or just a single donut. But he said it was best to stay away from them. Was he only joking?

In her rush to get to mom's, she hadn't had breakfast. She stopped at the Wawa convenience store and bought two bear claws. If Russ didn't want one, maybe Mindy or Grant would take it. She also got the largest coffee they sold. Black, with nothing added. No cream, no sugar, no vanilla or caramel. Pure caffeine. Gross and bitter, but effective.

Today she needed to be a machine. A paragon of productivity. No distractions allowed.

Again, she was the first car in the Veloma parking lot, except for the cleaning crew.

She got straight to work. Around seven, more voices punctuated the room. People were chatting about things…being social. At eight, Mindy's unmistakable voice pierced the din. She was in a political discussion with Russ and George. Apparently winning by sheer force of conviction. Something about universal basic income and health care. But no, Jenna thought, she shouldn't be listening. She reached for her headphones, not that they were connected to anything. But they buffered the noise and people would leave her alone.

Delving into the warranty claims, she uncovered something. More often than not, claims were refuted because the coverage period lasted only two years. Then a realization came. What percentage of users opted to throw out their printers when they broke? The company made most of its revenue—at least in the home user division—from selling new models. Were they designed to fail? And if this was the case, why would Grant let her go through this exercise? And what if…the most economical solution was to not give *any* kind of customer support?

Her brain froze.

No, that would put most of the people in her division out of jobs.

But also, from a purely marketing perspective, that would be ludicrous.

She needed to talk this through with someone before continuing on.

Swiveling in her chair, she noticed the Wawa bag on her top shelf. She'd completely forgotten about the pastries. Maybe she could bring Russ his and ask him to brainstorm with her.

She walked to Russ's cube. It was empty. Mindy was sitting in her cube across the aisle and asked, "You looking for him?"

Jenna noticed something odd in Mindy's cube. "Yes. Hey, what is that?" The item in question was like a tall white basket with a roof made of white satin fabric and large pink paper flowers attached.

"Russ is at the dentist. He'll be back after lunch. This…" Mindy patted the roof, "is a wishing well. For your shower. A friend of mine had one. Thought you might like it."

"A wishing well?"

"For small gifts. It's a thing."

Jenna looked at the well, estimating its dimensions in her head. Would that fit in Mia? Certainly not in the trunk. Possibly in the passenger seat with the back down? "Um, I'm not sure I can get that in my car."

"Well, if you can't, I can drive it over in my truck."

"Thanks. Hey, I'm having a problem. Not a problem, more of a sensitive question. Do you have a few minutes?"

"Sure. What's in the bag?"

"Bear claws. Want one? Let's go sit in atrium."

Mindy took her thermos with her and followed Jenna to the atrium. The space was a sterile-looking, three-story open hallway with a wide zig-zag staircase overlooking full height windows. With the building's elevator always out of service, it was the best way to reach other floors. Because of the ample unused floor space, people dumped their broken keyboards, monitors and other electronics in the corner of the atrium, stockpiling them until the recycling company made its quarterly pickup. Pictures of the company's president and other high-level officers adorned one wall, like they were watching their employees.

Mindy took a seat on a bench under the stairs. "What's on your mind? It isn't Jared, right? He's such a tool."

Jared was the office flirt. No, that was being kind. He was a creep who called women 'baby'. Luckily, she was not on Jared's radar.

"No, it's a work question. Are our printers designed to fail?" Jenna noticed her voice echoed through the open space, audible to anyone on the floors above. She continued in a whisper. "As a business strategy? I really need to know."

"I don't think so. Why do you ask?"

Jenna sighed. She bit into her pastry, mumbling, "I was beginning to think everyone is evil." She kept chewing.

"That's not a bad life philosophy." Mindy chuckled. She put down her bear claw and licked her fingers.

"I don't know if I can finish my special project. I need to think about it more."

"Just ask Grant for an extension. You know he's visiting his son at college next week. He won't get around to read your white paper."

"What?" Her voice was louder now. "He wanted it Friday morning for the Tuesday management meeting."

"All I know is he told me yesterday he'll be out most of next week. He probably forgot to tell you."

"Unbelievable." Jenna stuffed the last morsel of dough into her mouth. "I'll go talk to him."

"Hey, did you ever finish telling all the party guests to wear white?"

"I emailed about half. The sorority knows. Still need emails for some of

Blanche's family. I don't know if the nun has e-mail. But don't nuns wear white anyway?"

"Not all nuns are the same. Well, with Grant away next week, you'll have more time to work on stupid party games. Weren't you supposed to do some crafts?

Jenna sighed. "I'm supposed to make a life-sized cutout of Jack for some kind of pin the ring on the groom game. But I don't want anything to do with him."

"Look, just make a cutout the approximate size. I bet you could find a willing guy to help. What else?"

"Raven wants a bunch of poster boards with pictures. She sent me box of photos. But I have to make them pretty. Whatever that means."

"My after-school kids need a project. Come over after work."

Kids? Mindy was single and never mentioned motherhood. Jenna gave her a blank stare.

"I volunteer at the YMCA one or two days a week. I run an after-school arts and crafts program." She opened a picture on her phone. A group photo of middle-grade kids.

"Huh. Is that why you have the spray paint in your car?"

"What? Did you think I was Banksy? Or tagging overpasses?"

Jenna laughed. Yes, she had wondered about the overpasses. The offer sounded too good to pass up. "I would love help. What time?"

Having a crew of helping hands and creative minds would solve many problems. They worked out the logistics. Jenna would need to pick up craft supplies first.

Before Jenna returned to her desk, she visited Grant's office. He wasn't there, but his wall calendar marked out the next week with orange marker and the words *Out of Office*. Her mouth hung open. *Why didn't he tell her?* With more time for her project and the help of Mindy's kids, she might have a relaxing weekend for a change.

Well, except for Ava's visitation service on Sunday. That would be a sad occasion.

But so far, mom was alive, her workload got easier, and she had helpers for the party games.

She walked back to her desk with a spring in her step.

Checking her phone, a new text message arrived from Blanche.

No, this could not be good.

> Why didn't you introduce yourself at the dealership? Were you spying on us? Like a sneaky meatball. Whatever you heard is wrong, so don't dare mention anything to Raven. Consider this a warning. If it were up to me, you wouldn't come to the shower.

Consider this a warning? She would love to be dis-invited from the shower. She'd gladly hand over all the responsibility to Blanche.

Could it be that simple? Just tell Blanche and Raven to go pound sand? It was just a stupid party.

She closed her eyes and tensed her muscles. The party was in a week. Surely, she could get through a week.

Without Marcelo, Raven was the only real friend left in her life. Someone that accepted her and loved her unconditionally. Once the party was over, everything would go back to normal.

Still, the pit in her stomach begged to differ.

She'd been through worse things.

And could survive.

Chapter 12

Saturday morning, Jenna slept in and woke up feeling good. Almost great. Making crafts with Mindy and the kids yesterday afternoon was joyful. Mindy was a force of nature. All the kids loved her; hugging her goodbye when their parents arrived.

Together, Mindy's group helped make the poster boards with all of Raven's photographs, accenting them with paper frames and colorful hearts. One girl thought Jack was so handsome, better looking than Channing Tatum. Jenna didn't have the heart to tell her that Jack was human scum. At pick-up time, one kid's father offered to lie on the wide roll of craft paper to create the groom outline. Mindy made all kinds of off-color jokes, like calling him a great lay. Thankfully, the kids didn't get that joke.

Jenna was toasting waffles for breakfast when she got a text. It was Ben, the man she'd met at the dealership. He asked if Jack Forero drove a red Audi.

She wrote back, "Yes."

Ben texted back.

> "Did he mention a 1976 Firebird?"

These were very specific questions about vehicles. It piqued her curiosity. She wrote back what she knew, that Jack had crashed a Firebird before getting the Audi.

Her phone rang. She popped up the waffles before answering it.

"Hi, Ben."

"Jenna, thanks for the quick replies. I'm wondering…would you be available to meet me for lunch today? It's very important."

What was so important about Jack's cars? Ben sounded somber. Like this truly was important. She looked at the clock on the stove. "What time?"

"You live in Cherry Hill? I can meet you at Attilio's on Main Street in

Maple Shade at noon. I'm buying."

She reviewed her schedule in her mind. Last night she finished sending the remaining e-mails about the stupid 'wear white' rule. With the help from Mindy and the kids, she had room in her schedule to relax. A combination of pizza and intrigue sounded like a much better afternoon than watching television and trying not to call Marcelo. "I'll be there."

After hanging up, sat down on the sofa beside Thumper and ate her waffles. The morning was clear and bright for a change. Not like the persistent gray dismal days of the last month. *Could Spring come early?* On the first over 60-degree day, she wanted to put down the top and drive to the shore. Walk along the boardwalk and feel the ocean breeze. Surely a day like that would help her forget Marcelo. And there were always young guys running on the boardwalk. Perhaps she could take up jogging.

She checked the temperature on her phone. A new email arrived with the subject line "RSVPs".

Blanche finally got around to sending her the final count and list of party guests. Candy had been on her case for two days, needing the list to complete the gift bags, table rentals and catering contract.

Jenna opened the attachment. The list was three pages long. She began counting. A hundred and forty-one. Although some had asterisks indicating that those were 'very likely to attend but unconfirmed', but Blanche insisted they include them in the tally. But no, this number didn't include Blanche, Raven or herself or the caterers. She counted on her fingers. A hundred and forty-eight.

Jenna slammed her forehead with her palm. All she could do is forward it to the caterer and Candy and hope for the best. But her worst fear was realized. The total count exceeded the dreaded fire watch threshold.

She googled the Altoona Fire Department and dialed their non-emergency number.

A man's voice answered. "Chief Roberts, if this is an emergency, dial 9-1-1. How can I help you today?" His voice boomed, probably to carry over the background noise that sounded like a televised football game.

"Hi, I'm calling to find out about a fire watch?"

"Come again? You have a fire?"

"No. I'm calling about a party. It may need a fire watch."

"Normally, parties don't need those. We only do those for big concerts or venues that don't have functioning alarms or sprinkler systems."

"It's at the mansion off of Sargent Road. I was told approved occupancy was 130. We have 148 people attending. That includes the catering staff."

"Woowee! That's quite a gathering. I know the place. How are you going to do parking?"

She hadn't thought about parking. The driveway was long and the actual parking area might squeeze in ten cars. Another problem to add to her list. Sure, there were the buses for the sorority women coming locally, but they would probably need off-site parking with a team of valets or shuttles.

A pit formed in her stomach. "It's being worked out. What about the watch? How does that work?"

"Well, miss, one of our inspectors will come by the property the night before to scope out the egress and capacity situation. Test the fire alarms. We'll give you a set of written instructions for the number of watchers and reporting requirements. There are a couple private companies we work with and recommend. When is the party?"

She held her breath. "Next Saturday."

"Woo doggie." He whistled. "Cutting it close. You working with Candy Morris on this?"

"Yes, I booked the place through her."

"Fine, but you still have to fill out an application. Can you come by today?"

Jenna shook her head. "I live in New Jersey. Can I send it electronically?"

"It requires a handwritten signature, but I'll make an exception. What's your email?"

She gave him her contact info.

With that out of the way, she needed to work out the parking situation. Why hadn't she thought of that before?

Right. Because she was too busy dealing with champagne fountains and party games. And everything else in her life.

Next, she called Raven.

Raven answered with a faint giggle. "Stop it!" More giggling.

"Rae?"

"Sorry. Jack was tickling me. Stop. Hold on."

Jenna heard some rustling and a thud of a pillow. Raven came back on, short of breath. "Sorry. I had to go into the living room. What's up?"

What kind of romantic morning did she just interrupt? A dagger in her heart, now that she lost Marcelo. "There are some issues with the party."

"Oh, Jenna. Lighten up. Don't get so worried. Let the planner and caterer work it out. That's what they're paid for."

"There are a few big things out of scope." Jenna chewed her nails.

"Like?"

"We need a building inspection from the fire department, and a company to do something called a fire watch. Because there are too many guests. There's no guarantee they'll approve the application in time."

Raven sighed. "J-Bear, I appreciate everything. Really. But you are the smartest person I know. It will all work out. It has to. God, I feel like my blood pressure is going crazy just thinking about this. Please don't worry. When you worry, then I worry, and well, it's not the best thing for me right now. I'm getting my pre-admission lab work done this Monday."

Jenna wished Raven would confide in her about her surgery. As her best friend, she should help Raven with her illness—whatever that entailed—not relegated to dumb party planning. Why was Rae doing this to her? Why couldn't she trust her enough to talk about it?

"I'm sorry. I'll try not to burden you—"

Through the phone, more giggling. Jack's voice, "I got you."

Raven said, "Oops. Talk to you later. Love you." The call ended.

Jenna wondered if Raven's wedding would mean the end of her friendship. They'd already lost so much time together during college. Would they continue to slowly grow apart? Or would it be like walking off a cliff? Raven would spend all her time with Jack, doing married things.

She wanted Rae to be happy. But could she really be happy with a guy like Jack? And if not, would Raven come to her when it all fell apart?

The cartoon cut-out of Jack stood in the corner of her living room, by the front door, staring at her with a crooked, red crayon smirk. She wanted to tear cardboard Jack to tiny bits. Or have Thumper vomit on him. These, and other very dark thoughts, crossed her mind.

Still, she busied herself going through her closet, looking for something white to wear to the party. Her five white cotton button-down shirts for work hung side by side, but no other white attire. There was a second-hand shop across the street from Attilio's. She would go shopping after meeting Ben.

As she closed her closet door, her eyes landed on the red dress, still in its plastic bag. It was so pretty. She tried it on.

Fred had been spot on. It fit her perfectly. The color did amazing things for her skin tone, and it gave her an hour-glass shape. She tried her hair up and regarded her look in the mirror. Very Audrey. With a hint of sorrow, she knew Marcelo would have loved it.

She didn't believe in selfies as a general life rule, but was tempted. It was a travesty that she couldn't wear red to the bridal shower. Putting the dress back on its wire hanger, she ran her hand over the satin fabric, like petting a delicate, injured bird.

Perhaps next year on Valentines, she'd have a new beau who would appreciate it.

And, more importantly, appreciate her love.

* * *

A couple hours later, it was time to meet Ben. She parallel parked Mia at a numbered space on Main Street and put four quarters in the meter.

She recalled something. On the phone, Ben said, "you live in Cherry Hill". But *how* did he know that? All he had was her cell phone number. In fact, she hadn't even given him her last name.

Who was this guy?

Still, he was obviously an adversary of the Forero's. And the enemy of my enemy is… an ally? Sounded close.

For a Saturday afternoon, Attilio's was unexpectedly empty. A man and woman sat in a booth near the back. She looked around; the man waved. It was Ben. *But who was with him?*

The woman moved to sit next to Ben and offered Jenna the empty red-laminate bench. It appeared they had been there a while. Their slices were half-eaten, with crumpled grease-stained napkins next to their plates.

"Am I late?" Jenna asked.

"Not at all." The woman extended her hand. "Hello, Jenna, I'm McKenzie but call me Mack."

"Hi." Jenna sat down but kept her coat on. She squinted at Ben. "What's this about?"

Ben cleared his throat. "Do you want to order first?" He waved at the man behind the counter who was busy folding pizza boxes.

The pizza smelled delicious, and Ben said he was buying. To the pizza guy she said, "Two plain slices, a small Caesar salad without croutons, and a bottle of cherry coke." After the man departed, Jenna glanced about,

"Why are we the only ones in here?"

Ben crossed his arms and leaned forward. "How well do you know Jack Forero?"

"He's my best friend's fiancé. I met him three times. Why?"

Ben looked at Mack. She stared back and tilted her head as if to say "go ahead."

He took a deep breath. "Your friend is Raven West? You go back quite a ways, I hear."

"You hear?" Jenna shook her head in disbelief. "Who are you and what's going on?"

Mack put her hand on Ben's arm, and leaned forward. "Your friend Raven is engaged to a criminal."

"What? Because he lies about car prices? Don't all salespeople do that?"

Mack stabbed the table with her finger. "No, because his family does very criminal things for the Philadelphia mob. Money laundering, criminal conspiracy, bank fraud, accessory to murder...I could go on."

Jenna clasped her hands over her mouth. "What? No...come on...I don't believe..."

Mack's voice softened. "You'd better believe it because your friend is in serious danger if she marries Jack Forero."

Jenna froze. *The mob? Did Raven know?* "I need you to back up. Who are you and why are you telling me this?"

Ben said, "I'm a Special Agent with the Internal Revenue Service. The criminal division." He pulled out his badge. It looked real, not that she'd seen a real badge before, but it seemed weighty and professionally manufactured. "I've been going through the dealership paperwork and assets to lay the groundwork. Mack is with the FBI, she's the actual lead on the case."

He continued, "And we're talking to you because the bridal shower gives us a perfect opportunity to get Mrs. Forero alone. With your help, we'll stake out the party and give Jack's mother the opportunity to cut a deal with us. The Forero's are small potatoes; but we need to leverage their cooperation to reach the mob itself."

"You know about the party?"

Mack said, "We've been monitoring the family's cell phones for the last three months. Mrs. Forero has been texting you often."

Ben added, "When you introduced yourself at the dealership, I said to myself, 'It's got to be the same Jenna.' And sure enough. Oh, by the way, I can't believe how restrained you are in your replies to her. I mean," he chuckled, "if I received a dozen bossy emails every day about party favors and decorations, I wouldn't be so nice. Anyway," Ben waved his hand, dismissing that train of thought. "Mack came up with the idea and the reason we're talking to you today. I mean, surely you don't want your closest friend marrying into a crime family, correct?"

Jenna shook her head. "This is nuts. So, you want to crash the party and interrogate Blanche?" She visualized armed agents tying Blanche to a chair, shining a spotlight in her face. Actually, she kind of liked the idea. Maybe some waterboarding…

"No, we were thinking something more subtle," Mack said. "We just want to get her away from her husband. To talk to her alone, on neutral ground. Apply some pressure. Did you know all the family assets are in her name? We believe her husband is the primary criminal. But on paper, she's the one that has the most to lose and who would receive the longest sentence. We believe we have an excellent shot at this."

Giving Blanche small electric shocks in a dark room sounded pretty good. The more reserved, quiet conversation Mack proposed seemed less enticing.

"You have to give me more than this. Why should I believe you?" Jenna crossed her arms.

Ben gave Mack a side-look. Mack said, "Hmm."

Jenna hit her fist on the table. "Well?"

Mack said, "Jenna, I can't give you all the details. But I'll tell you this. On a few occasions, John Forero 'sold' vehicles to mob hit-men, who used them for a day or two for some nasty business. In their scheme, the mob 'returns them' to the dealership where Mr. Forero changes the VINs and the odometer readings. The family uses them as personal cars for a few weeks. Later, his son, Jack, re-sells them off-grounds, posing as 'a private seller' to unsuspecting buyers. A process called 'curbstoning'. The Forero's, especially John and Jack, have deep knowledge of the mob's operations and tactics."

Jenna said, "Wait, so Jack is aware of all of this and is actively criming?"

Ben said, "Yes. Besides the illegal car activity, Jack has been branching out, transporting illegal substances for the mob."

"Jack and illegal drugs? Why am I not surprised? He's such a dick-weed." Jenna huffed.

Mack said, "But there's more. The dealership took out substantial loans from the mob. Mrs. Forero has lavish tastes and maxed out their family's credit cards, digging themselves into quite a hole. We know they are behind in repaying their, let's say, benefactors."

Jenna said, "Hmm, somehow that sounds like Blanche."

Ben said, "We have recordings of her and Jack discussing how they plan to take your friend's trust fund to pay off these loans."

Jack was after Raven's inheritance after all? "What do you mean, 'take'?"

Ben folded his arms. "It isn't clear. We suspect Jack looks to inherit Miss West's fortune as soon as possible."

Inherit? That part took a couple seconds to sink into Jenna's brain. Was Jack going to kill Raven to get her money? Or was Ben only trying to scare her into helping them?

Jenna's food arrived. But now she didn't feel hungry. She turned to the pizza guy. "Could you make that a to-go bag?" The man nodded and left again.

Ben said, "Jenna, I know you want to protect Raven. We do too. But we can't risk her telling Jack. Once we get Mrs. Forero to cooperate and fulfill her part, we'll be glad to tell Miss West everything we've told you. All you have to do is help Mack pass for an invited guest and keep us posted on her movements."

Jenna looked at Mack. She was certainly young enough to pass for a sorority sister or college friend. It could work. She scrunched up her face. "I still don't understand…"

Mack said, "Understand what?"

"Why not just arrest all of them?"

Mack said, "We could, but all we have right now are some strong theories and some minor drug charges. And an arrest would put the mob on high alert. But if we can divide and conquer? Get their cooperation without the mob suspecting? It could be a game changer."

"Why can't you just go talk with Blanche at her house? Or intercept her at the grocery store. Why does it have to be the party?"

Mack wrung her hands. "We tried that. Last week. My partner, Jay, went to their house. Did Raven ever mention the Forero's dog, Wolfie? Long story short, Jay lost a finger to that maniac dog. And since then, Blanche doesn't go out in public without her husband by her side."

"Whoa."

"Yes. Therefore, the shower is the best opportunity. I mean, alternatively, we could storm their house with fifty agents—and it could still come to that—but our director is trying to avoid another Waco."

"Waco?"

Ben shook his head. "It was a long time ago. Google it."

Her stomach felt sick. "I need a little time to process all of this. Can I get back to you? In a couple days?" She slid across the bench, standing to leave.

Mack stood, placing a hand on Jenna's shoulder. "Fine. Call Ben no later than Monday night." Mack's eyes bored into Jenna's. "But you understand you can't say anything to Miss West or the Forero family? If you compromise the investigation, you could receive five years in Federal prison for obstruction of justice."

"I understand." Jenna walked up to the pizza counter and took the large paper bag. "I'm going to a funeral service tomorrow. But I'll call you." She nodded to them and strode to the exit. Her heart was beating out of her chest.

Once on the sidewalk, she couldn't remember where she had parked. After scanning up and down the block, she saw her car parked across the street. She stepped off the curb. A black sedan whipped by, inches from her. Her heart leapt to her throat; she blinked to clear her vision. The paper bag landed on the blacktop, still intact. Picking up the bag, she looked both ways this time before proceeding.

She started her car, took the soda can from the bag, and popped the top. It exploded, fizzling red soda down her coat. Not caring, she drank in large gulps. *Jack was an accessory to murder?* A drug lord? He wanted to steal Rae's money? Did he love Raven at all?

How could she warn Raven without spilling all the beans?

If planning a party was too much stress for Rae, she would have a stroke if she knew about the mob stuff.

Jenna drove back to her apartment to eat and to think.

Or to eat and sleep.

Or probably just sleep.

She wanted to call Marcelo so badly.

As she crossed the township line into Cherry Hill, a Sarah McLachlan song came on the radio. Normally, she would have sung along, knowing all the words by heart.

Instead, she bashed the knob, turning it off.

She had to stop Raven's wedding. *Talk some sense into her.*

Surely, Raven would do the same for her. They were sisters for life.

Eventually, Raven would forgive her. Perhaps thank her.

Because losing Raven would mean losing the only person who really loved her. Losing the best part of herself.

Keeping her gaze on the road in front of her, she blinked repeatedly, breathing in rapid, shallow pulses.

The tears she tried to hold back flowed anyway.

Chapter 13

The temperature was just above freezing with a dusting of snow on the roads. Jenna arrived at noon and the parking lot had only ten cars. An elderly couple shuffled to the front door.

The white, single-story building was squarish and plain except for some symmetrical fluted columns near the entrance, punctuated with a life-size, concrete statue of an angel to the right. Mansfield Funeral Home had been around since she was a kid. She'd never been inside before, but during her childhood, she had witnessed its Sunday processions.

She wore a work outfit, black slacks, jacket and a navy blouse. The only black dress she owned was a summer dress with thin straps and dainty pink flowers; not suitable for winter, nor a solemn event. Plus, it was crumpled in a bin of summer clothes jammed at the top of her small closet.

A thin, older man in a black suit and tie—standing still with excellent posture with his hands clasped below his waist—greeted her. "Are you here for the Blesky service?"

She nodded. He directed her to the room on the left.

A couple dozen people milled around. She signed the visitor book. Rows of white-painted wood chairs filled the center of the room, with an urn on a table at the far end and a large black-and-white photo of Ava, surrounded by flower arrangements. A chill cut through her. She'd forgotten to send flowers. She hoped Fred wouldn't hold that against her.

What did one do at a visitation? What do you say to people?

She felt like a five-eyed mutant alien who just landed at the Met Ball. Which meant, on the surface, she wouldn't look completely out-of-place given the outrageous outfits worn, but once she opened her mouth, they would know, in an instance, she didn't belong.

Near the urn, she saw Fred talking with a man and woman. Not wanting to disturb them, she inspected a table of photographs along the side wall.

Pictures of their family. Fred and Ava holding their baby son at the hospital, Ava tending a vegetable garden wearing an apron, a picture of a vacation at the Grand Canyon when their son looked to be in middle school. The next picture broke her heart. Their wedding photo, in sepia tones. Smiling and young, a gorgeous couple. His wife had been so radiant. In their eyes, she could almost feel the depth of their love. Then another wedding photo—their son's. For some reason, Fred wasn't smiling.

She now recognized the couple he was speaking with.

Not knowing what to do, she took a seat in the back row. She checked her phone. A message from Blanche about Sister Mary wanting a microphone for her benediction at the shower. Jenna turned off her phone.

When Fred was free, she went over to him and placed her hand on his arm. "Fred, how are you holding up?"

"Jenna, I'm glad to see you. I'm fine. Just fine."

She pointed to a skinny man with scraggly facial hair next to a woman with long blond wavy hair standing in the corner. "Is that your son? From Minnesota, right?"

Fred sighed. "Come with me."

They walked up to the couple.

"Jenna, this is Gabriel and his wife Patricia. Patricia is a nurse and Gabriel is…"

Gabriel said, "A builder."

Fred said, "Oh, is that what you are these days? Well, anyway, this is Jenna. She's my neighbor. A good kid."

Patricia said, "Nice to meet you. How long have you been a friend of dad's?"

Before she could respond, Fred shook his head. "Why do you care? I tell you, I've only known her a short time, but she cares about me more than you *ever* did."

What was going on? Jenna wanted to back away slowly, fade into the walls.

Gabriel waved an arm over his head, "Here we go again. Dad, you know I care."

"Yeah, so where's Timmy? You know I wanted him here."

Jenna took a step back, trying to distance herself. Fred, without looking, grabbed her arm and locked her in place. "No, stay. *They* are the ones that should leave."

Patricia trained her eyes on Jenna and said in a low tone, "Hmmf. Is she the one you gave mom's dress to? It belongs with me. I'm her daughter-in-law." Patricia leaned in with a scowl.

Fred let go of Jenna and raised his voice. "So, Gabriel, now that you're a builder, how are those child support payments going? Or are you still a rotten deadbeat?"

Every head in the room turned towards them.

Gabriel scowled, took Patricia's hand, and they strode out of the room toward the exit.

Fred yelled, "Yeah, I thought so." He cleared his throat and in a controlled, subdued tone, said, "Sorry, folks. I'm…I'm going to go get some air."

People went back to talking among themselves.

Fred said, "Jenn, I'm sorry. Family crap, you know how it is. I'm going to clear my head. Come with."

Once they got to the center hall, Fred craned his neck, peering into the other viewing room. "In here."

She followed behind him and asked, "Who's Timmy?"

They sat down on a brocade sofa in the adjacent empty parlor.

"He's my grandson."

"You've never mentioned him."

"My son is a horse's ass. Timmy was from his first marriage. But then he fell in love with Patricia and left them. I swear, when he told Ava she couldn't visit Timmy anymore, it made her sick. Who does that? Abandon's their infant son? And tells the grandparents they aren't allowed to see him? Gabriel was always a dumb-ass. But I also blame Patricia. She's a jealous, spiteful type. I think she's the real reason Gabriel won't see his kid."

"That's terrible."

"I pleaded with Gabriel to bring Timmy to his grandmother's funeral. God, he's ten now and I haven't seen him in the last five. Gabriel hadn't paid child support in years. I've been sending Timmy's mother cash whenever I have some extra. I'm so fucking mad at them I could spit."

"I'm so sorry, Fred. I had no idea. What can I do?"

With soft eyes, he said, "Dear heart, there's nothing to do. But let me tell you something. And I want you to remember this. You can't pick your family. But you can pick the people you keep in your life. Sure, you need to stand by family. But you also need to surround yourself with people who really care about you, who deserve your love. You understand what I'm telling you?" He placed his knobby hand on hers.

He didn't seem to be talking about his own family anymore.

"Yes, I understand."

He took his hand away and straightened. "Good. Enough about that." Standing, he stretched his back and walked out of the room.

She sat there in the empty room for a few moments, digesting all that just happened.

Gabriel married the wrong person, and it devastated their family, perhaps for generations.

And now Raven was on track to make a similarly grave mistake.

Jenna had to try to make Raven see the light.

With a deep breath, she got up and left the funeral home.

Her next stop would be Raven's.

And she had renewed courage to speak her mind.

* * *

"Jenna, what are you doing here? You should have called. We were just about to go to a movie and dinner."

"I need to talk to you."

Jack came over to the door, his coat on. "Hey, Jenna. What's up?"

Raven said, "Can it wait until tonight? I'll be back around six."

Jenna closed her eyes. Would she have the same fire in her belly in five hours? Or would she chicken out and not say what she came to say?

"Um, if I come back, will it just be the two of us?" Having Jack lurking around would hamper her ability to raise certain questions.

Raven looked at Jack.

Jack said, "I can take a hint. Sure, I have other stuff to do, anyway. You girls have an evening together."

Raven turned to Jenna, "Come back at six-fifteen. We'll make brownies and talk about the party. But don't tell me too much. I want some stuff to be a surprise."

Jenna gave a quick smile. "Sure. See you then." She stepped back off her front step and left, wondering if Jack would notice her new car parked on the street outside. She hoped he would, to rub it in.

On the way home, her phone rang. She hit accept on the car's Bluetooth.

"Hello?"

"Jenn, you have lots of nerve."

Mom was drunk again, sounding both sad and hostile.

"Yes."

"Yes, what?" Mom said.

"I'm agreeing with you. I have nerve. Why are you calling?"

"Why didn't you invite me to Raven's party?"

"Wait, how do you know about that?"

"I saw one of your old high school friends at the supermarket."

"Mom, I'm in the car. I can't talk to you right now."

In a child-like voice, she said, "You never come see me."

"I saw you two nights ago."

"No, that was different. I was sleepy. Come over and talk with me. I'll cook dinner."

"Did dad come home?"

"No. He comes back tomorrow." Mom began weeping.

"Bye, mom." She ended the call. There was no way on earth she would consent to visit mom without dad at home. He needed to be there to referee or simply witness how bad things had become. No, she wasn't going there, into the lion's den, without backup. Her own mental health depended on it.

Back at her apartment, she found some lined index cards and began listing things she would ask or say to Raven. To make her reconsider her plan to marry Jack without violating the FBI's instructions. Just like the script for customer support, she needed to steer the conversation to the most constructive resolution possible. But in this case, she'd have to memorize her questions and responses, using them like chess pieces.

At four o'clock, someone knocked on her door. It was Fred. He was holding a paper grocery bag.

"Do you want to have dinner later?" he said.

"Um, sorry, I'm going to Raven's. But I could use your help with something."

He followed her to her dining table now filled with notecards. The wall next to it was covered in flow charts.

"I see you have a new boyfriend."

"What?"

Fred pointed to cardboard Jack.

"Very funny. It's for the shower. What's in the bag?"

"I brought over some of Ava's old photography magazines. Your friend Raven is into photography, right? Thought she might get a kick out of them." He looked around for a place to put the bag.

"That's so nice." Jenna placed the bag on the couch. "I'll bring them over tonight. In the meantime, um, can you keep a secret?"

"Sure, I can keep a secret. What's going on?"

Jenna relayed everything that Ben and the FBI woman told her about Jack and his family.

"Wow. And I thought my family was eff'd up."

"I have to warn her. But I can't divulge everything I know. I've been writing what I'll say and anticipating her questions and arguments. I have to leave in half an hour. Can I try this out on you?"

"You want me to pretend to be Raven? Ha. Okay."

"Good." She cleared her throat. "Raven?"

In a high-pitched voice, "Yes, Jenna?"

"How well do you know Jack?"

"What are you getting at? I'm marrying him. Obviously, I know him."

"But, like you said, you're both young. More than half of marriages don't last. It makes sense to protect yourself. Did you ask Jack for a pre-nuptial agreement?"

Fred put a hand on his hip and fanned his face with the other. "I do declare, Jenna, I think you are jealous of me and my man-muffin. We don't need a pre-nup. Our love is for the ages. How dare you?"

"Fred, you sound like Scarlett O'Hara. I don't think Raven would be that dramatic."

"Oh, really? But you said you wanted to prepare. And Scarlett was a master manipulator. I'm doing you a favor."

"Sheez. Fine. Um. Well, Raven, because Jack loves you, he would be fine with a pre-nuptial agreement. Lots of couples have them."

"Jenna, why are you so worried? Jack's family has ten times my net worth." He swept his hands in the air, 'making it rain'.

Jenna laughed. "Stop that. Um…what if I told you I think the dealership has some financial problems?"

"How would you know that? I don't believe it." Fred pantomimed applying lipstick.

"Shoot, I can't say I talked to the IRS auditor, right? Um, I'll say, 'you should look at their tax returns'. What do you think?"

Fred stopped fluffing his imaginary long locks. In his regular voice, he said, "You won't convince her. No one wants to believe bad things about their fiancé. All these notes and charts aren't gonna work."

Jenna sighed. "Might not. But I'm still going to try."

"And if you don't succeed?"

"Then I help the FBI and they come to the party. If Blanche takes their offer, Raven would feel hurt by the breakup, but her life will be spared."

"Now *that* sounds like a better plan."

Fred was probably right. But if she could extricate Raven now, before the shower, before the FBI swooped in, that had to be better.

Fred said goodnight and Jenna got ready to go to Rae's.

She picked five note-cards and put them in her coat pocket. Not that she would actually read from them. But it bolstered her confidence knowing they were close by.

Jenna fed Thumper and left her apartment.

It was now or never.

Would she risk jail to convince Raven and save her?

Would Raven do the same for her?

She knew the answer and didn't like it.

Loyalty was a funny thing.

Everyone thinks they are loyal until they aren't.

* * *

At six-fifteen, Jenna knocked on Raven's door. She hoped to the heavens that Jack was gone. A flood of anger washed over her. If she saw him now, she'd spit in his face.

Raven answered the door. "I'm glad you're here."

Jenna took off her coat and headed to the sofa. She heard the door slam behind her.

Raven's eyes were like daggers, her arms crossed.

"What's wrong?"

"Your mom called me. Fifteen minutes ago."

Jenna knew what that meant. But she asked anyway. She sat on the couch, hugging her coat. "Was she…?"

"Plastered? Obviously. Why didn't you tell me you and Marcelo broke up? And you told your mom you think Jack's family is after my money?"

Jenna froze. She shut her eyes tight, trying to recall.

Raven stood over her and glared. "Well? What the hell?"

"I don't…let me think." She took a deep breath. *Was it possible her mom wasn't completely passed out the night she and Fred came over?* It was the only answer.

Raven sighed. "J-Bear, this isn't like you." She sat on the other end of the sofa, cross-legged, facing her.

"I didn't tell mom anything. She overheard a conversation. I thought she was blotto. You know how she is."

Rae's eyes narrowed. "So, you're saying she completely made those things up?"

Jenna's mind raced. She decided on a half-truth. "Okay, yes, Marcelo and I broke up. I think. Probably."

"Aw, sweetie." Raven leapt forward into an embrace. She rubbed Jenna's back. "You should have told me. Here I was going on about my engagement." Rae released her, placing her hand on Jenna's. "Are you okay? Do you want to talk about it? Is that why you came over tonight?"

It would have been so easy to say yes. Get comfort from her dearest friend. Avoid the subject of Jack forever. But she needed to give Ben an answer soon.

"I'm trying not to think about Marcelo. Let's not talk about him. We need to discuss Jack."

Raven pulled her hand away. Her eyes narrowed. "What about him?"

She told her the story of the green VW bug and how Jack lied about the price and flood history. Then told her about him smoking pot while driving and getting pulled over. She finished with, "I'm sorry, Rae, I don't see him as a trustworthy person and I'm concerned. I'm your best friend. If he treats me with that kind of disrespect, I worry he won't respect you either." She let out a long breath. Surely, Raven couldn't argue with these facts.

Raven knitted her brows. "Oh, J-Bear, I'm sure Jack was just on autopilot, acting the salesman on reflex. Jack wouldn't try to cheat you. I'm sorry if you thought he tried to sell you a lemon. But how do you know they didn't fix the damage? Maybe that's why it cost more. Did you ask him about repairs?"

Jenna's brain was on fire. *Why couldn't Raven see Jack for who he truly was?* No, she had chickened out of asking because, with Jack, she expected only lies. But the mere fact he didn't mention the car's history was itself illegal. "No, but it's still dishonest. There are disclosure laws…"

"He said you left without explaining why you changed your mind. You didn't even give him a chance. And you didn't introduce yourself to Blanche when you ran into her. If anything, you were the one who was rude." Raven crossed her arms again.

This was going sideways fast. There was something else on her notecards, but she couldn't remember what it was. In a last-ditch effort, she took the nuclear option.

"Raven, did you ever consider a prenuptial agreement?" There, she said it. No turning back now. It was going to get real.

Rae rubbed her face with both hands. "So, you *do* think he's after my money."

"Yes."

Raven yelled, "Based on what? Look, just because Marcelo broke up with you, maybe you think all men are bad. Or you're just jealous." Raven sighed, her voice softer. "Jack and I have something great. His mom has treated me like her own daughter. I've told you. His family is far wealthier. They keep three million in inventory at all times. Plus, they own the dealership building with ten acres of prime commercial land."

"I get it, but—"

Raven shook her head. "Do you know what Mr. Forero gave Blanche last Christmas? A four-carat yellow diamond. My paltry two million, if it's still worth that next year, is nothing to them."

Paltry? Jenna almost laughed. Except she saw the disgust in Raven's eyes.

"I'm just saying—"

Raven stood up. "I think you should leave."

Were there tears in Raven's eyes?

"I'm sorry, Rae. Like I said, I'm worried. I want you to be happy."

"I have my pre-admission blood tests tomorrow. Just go. I don't need this kind of negativity. I will try to forget you said this." Raven's eyes gestured toward the door.

Jenna knew it was time to leave. Before she left, she donned her coat and added meekly, "I'll call you tomorrow."

Stone-faced, Raven said, "Bye," and closed the door behind her.

Jenna put her mittens on. The temperature had dropped into the twenties. In the crisp air, she could breathe again. Thick snowflakes wafted down.

The confrontation had gone about as badly as she thought it would go.

Hopefully her words planted a seed of doubt that would grow later. The bridal shower was in six days and the wedding in four months. She needed some magic beans of truth and revelation to sprout quickly.

And in this nightmare of a fairy tale, she needed to cut down both Jack and his evil beanstalk of a family. That image made her smile.

The FBI would become a very convenient hatchet.

Chapter 14

It was mid-morning on Monday. Jenna was just about done with her white paper for Grant. Now the missing piece was customer loyalty. Did having a reliable printer translate to repeat customers returning to their products in the future? Because, if that didn't matter, her entire premise was off. She had to believe higher product quality would be rewarded. Otherwise, why bother trying at all? Was the current throwaway culture too pervasive?

Another problem plagued her. If Veloma made a better product and had fewer customer complaints and trouble calls, would she work herself out of a job? Would her entire division be slashed?

Lost in thought, she looked up and saw Russ walking by. She called, "Hey."

He stopped and came back. He was holding a Scooby-Doo mug, with an image of the Mystery Machine with the cast's faces behind the windshield. "Hey, how was your weekend?"

That was a loaded question. Being interviewed by the Feds, a funeral, a confrontation with her best friend. "Fine. Hey, I need your opinion." She explained her conundrum. "What if my project eliminates jobs? Or kills off our entire division?"

Russ laughed. "Well, think about it this way. What happens when you build a better product?"

"People buy it? Or I hope they do."

He nodded. "And?" He sipped his coffee.

She shook her head, "And what?"

"Does the company expand or contract?"

"The company has to build and ship more of the good ones. Oh. So, they'll need more jobs in those areas."

"Exactomundo." He tapped his nose.

She sighed with relief. "And they might retrain or transfer people instead of firing them?"

He nodded.

Her face brightened. "I'm glad we had this talk."

"Me, too. What are you doing for lunch?" He downed the rest of his coffee.

"I brought a sandwich."

"Well, George and I are going out. Want to ditch the sandwich?"

The thought of food reminded her of the meeting with the FBI. She needed to get back to Ben today.

"I wish I could. But I'm swamped. Maybe next time. Hey, I like your mug."

"Thanks." He lifted it, inspecting the image. "When I turned thirteen, I had a voice like shaggy." Russ laughed, "My best friend in middle school gave me this as a joke. But, from the beginning, I was always a Velma fan. Daphne was gross."

Jenna nodded. "I agree."

He waved and walked away.

She closed the binder of financial data. There was no better time than the present. She wrote out a text to Ben. "I'm in. What's next?" She paused her finger over the send arrow. Allowing armed agents to stake out a bridal shower seemed excessive. But if the Forero's were involved, even tangentially, with murder, she had little a choice. She hit send and placed her phone face down on her desk.

A minute later, her phone dinged. A new text from Ben: "Good. Mack will call you tomorrow with instructions. Splendid news about the fire watch."

She stared at the text. *Were the Feds monitoring her phone now?* Because she hadn't emailed or talked with Blanche about the fire watch. But she'd mentioned it to Raven on the phone. *Were they also monitoring Raven's phone now?* Whatever the answer, it scared her.

Her phone rang. Startled, she flipped it in the air and it bounced off her shelf with a bang before hitting the floor. She heard Mindy call out, "You okay, Jenn?"

"Fine," she answered in a low voice through the partition.

She picked up the phone, still ringing. A sliver of a crack on the top left portion of the screen. It was Blanche the B. Her body stiffened. With her best customer service voice, she said, "Good morning, Blanche." She grabbed a pen, assuming Blanche was planning to give her some new ridiculous instructions about the party.

"Jenna, I want you to stay away from Raven. You are not coming to the shower."

"Wha...what? Why?" She dropped the pen.

"Raven called me last night in tears. You're supposed to be her best friend. I knew the first time we talked you were a spiteful, two-faced, jealous brat. You've had it out for Jack from day one. Well, I won't let you break up this beautiful couple. Send me all the party information. I'll deal with Ms. Morris from here on out."

A wave of panic. *Think*. What did she do when a hostile customer called? Right, *eat shit*.

"You know, Blanche, you are absolutely, a hundred percent right."

"What?"

"I've been doing some soul searching. And you and Raven are right. I *have* been jealous. My breakup with my boyfriend really messed with my head. Have you ever had a bad breakup?" Jenna picked up the pen and started stabbing the partition wall. She imagined how good it would feel to stab Blanche in the face. The motion was cathartic.

"Well, that was a long time ago. But that doesn't give you any right..."

"I'm so ashamed. You have every right to be angry. Not angry, furious. I can't apologize enough." Was she laying it on too thick? In this situation, maybe not thick enough. She needed to add some compliments. She put down the pen and summoned her strength. "Blanche, Raven told me you are like a mother to her. It was so awful when her own mother died. I'm glad you are in her life, caring about her, protecting her. Being the mother she desperately hoped for. You have a big heart."

"Well, I...I appreciate you saying that."

"I want Raven to be happy. Jack is a fine person. So handsome and charming." Jenna cringed, hearing her own words. "I can tell how much they love each other. And I've messed up completely. If you don't want me at the party, I'll understand. But I need to make things right with Raven. She's like my sister. The only one who's ever really been there for me. I couldn't forgive myself if I lost her forever." This last part was true. Jenna's eyes teared up. She planned on fake tears. But, in truth, the thought of losing Raven pained her heart.

Mindy appeared at her cube. She mouthed, "Mrs. Forero? Oh-My-God." She stuck out her tongue and extended an aggressive middle finger to the phone.

Jenna suppressed a laugh. She blinked back the moisture in her eyes.

Mindy grabbed a stack of Post-It Notes. In black magic marker, she scribbled,

'Tell her to Eat a Bag of Dicks!!'

Jenna's body spasmed with laughter. She crumpled up the note and whispered, "Shoo."

She clasped her hand over her mouth, swiveling in her chair to hide her eyes from Mindy's antics. If Blanche heard her giggling, it would all be over.

Blanche said, "Are you still there?"

"Um, yes. I'm at work, so it's difficult to talk. Just know that I want to make everything right. I'm so sorry. I hope you can see your way to forgiving me someday." She saw some movement on the edge of her vision.

Mindy was gesturing a blow job, her hand bobbing toward her mouth. Jenna slapped a hand over her eyes. It was too much.

Jenna added quickly, "Blanche, I have to go. Hope we can talk soon. Bye." She ended the call.

Mindy laughed. "What did Mrs. Fuckface want? And why were you apologizing to her like that?"

Laughing, tears streaming down, Jenna said, "Min…you—" She gasped for breath. "I can't believe…that was awesome." She rocked back and forth, convulsing.

"You're welcome." She curtsied. "I'm going to lunch with Russ and George. Come with."

Jenna looked around her cube. Her project binder and the printouts of financial data didn't seem important anymore. She needed fresh air in her lungs and to stretch her legs. She nodded. "I think I will."

"Good. We're leaving in thirty. Can I ride with you in the Miata?"

"Yes! Excellent."

Mindy left and Jenna got up to walk to the break room. In the refrigerator, she located her insulated Godzilla lunch tote and retrieved her PBJ sandwich. With a sweeping gesture, she tossed the PBJ in the trash can in the corner.

She hummed all the way back to her desk.

Back at her cube, she regarded Mindy's crumpled post-it note. She smoothed it flat on her desk, running her hand over it several times to remove the creases. It wasn't perfect, but somehow it was more than perfect.

With glee, she taped it to the bottom of her monitor.

* * *

On the drive home from work, Jenna sang along to all the songs on the radio. Overall, it had been a good day. Lunch with the gang was fun. She wondered why she hadn't gone with them before. After lunch, she had a break-through on her project; the sales projections and cost avoidances more than offset the extra cost of improving initial product quality. She just needed to do some tweaks and her findings would be complete.

The next season of her favorite show began tonight and she bought milk duds to enjoy during her watch party. Of course, it was a party of one. But without all her normal worries, she felt in good company for a change.

But before she could settle in for the evening, she needed to talk with Raven. Obtain forgiveness. And above all else, ensure she was still invited to and in charge of the bridal shower.

When she walked through the door to her apartment, Thumper was sleeping like an angel on the couch. She put food in his bowl. Cleaned his litter box. Took out the trash.

In her bedroom, she combed her hair, brushed her teeth, changed into her pajamas, shut the door and then sat cross-legged in the center of her bed, holding her cell phone. Before she called Raven, she closed her eyes and went through her mental list of all the things she wanted to say. What were some good things she could say about Jack that wouldn't ring false? That was the difficult part. She'd told Blanche that jealously was behind her 'two-faced' ways. Could it be possible? Was there some fiber of truth to the idea that she resented Raven's happiness?

In fact, had she resented Raven *for years*?

Rae had always been prettier, more popular, more daring, more confident. She had no student debt and a trust fund to fall back on soon.

Jenna had none of these things. All her life, she'd been the side-kick, the doormat, the loyal follower. She had intelligence and a work-ethic, but didn't know how to enjoy life.

And there it was. She resented Raven's entire life.

Despite the grief of losing her mom, Raven didn't wallow or hold herself back. She embraced life.

That was the cruelest cut of all.

Still, despite the undercurrent of real jealousy, she couldn't let Raven fall into the hands of those people. She remembered the times they played in the sandbox for hours and rode bikes to the junkyard. And the Saturdays staying up all night in sleeping bags on the floor of Raven's den; watching TV, talking about getting their periods for the first time, or which boys they liked, or how much Raven missed the smell of her mom. She recalled the more serious times, like the fight where Helen hit her face with a frying pan and Raven and her dad picked her up so she could stay with them for the night.

Holding back tears, she called Raven.

"Raven, can you talk?"

She heard a pause on the phone. "Are you crying?"

"I just want you to know that I love you and you're the only person who really knows me and I'm very sorry."

Rae sighed. "Aw. Stop crying. You're going to make me start."

"Can you [sniff] forgive me?" Water streamed down her nose.

"Oh, Jenna. Yes, I forgive you. Blanche told me what you said. Your apology really touched her."

"I've been an awful friend."

Raven laughed. "Yes, but I still love you."

Jenna laughed and wiped her eyes. "I love you, too. So…we're okay?"

"We're okay. Sisters forever, right?"

After she composed herself, Jenna said, "Hey, the new episode of Monster-Beast Galaxy 9000 is on tonight. Do you want to watch it together over the phone?"

"Sounds good. I'll call you at nine. Did you get milk duds?"

"Yep." Jenna grabbed a tissue from her nightstand and blew her nose. "Did you?"

"What do you think?"

Jenna laughed. "Great. Talk to you later."

They hung up. The tension in her shoulders eased. She ran into the living room and picked up Thumper. She held him tight to her chest and danced, swaying back and forth, pretending to dip him, which he didn't like very much. Thumper squirmed to get free. When he gave a low growl, she put him on the floor, then continued her dancing and singing the lyrics to 'Moves like Jagger'.

She made herself some boxed mac and cheese and heated a frozen chicken cutlet for dinner, and ate it watching the early news. She cut a piece of chicken for Thumper and threw it across the room to him.

Her doorbell rang. It was only seven now. *Perhaps Fred?*

"Hold on." She put down her fork, found a long gray sweater to wear over her PJ's and went to the door. Looking through the peep-hole, the figure was dark. Her outside light wasn't working. Another thing to fix. "Who is it?"

"Your mother. Open the damned door."

Jenna unhitched the chain and turned the knob. It was mom all right. With a quick visual inspection, Jenna rated her at five. Not entirely sober like a zero and not falling down, almost comatose like a ten. Her mom was apparently functional enough to drive and not kill herself but had crazy eyes, messy hair, her blouse mis-buttoned, no coat despite the thirty-five-degree temperature, and showed up without warning. A solid five. Possibly borderline six or seven. She would find out soon.

"Did you drive yourself here?"

"Oh, like you care." Her mom brushed past her into the living room. "Fuck, it's cold out there. Taking your sweet time opening the door. You trying to kill me?"

"Where's your coat?"

"Don't change the subject. I want my invitation to Raven's bridal shower. I was like her goddamned mother back then. You remember. All the times she stayed over? Why are you keeping her from me?"

"I'm not keeping her from you."

Her mom surveyed the small living room. "Your apartment is ugly. Just like you. You deserve each other."

"Just go home. She doesn't want you there, and neither do I." Jenna held the door open. Thumper began walking toward it, then sped up. Jenna yelled, "Thumper, don't you dare."

He froze, his ears back and tail down; he turned and ran toward Jenna's bedroom.

Helen sat on the couch. "You stupid little bitch." Her gaze traveled around the room. "Do you have any beer?"

Jenna closed the door and stalked over to Helen. Standing above her, she crossed her arms, "Mom, I don't care anymore if you drink yourself to death. I'm done with you. Now get the hell out of here or I'll call the cops."

"You don't have the guts. That's why Marcelo left you. You're a spineless worm. Ugly and worthless. No one could ever love you." Her mom turned her attention to a commercial for mouthwash on the television.

"That does it. Get up." Jenna turned off the television and threw the remote across the room. The remote's battery cover popped off during impact and two AA batteries rolled across the floor. She grabbed Helen's arm and pulled. But she didn't achieve any progress or upward motion.

"Ha. Can't make me." Mom smirked and crossed her arms.

"I'm calling Dad." She snatched her phone off the kitchen counter and took it to her bedroom. As she closed her door, she heard Helen yell, "He's worthless, too. Both of ya."

She dialed. He didn't pick up. Maybe he *was* worthless.

What were her choices? She could leave Helen on the couch and hide in her bedroom. The other option was to actually call the police.

As she contemplated her next move, Thumper popped out from under her bed and joined her. He licked her hand. After a couple of minutes, she decided what to do. She returned to the living room. Her mom was stabbing the couch cushion with Jenna's dull dinner knife, like she was in a deranged trance, humming to herself.

"Mom. Mom! Look at me."

Helen looked up.

"I called the police. They should be here in five minutes."

"Shit." Helen looked around. "Shit. Fuck you."

Hands on her hips, Jenna said, "Fuck you back. You're the reason Dad leaves all the time. He hates you. I hate you, too."

Helen dashed to the front window, still clutching the dinner knife, and pushed back the edge of the drapes, like she was looking for police lights. She opened the front door. Before she exited, she turned her head and said, "Yeah, well, don't be asking me for any handouts. You are not my daughter anymore. You are dead. Dead to me. DEAD TO ME."

Jenna slammed the door closed. She yelled, "Drive safe, shit-head."

She let out a deep breath and slumped to the floor. Then she started giggling. A nervous, boisterous giggle that seemed like an out-of-body experience. She barely recognized the voice that said that last part of 'shit-head'. Maybe she was finally cracking up. But it felt deliriously great at the same time.

She considered the loss of the knife. At least it wasn't a spoon. She was dangerously low on good spoons.

Thumper waddled out of the bedroom and chewed the food in his bowl. His munching rattled his stainless-steel dish; the noise echoed off the linoleum floor through the otherwise quiet apartment.

Jenna inspected her sofa cushion where her mom had stabbed it. Clearly, Mom was off her rocker. Being dead to mom sounded promising. Like she could finally get on with living.

She envisioned her mom hitting a patch of black ice on the way home and careening into a telephone pole.

For once, she'd be okay with that.

Or would she? She had lied about calling the police and felt some satisfaction her ruse worked. But, in actuality, she didn't want mom to collide with other drivers. Maybe she should have let mom sleep it off on her sofa.

She looked out her front window down at the parking lot below. Her mom backed her car out slowly, avoiding hitting other parked cars and the wood fence surrounding the dumpster. Backing out as a normal, *non-intoxicated* person would.

A three? Mom wasn't as plastered as she originally thought; sober enough to drive. This time.

Jenna closed the drapes.

For the next half hour, she wrote out a long email to her dad. Telling him about mom's visit. Insisting he deal with the situation; otherwise, he also would be dead to her. That part stung. But it rang true in her soul. They weren't a family anymore. Just a disjointed group of individuals avoiding each other and dreading any talk about real issues. Something had to give.

And Jenna was about to give up.

* * *

She met Mack after work at their last meeting place. The party was in five days. It occurred to her that Mack never gave her last name. It didn't matter, she supposed, but it seemed Mack knew everything about her and that seemed unfair.

Mack was at the same table, studying something on a laptop. Jenna slid into the same bench as before. Two slices and a cherry coke were already waiting for her. *An attempt to butter her up?*

Mack was wearing a navy suit with a black collared shirt, with the top three buttons undone. Her medium length, dirty-blonde hair was up in a clip, no make-up except a little eyeliner. To Jenna, she looked cool, confident, kind of sexy in a bad-ass, take-charge way. In that moment, Jenna aspired to be just like Mack one day.

"Hi."

Mack looked up and closed her laptop. "Glad you decided to join me. I got you some dinner."

"Thanks." Jenna wasn't sure how this was supposed to go. She assumed she would speak when spoken to.

Mack folded her hands on the table. "We need to go over details, logistics. I have some homework for you."

Jenna's mind raced. *Homework?* "Sure, but first, I have some questions." She picked at her nails below the table.

"Like?"

"Are there any risks that the mob or the Forero's will know I helped you? That is, I don't want to be murdered. And I want Raven to be safe. And the guests. What if things go badly? Does Blanche carry a gun? Will your agents have guns? What if she doesn't cooperate, and she knows I helped you? I'm too young to go into witness protection." She was rambling. She looked down at her hands. One of her fingers was bleeding, where she'd ripped off a sliver of skin.

"All valid concerns."

"So?

Mack pulled a thin folder from under her laptop. From it, she selected an aerial image of the mansion. With a black pen, she marked the exits. "I'll start from the top. If you have questions afterward, we'll go through them."

Over the next ten minutes, Jenna learned a few key points. Mack was going to pose as a guest, armed only with a taser. After the party ended, she would get Blanche alone, preferably upstairs, to offer the deal. By that point, Jenna could leave. During the party, two other agents would pose as fire watch officials, where they would stand by exits, conduct walk-throughs every half hour to inspect for ignition sources, and case guests movements.

Monitoring the ballroom during the party would be tricky. One agent would cover the front door area, another the rear French doors, and Jenna would need to keep watch at the entrance adjoining the kitchen.

Jenna finished her second slice and said, "What's the homework?"

"We need a minute-by-minute schedule of how you'll be running the party. Arrival times, meal times, when the cake will be served, activities, opening presents, all aspects that involve guests moving around or congregating in specific rooms. That will give us a guide on how to keep tabs on Mrs. Forero and when we'll make our move."

"I have an agenda. Or whatever you call a shower schedule." She pulled it up on her phone and showed it to her.

Mack squinted at it. "That's a good start, but I want you to take a day or so to refine it. And add the movements of the catering staff and valets, too. We need to orchestrate this with military precision. With backup plans as things shift on the ground."

Mack sighed. "Normally, we'd have a half-dozen or more agents involved. Because of cut-backs, I'll need you to assist and keep me posted throughout the party. You'll have a small radio to report updates to the itinerary and help us track Blanche's whereabouts. Most importantly, you need to ensure Blanche has a parking space at the house and make sure the main gate at the driveway remains locked until we give the go ahead. You must herd these women to keep to the schedule."

Jenna sighed. *Could she keep a hundred and forty-eight people on a schedule?* Especially women drinking champagne and gossiping? Could anyone?

Mack leaned forward. "Are you up to that? Because if you aren't, we need to know now."

She furrowed her brows. At the after-school program, Mindy had those kids eating out of her hand. She ruled that place like a prison guard but a really nice one, where all the inmates adored her. Could she emulate that kind of leadership? Or was it construction paper and modeling clay that kept Mindy's posse in-line?

"I'll do my best. But you haven't answered my biggest question."

"That Blanche will suspect you?"

Jenna nodded. She took a sip of soda.

"It's possible. This is the reason we have to act quickly. After my

135

partner's mauling, they hunkered down. However, from our surveillance, she doesn't seem to suspect anything might happen at the party."

"What about Raven?"

"She's still in the dark, right? Keep it that way."

"If you want my help, you have to do something for me." Jenna leaned back and crossed her arms.

"I'm listening."

"The deal with Blanche? It has to include a provision that Jack calls off the wedding and cuts ties with Raven completely."

Mack wrote some notes on her laptop. "Done." She placed her computer in a case and gathered her things.

Jenna smiled. "Cool. How do I get you my homework?"

Mack slid her feet around and stood. Jenna glanced down, noticing her gorgeous black patent leather high heels. "I'll send a courier to pick up a hard copy from your apartment on Wednesday night at nine. He'll use the code-word *meatball*."

Had Mack read the text from Blanche that called her a 'sneaky meatball'? It couldn't be a coincidence.

Jenna stood and put on her gray coat. The soda stain hadn't come out completely, leaving a dark maroon splotch on the front. She winced at how sad it must look to Mack, who was sleek and polished. They said goodbye.

A code-word? Spy stuff was pretty awesome. And Mack's pumps reminded her she needed elegant shoes of her own to wear to the party. Something to wear with the red dress. Screw the 'wear white' nonsense.

She decided that if Raven didn't like it—in the words of Mindy—she could go eat a bunch of dicks.

Chapter 15

Wednesday was a busy work day, but Jenna found time to jot down all the relevant party details for Mack. She included a rough floor plan of the mansion.

Jenna also arranged for two valets with the help of Candy and obtained approval to stay the night before so she could meet the Fire Chief and also decorate. With a series of calls to various branches of the Altoona public works department, the city granted permission to park guest's cars along the road on Saturday.

She had to decline Raven's offer to stay with her at the sorority house Saturday night and take part in the Walk-a-Thon. *But wondered if she dismissed the idea too quickly?* It might be a chance to repair their friendship before Rae's surgery. And when Raven found out the truth about Jack and his family, she would need a shoulder to cry on.

But no, her exhaustion was too great. Walking ten miles in the cold with chatty strangers after these weeks of turmoil was a non-starter. Despite whatever Raven was going through, Jenna decided she needed a break for own health.

It was all coming together. But she needed more help. Raven didn't act interested in helping. And perhaps that was for the best. Because spending time together might cause her to crack and spill information. Besides, Raven needed to save her strength for her upcoming surgery or chemo or whatever.

At lunch, Jenna visited Mindy's cube.

"Hey, Mindy."

Since the day before, Mindy had dyed her hair dark purple with pink highlights. She was wearing a voluminous lavender dress with puffy sleeves and her black combat boots, a thick black chain around her neck with a large, blue enameled and gold scarab pendant. Kind of chic meets

Punk. Only Mindy could pull off this outfit.

"Yo, howz it hanging?" Mindy swiveled toward her and smiled.

Jenna plucked at the strands of unraveling fabric on the partition wall. "Good. Are you busy this weekend?"

"Not too busy. What's up?"

"I hate asking for favors, but I could really use your help at the party. To keep things on track. Like make sure we finish the games before the champagne toast and round folks up for the group photo. If I don't keep things moving, it could be a disaster."

"Huh. Interesting." Mindy rubbed her chin.

"I can drive. But…um…I have to be there Friday night. So, it would mean an overnight. But the mansion is amazing and there are seven bedrooms, each with their own bathroom."

Jenna winced. Hearing this out loud, it seemed crazy to ask someone to help her out for a full twenty-four hours in the middle of nowhere, babysitting a bunch of cackling women as they got drunk on champagne and 'ooh'd and ah'd' over lingerie and other naughty bride presents.

Mindy said, "If you drive, how are you getting everything in your car?"

This is precisely why she needed someone like Mindy. Because she'd completely forgotten about bringing the wishing well and cardboard Jack and the myriad of posters, toilet paper rolls and decorations amassed in her living room.

Jenna said, "I guess I could rent a van?"

"I'd be up for a road trip. Count me in. Tell you what, I'll drive. No need to rent a van." It was true. Mindy's RAV4 had real cargo space, especially with the back seats folded flat.

"Really? That would be awesome. But I can manage by myself if you're busy."

"It might be a blast. I mean, I might get wasted during the party if it's lame, but, somehow, it could be entertaining. Like watching Real Housewives, but up close. God, I hate those people."

"Wait, you *hate* them but you *watch* them?"

"Yeah, hate-watch. Those shows inspire my anti-establishment art process. Did I ever show you the painting I did last year?" Mindy reached for her phone.

"No…."

Mindy showed her a picture. It was a painting of a donkey with long glamorous hair, wearing a push-up bra, holding a Gucci bag. It was bizarre, but very well done.

Jenna studied it. "Um. Nice."

"Wait, check this out." She swiped to another photo. It was a cake that looked like an elephant taking a dump on an election sign.

Jenna laughed. "I didn't know you baked."

Mindy whistled. "I dabble in many things. Last year I sewed a quilt promoting transgender equality."

"I'm glad you can help. I'm hopeless when it comes to decorating."

"It'll be fun. Tell you what. You can repay the favor by helping me run the classes at the 'Y' for the next month. I'll feel less outnumbered. Deal?"

It wasn't like she had a roaring social life, Jenna thought. In fact, it was an easy decision. "Yes. Deal." She returned to her desk. Volunteering would be fun. She had to admit spending time with Mindy's kids got her out of her own head and away from her troubles. Little kids were unfiltered. Genuine. Without ulterior motives. Not that they were all perfect angels, but being with them felt refreshing. Yes, she could really enjoy spending time with them.

She wondered if she should tell Mindy about the FBI stakeout. But, concluded it was best to keep it under wraps. Knowing Mindy, she'd ask the agents to give her shooting lessons, or ask them awkward questions about the militarization of today's law enforcement agencies. No, the less Mindy knew, the better.

Only two more days left before the party.

With Mindy's help, it just might work.

* * *

Jenna had all her lists ready. Boxes were lined up and labeled at her apartment. Her overnight bag was packed for the camp out at the mansion. It was Friday. She arrived at the office at seven. She and Mindy planned to leave by three o'clock to avoid Philadelphia commuter and weekend traffic.

At ten, her cell phone rang. It was the caterer, Tanya.

"Hi, Tanya. How are things shaping up?" Jenna doodled on her desk calendar.

"Ms. Mott, I'm so sorry. I have to cancel." Tanya sounded hoarse.

"What's wrong?" Jenna stopped doodling and dropped her pen. It rolled and landed on the floor.

"I'm in the hospital. I won't be able to cater the party tomorrow."

The words registered slowly. *She won't...* "What? I mean, that's awful. What about your staff? Can they still come?"

"Yeah, um, no. I may have a form of meningitis that's contagious. Until I get the labs back in two days, the doctors said we should all quarantine ourselves."

"Oh, no. I hope you're okay." Jenna's mind blanked. A hundred and forty-one guests and no food or cake?

"If it helps, all the food and materials are being delivered by the grocer directly to the house tonight. Candy is letting them in. If you can find another caterer, they can use what's there. It's already paid for. Hey, the nurse is here. I've got to go."

Jenna's brain was on fire with questions. Could she find another caterer in the next twenty-four hours? That didn't seem likely. What could she say? "Feel better soon, Tanya."

"Thanks for understanding. Tell Mrs. Forero I'm sorry. Bye, Ms. Mott."

Jenna said, "Bye," and hung up. This couldn't be happening, could it? After all the days planning, all the phone calls, the meetings with the FBI, getting permits and stuffing envelopes, it couldn't fall apart.

Inconceivable.

She scrolled through the contacts on her phone. She dialed Candy Morris.

"Candy, I just got a call from Tanya." She looked at her finger nails. There was blood. She realized she'd been unconsciously scratching her scalp, breaking the skin. A disgusting, terrible side-effect of her raging anxiety.

"Jenna? Yes, I told her to call you. Poor thing."

"You must have a backup plan, right? I mean, you work with catering firms all the time. Who's replacing her?" Jenna found a tissue and held it to her bleeding scalp.

"I don't know. You'd better start calling around."

"What? You're kidding me. Tell me you're kidding me. This is your *job*." She said that last part louder, unconcerned if others in the office heard. "This is why we're paying you to organize this thing." Her heart pounded.

"Ms. Mott, don't take that tone with me. The contract is clear. My job is to coordinate with the caterer. Tanya is an independent contractor and you have a separate contract with her. It's not a requirement that I provide a caterer."

Jenna's jaw fell open. *It couldn't be. Could it?* She grabbed her party folder and began rifling through all the documents. "Wait, hold on."

Candy said, "Read it, you'll see. Second page on the bottom."

"I've got it, hold on. I'm reading…"

"Look, I don't have time for this. Have a good day." Candy hung up.

Jenna dropped her phone and kept scanning page two. Her lips moved as she read. There it was, in italics. Candy was correct. Which meant the party was screwed.

Should she just tell Raven her fiancé was planning to murder her? Just cancel the party altogether?

Then it occurred to her. Perhaps Ben or Mack could help. They had the resources of the Federal government. Surely, they could help find a caterer, particularly since their sting operation rested on this event.

She called Mack and explained the whole situation.

"Sorry, Jenna. I can't help you. But, honestly, just go to Costco and get a sheet cake and some platters. The guests won't care. The party has to go on."

Jenna thought about Costco. It could work. Just put stuff on pretty plates. *Could anyone tell the difference?*

"Mack, if Raven's life is in danger, why not arrest Jack and his parent now? Why bother with this stupid party?"

Mack sighed loudly. "Jenna, if we had prima facie evidence of a murder plot…yes, we could arrest them now. If you want to back out, let me know now. Look, in another twelve to fifteen months we could have enough evidence to get the mob *and* the Forero's. But, as you know, your friend may not have that much time, and if she survives her wedding to Jack, she could also become implicated and arrested in this whole ordeal."

It hadn't occurred to her that Raven might become entangled in this mess. Jenna scratched her chin. "No, I'm in. I'll make it work. See you tomorrow." Jenna hung up.

She looked through the contract with the caterer. The deposit covered the cost of the food and supplies. Which they were receiving. The labor costs would be paid after services rendered. Which wasn't happening and meant that there wouldn't be a refund coming to cover the costs of additional labor or prepared foods. No, if she needed money, it would have to come from Blanche. The last person she wanted to beg to. And she couldn't tell Blanche she needed money for food from Costco, because it would be so beneath her snooty standards. So, unless she found new chefs, she was stuck.

Adrenaline surged through her veins. Her mind blanked. She was back to square one. All the days and nights planning and preparing wasted. Part of her wanted to search the internet for catering companies. Another part wanted to go home, crawl in bed and stay there for a week.

As a compromise, she walked over to Mindy's cube. Mindy was on a phone call. Instead, she dragged herself over to Russ's cube.

He was reading e-mail. A bowl of M&Ms sat on his desk, near the cube opening. She wanted to grab a fistful and smash them in her mouth. "Hey, Russ."

He swiveled to face her. "Hey. What's up?" He had a grease stain on his blue plaid shirt, right where his belly jutted out slightly.

"You won't believe it."

"What?"

She slumped against the partition. "The caterer for tomorrow's party just cancelled. I'm so…I'm going to have a break down."

"It's just a party."

"Ha!" Jenna began giggling. A nervous, crazed giggle she didn't recognize in herself.

"Whoa. You need to calm down. Take a seat."

She took a seat in his guest chair, wedged next to hanging file drawers. But she grabbed a handful of M&Ms first.

Mindy came over. "Sorry, I was on the phone. Did I just hear you say the caterer cancelled? Like not coming at all?"

Jenna chewed on a dozen chocolates. With her mouth full, she said, "Yep."

Mindy said, "That's crazy. Can you hire a different company?"

"I don't know." Jenna finished chewing and closed her eyes. "Maybe I don't care." She ran a hand through her ponytail. A few dark, long strands of hair came out, now interwoven through her fingers. She picked the hair off her hand, dropping it onto the floor. "Great. I'll be bald soon."

Russ said, "Like a hairless cat. Or a naked mole-rat." He smiled.

Jenna looked at him with narrowed eyes. Why was he making fun of her?

He said, "Sorry. Just trying to make you laugh. Why don't Mindy and I help you call around? I'll print out a list of all the caterers within a twenty-five-mile radius, including restaurants, and we'll split it up?"

Mindy said, "Absolutely. We can even try culinary schools and private chefs. Jenna, why don't you go relax at your desk? Get a snack or take a walk. Inhale some fresh air. Russ and I will work on this. It will be fine. I promise."

Jenna looked at them. "Really? Okay." She got up and ambled over to her desk. How was she going to relax? Her heart was still pounding, but she had an eerie stillness in her brain at the same time. She wanted to vomit.

A few minutes later, Mindy's purple hair bounced above the partitions toward her.

Jenna balled her hands into fists and squeezed her eyes shut. "Tell me you found someone."

"Nope. We called around. There's a caterer free next weekend, but I'm guessing that's a non-starter."

"All the groceries are being delivered to the house. I don't suppose you know how to bake a fancy cake?"

"Sure, I can make a cake. In fact, with some help, I bet together we could prepare everything. Wait here."

Wait here? At my own cube? "Sure."

After a couple of minutes, Mindy came back with Russ behind her. "He's in."

Russ grinned, "I love a road trip."

Jenna chewed her nails. "You can cook?"

"No," he said, "well, I can boil water and stuff. I'm good at taking direction and being bossed around. And I could use a change of scenery."

"Really? Thanks. We're leaving at three. Wait, Mindy, will we have enough space in your car?"

Mindy rubbed her chin. "We should take both my car and yours." She turned to Russ. "Go home and get a change of clothes at lunchtime. I'll do the same. After work, we'll convoy to Jenna's to load up the cars. Sound good?"

They agreed.

Mindy and Russ returned to their desks.

Jenna took a deep breath. Could they really cook for a party this size? It was a crazy but intriguing plan.

She texted Raven.

> "I'm going to Altoona tonight to prepare. Could really use help.
> Can you meet us there? A sleepover like old times?"

Raven texted back that she had a hair and make-up appointment early on Saturday and she might be a few minutes late to the party.

What? She wasn't even going to be on time to her own party?

Rae was no help. Somehow, this didn't surprise her.

But she had another ace up her sleeve. She made the next call to someone with the right experience.

* * *

At 3:20, the trio converged on Jenna's apartment. Russ took the heaviest items down the metal stairs and loaded Mindy's SUV. Jenna piled food in two bowls for Thumper, plus extra water dishes. Then she ran downstairs to knock on Fred's door.

"Are you ready?" She gasped for air, holding her side.

Fred had his coat on and a small backpack on one shoulder. "Sure 'nuf. It's been a long time since I spent a night out of town."

"Great. We're leaving in two minutes."

They walked to Jenna's car. She said, "Fred, you're with me."

Next to her car, her coworkers were readjusting items in the back of the RAV 4. "Fred, meet Mindy and Russ."

Fred gave them a salute. Russ saluted back.

Mindy smirked. "So, this is famous Fred. Jenna says you're the bee's knees."

"Or a bee that knows how to cook for a submarine full of sailors." Fred chuckled.

"Fred will be your First Mate," Jenna said. "Come on, let's go."

Russ got into Mindy's SUV and Fred drove with Jenna. If they were lucky, they would arrive in Altoona by seven-thirty.

Jenna tried to focus on the road, but her mind kept going over all the things she needed to do once they arrived. First, get let in by Candy and receive keys to the doors and keycard for the gate. Second, call the Fire Marshall to let him know they arrived and set up the walk-through. Third, look through all the groceries and match them up to the dishes to be prepared. Fourth, make a list of anything missing and send Fred and Russ to the store. Fifth, get Mindy working on the cake.

Oh, and text Mack to let her know they were "in". Like a bank heist. Or a different kind of heist. She hadn't worked out the logic of that one yet.

Then came any food prep that made sense to do ahead of time and, of course, decorating. All this was just the 'night before' list. The 'day of' list was worse.

So many moving parts.

And what exactly was Candy doing to help? It wasn't clear. In fact, Candy acted like her job was done: delivering the party favors; setting up the tables and chairs, plus linens, place settings, and centerpieces; delivering the champagne fountain and a helium canister. These were all good things. Necessary things. But they were the window dressing. Not the stuff that required real coordination. Real planning. Actual back-breaking labor.

Fred broke her from her crazed thoughts, saying, "I'm guessing it's okay if I don't wear white?"

Jenna smiled. "You wear whatever you want. In fact, I decided to wear Ava's dress."

"Good for you."

"In truth, I didn't have many other options." Her earlier idea to go clothes shopping had completely escaped her mind after the meeting with Ben and Mack. A reasonable person would look at her clothes closet and assume a depressed Amish person lived in her apartment. All black, gray and navy clothes, with some white dress shirts for work. Nothing with bright colors, pastels or frills that would convey femininity or fun.

"Well, I think Ava would be happy her dress is getting a new life."

A wave a sadness overtook her. Maybe it was just stress. Or his phrase "new life", reminding her of Fred's loss and how she bullied him into helping her, when she should be helping him. Not that she actually bullied him. But just asking him for his help now felt like a crime. She wiped her eyes.

"Hey, Jenna, did I say something wrong?"

"No, Fred. I'm…I'm just happy to have a friend like you."

"Well, stop 'yer waterworks. How about some music?"

This time Jenna was prepared. All the presets were fixed on her radio. She hit each button. But instead of her pop and soft rock songs, religious sermons, sportscasters and classical music stations came up. Now a half-hour drive into Pennsylvania, all the stations assigned to those frequencies were different.

Fred said, "Forget those. I made a playlist on my phone." He synched the Bluetooth to his phone and Bobby Darin came on. Fred began singing "Mack the Knife" along with Bobby. Fred wasn't bad as a crooner, but when he started swaying his shoulders and making silly faces at her, it was clear he was trying to cheer her up.

Jenna laughed. The real Mack the Knife was arriving in the morning. And hopefully, the real Mack was a shark of justice with rows of razor-sharp teeth.

Chapter 16

It was dark when they arrived at the mansion. Candy stood in the driveway, waiting for them, shaking her head. They were twenty minutes late.

Candy said, "I almost gave up on you. I have other clients to deal with. By the way, the food was delivered and placed in the kitchen." In a bitchy tone, she added, "You're welcome."

Jenna said, "Thank you," although she wanted to say something else. Something snide. But it wasn't worth getting into a fight. The schedule didn't allow for it.

Before Candy left, she said, "Remember, leave it as clean as you found it. Otherwise, I keep the security deposit."

They were still unloading Mindy's car when the Fire Marshall arrived. After a cursory inspection, he announced the fire extinguishers in the kitchen and the ballroom had expired and they needed new ones before the guests arrived. It was nearly eight at night. The only home improvement store would be closed by the time they drove there. Jenna added those to the list of things to buy.

So much to do, Jenna thought. She propped 2-D Jack against a wall in the ballroom. She gazed at the figure. *This is all your fault.* She tugged on his cardboard pinky finger and tore it off.

Jenna heard pots and pans clanking in the distance. Mindy was going through the grocery order and menu to determine if anything was missing.

"Jenn," Mindy said, her voice carrying from the kitchen. "I can't find any cake tins."

She tossed paper Jack's cardboard finger to the floor and stalked over. "Did you go through all the cabinets?"

"I hope I'm wrong."

They looked through the kitchen again, Mindy taking the cabinets on the left side of the stove while Jenna took the right. They looked high and low. In the oven, in the pantry. *Nada.*

Mindy leaned against the refrigerator. "Don't worry about it. I'll improvise." She pointed to an assortment of frying pans and sauce pots she'd assembled on the counter. "Besides, many sins can be hidden with frosting."

There were lots of sins that could never be solved with frosting. Although frosting helped in many situations. She looked around. "What are Fred and Russ up to?"

"They found the air hockey table in the basement. You may need to drag them away."

She sighed. "What do you need? I'd rather they help you. Decorating may not be their thing."

"I need potatoes peeled, lettuce, tomatoes, cucumbers and garlic chopped. I need, well… everything."

"Good. You focus on the cake. I'll send the boys up. I have a champagne fountain to assemble." A thought came to her and the blood drained from her face. "Oh, no."

"What?" Mindy began measuring out flour.

"I didn't get the champagne."

"Liquor stores might be open late."

Jenna checked her phone for store hours. There were three in town, one was open until ten. But she'd have to hurry. "I'll go over now. Should I stop at a store to find cake pans? Anything else I should get?"

Mindy tapped her fingers on the counter. "You know what? Stay put. We'll keep adding to the list and have Russ go out first thing tomorrow. If we don't consolidate shopping trips, we'll never get everything done."

Jenna's shoulders eased. "Yes, I suppose that would be more efficient. I'm a little tired."

"It was a long drive. Better to get to sleep at a decent hour tonight and hit it fresh tomorrow. I'll get the cake rounds done tonight and tomorrow I can frost and decorate."

Jenna took a seat at the island and rested her head on her folded arms. *Sleeping for a hundred years would be nice.*

Mindy coughed. "The boys?"

She bolted up. "Right. Get the guys. I'll be right back."

During her last visit to the house, she never found the basement door.

But this time, she found it next to the office near the foyer. The staircase was dark. No sound.

She went to the large ballroom. No one in there. Sounds came from a den in the rear of the house. She followed the noise and found Fred was making a fire in the fireplace. The den was one of the smaller rooms in the house. It was cozy, with dark painted walls and a stone fireplace that seemed rustic compared to the rest of the décor in the house. A luminous landscape painting of the Pennsylvania country-side hung above the mantle. The sofa and chairs were olive-colored with deep cushions and sumptuous throw pillows. In fact, in that moment, she decided it was her favorite room.

"Hey, Fred. Where's Russ?"

"I think he's in the bathroom."

"Um, why are you lighting a fire?"

Fred crouched by the fireplace, put some kindling on top of the logs. "Sorry. I'm a sentimental old fart. Had a fireplace in my old home. Ava always wanted a fire going on a cold winter's night. I guess I'm just saying hello to her."

That was the sweetest thing she'd ever heard. She kissed the top of his balding head. "You're a good man."

Fred laughed. "Well, if you say so."

Russ entered. "Hey, Fred. Mindy said she could use our help in the kitchen."

Fred dusted off his hands. The fire was small but seemed self-sustaining. "Sure 'nuf. Let's go."

The guys headed to the kitchen. Jenna stayed behind, mesmerized by the fire. All she needed now were some marshmallows. And a sleeping bag. And some good friends.

Life would be complete.

Her trance broke, and she ambled into the ballroom. She found the helium canister and began blowing up of pink balloons. So much pink. Pink streamers, pink ribbons, pink table cloths, pink napkins. The room was an explosion of Pepto Bismol. With a stupid champagne fountain in the center.

She only hoped this descent into a pink hell would be worth it.

Maybe Jack would go to prison.

Maybe Raven would come back from the precipice.

She tied another long ribbon onto a balloon and released it to the ceiling.

Her fingers ached from twisting rubber knots. She'd lost count of the balloons. *Did any of this matter?*

Mindy appeared. "You know, latex balloons deflate in eight hours. You should do that in the morning."

"Great." One more screw up. She released of the balloon in her hand and it screamed through the air with a prolonged farting noise. She hung her head, clapping her hands to her face.

Mindy said, "Come. Join us in the kitchen. Lots to do there."

"Fine." Her stomach grumbled. Despite her lists and planning, she realized none of them had dinner. She followed Mindy to the kitchen. Russ and Fred were laughing, chopping vegetables, peeling potatoes, and having a jovial time.

Russ said, "Jenn, we ordered some takeout. Should be here in fifteen minutes. But, ah, we may have also eaten some fancy chocolates from the gift bags."

Mindy raised an eyebrow. "We?"

Fred said, "Fine, it was me and Russ." He reached into the open confection package and took out two wrapped truffles. "Catch." He threw them to Jenna.

She caught one and the other bounced off her hand and skidded sideways across the wood floor. It rolled under the baseboard by the pantry.

Russ yelled, "Finders keepers!" and lunged for it.

Without thinking, Jenna raced to beat him. Like Thumper after a ping-pong ball. They collided on the floor, both reaching for the silver-wrapped orb.

She grabbed his wrist, trying to pry his fingers apart. But she was no match against his long reach.

He yelled in a silly voice that sounded like a vaudeville villain, "You can never win," twisting his body, extending his arm.

Instinctively, she threw herself across his chest to maintain her grip. The closeness gave her flashbacks of Marcelo when he teased her. She looked into Russ's eyes.

His eyes pierced hers with an odd recognition and he stopped struggling, releasing the candy. "Okay, you win."

She rolled to the side and regarded her prize. He laughed, got to his feet and extended a hand. She grasped his hand. It felt soft, warm. Rising off the floor, her knee buckled; she lost her balance, falling forward. He grabbed her waist. *Was she weak from lack of food again?*

His arms felt strong, solid. Heat rose to her face. When her feet found purchase, their bodies were close, facing each other, his face showing concern. Instinctually, she lifted her chin for a kiss, as if he were Marcelo. But no. She shook her head and backed out of his arms. "Um, thanks, Russ. I'm okay now." She unwrapped the candy, avoiding his gaze.

Fred gestured toward them with his knife. "Ok, you lovebirds, get with the chopping."

Lovebirds? She looked at Russ. He didn't say anything. No witty comeback or silly joke. He simply walked back to his cutting board, picked up his knife, head down, began cutting some tomatoes. *Were his cheeks red?* Hers felt warm.

Mindy cut the tension by asking her to get some eggs.

She walked to the fridge and retrieved a carton. Part of her wanted to stick her head in the cold compartment and keep it there. As she placed the eggs next to Mindy, Mindy kept stirring batter, but looked up and winked at her, nodding toward Russ. These subtle gestures meant something. It reminded her of high school, talking at your lockers, when a cute guy walked by and your friend hints, "he likes you."

And, the scary part was, she liked him too.

* * *

Shortly after eleven, glassy-eyed and lids drooping, Fred firmly announced it was time to call it quits. No one argued. He walked to the den to check on the fireplace. Jenna followed him.

The lights were off, but the fire illuminated the room in a warm glow. Fred poked the logs apart to dampen the fire.

"Don't do that," Jenna said.

"Why?"

"I like it. I'm going to sit down here for a little while. Decompress."

"Well," he rearranged the logs back into a mass. "I'll keep you company. Least for a bit. I turn into a pumpkin at midnight." Fred plopped himself in a cushy arm chair, which turned out to be a recliner, because he hit a button and the foot rest eased up with an electronic whir.

Jenna grabbed a wool throw blanket off the sofa, wrapped it around her shoulders, and sat cross-legged, about four feet from the roaring fire. She stared, trance-like, at the flames as they crackled and sparked. The woody smell reminded her of a family vacation in the Adirondacks when she was six. A rare good memory. Her own apartment was always on the chilly side to save money. Electric base-board heat was expensive. The fireplace radiated a kind of heat that penetrated her bones. Like a hot bath, or sunbathing on the beach in the middle of August. All the voices in her head shut down and shut up, all enjoying the glorious hot air.

Mindy and Russ poked their heads in the room.

"Whatcha'll doing?" Mindy asked.

Fred shimmied in his chair, arching his back. "I think you youngsters call it 'chillin'."

Russ said, "I'm heading up to sleep. See you in the morning."

Mindy grabbed Russ's arm. "Stay." It sounded like an order. Mindy grabbed two cushions off the couch and tossed them on the floor next to Jenna. "Sit."

Russ laughed. "Yes, ma'am." He sat on the cushion closer to Fred.

Mindy smiled. "Who wants to tell ghost stories?" She lay on her stomach, her torso propped up by her elbows.

Fred said, "I'm too old for that nonsense. Can't we just have a nice quiet conversation? Sheez. This ain't middle school."

Russ said, "He has a point."

Fred said, "Yep, right on the top of my head." He paused for laughter, but only received an eye roll from Mindy. He looked at Russ. "Young fellow, what's your story? Jenna never mentioned you."

Jenna winced. It was true Russ never came up in their conversations. But the way Fred phrased this statement, it seemed like an insult. Like Russ was a stranger, insignificant, a nobody.

Russ scratched his head. "My name is Russ. I'm an engineer. I work with Jenna and Mindy. Printing solutions are my true passion." He chuckled and shook his head. "What do you want to know?"

Mindy sighed in frustration. "Where are you from? What's your family like? Hobbies. Aspirations. Favorite color. Whatever. Come on. Spill."

He grinned. "I like the color blue."

Mindy hit him in the shoulder. "Pathetic. Fine, I'll go. I'm from New York, Queens originally. But grew up in East Windsor. I have five older brothers, all married with kids. I wanted to go to art school, but ended up in computer science. I've worked at Veloma for five years, but my real joy comes from working with kids on art projects. And fashion. And sewing.

Plus, sculpting, and painting. And fighting the establishment."

Fred laughed. "Is that all?"

Russ said, "I have to say, I'm not so interesting. But I had a challenging upbringing. Raised by wolves. Lived on cold cereal and kept to myself. Growing up, my only goal was getting into college. My dad died a few years back from heart disease. My mom is in a nursing home. She has schizophrenia. I have an older brother who lives in California. We don't talk much."

Jenna said, "Your mom has mental illness? I'm so sorry."

"Yeah, since I was a little kid. She didn't know who I was most of the time. Called me that 'nice boy who brings her food'. But I made it to college alive. Although, she almost burned down the house once. I had to disconnect the stove when I was eleven. We never used it again after that."

Mindy said, "Wow. No wonder you don't know how to cook. What about your dad? How did he deal with her?"

"He was a salesman. Gone from the house a lot. When he was home, he drank a lot. There were lots of drunken screaming matches. But I never felt in danger. They never hit me."

Fred said, "Jesus. Ha! I thought I had an awful childhood. Russ, you win."

Jenna studied Russ's face. He didn't convey anger or sorrow describing his early life. Instead, he was remarkably Zen-like. Had he forgiven his parents? How did he survive a worse situation and come out without a smidge of bitterness? Perhaps she could learn something from him.

"Well, that got heavy fast," Mindy said. "Hmm. Russ, you are shockingly normal. That's a compliment."

Russ laughed. "Sorry for bringing down the room."

Mindy turned to Jenna. "Whatever happened with your boyfriend?"

A total non sequitur. Jenna stared at Mindy. A wave of humiliation flooded her brain and her throat felt tight. "I honestly don't want to talk about him. We broke up." She fiddled with the ring on her finger.

Mindy pointed to Jenna's ring. "Didn't he give that to you? Why are you still wearing it?"

That cut to the bone. *Why was she still wearing it?* Was it too soon to close that door? "I, um, don't know. Haven't thought about it."

Fred came to her rescue and said, "Well, I'm plum tuckered. More tired than a possum workin' the day shift. I picked the bedroom at the top of the stairs." He pressed the button on the recliner to right himself. As he got up, he smiled and pointed to Mindy. "Don't you chickees think of seducing this old fart in the middle of the night. My ticker and other parts couldn't take it. And if you hear someone teetering around downstairs at three in the morning, it's probably me. I don't sleep much these days." He waved and ambled out of the room.

Jenna said, "He's right. Time for sleep." She got up and poked the logs apart like she'd seen Fred do earlier.

Mindy and Russ put their cushions back on the couch.

Russ said, "I'm heading to the store at seven. If you think of anything else you need, let me know by then."

Jenna said, "I'll be up at six. I can go with."

Mindy beamed at her. "See you in the morning." She blew them a kiss goodbye and left.

Jenna said, "Goodnight, Russ." She closed the glass doors on the fireplace, taking her time to put away the poker and straighten the room. Creating a delay so he would leave without her.

Russ nodded and left the room.

She glanced around the dim silent room. Tomorrow the house would be filled with dozens of women dressed in white, like a weird suburban cult.

Just sixteen more hours, she thought.

And her best friend would be returned to her.

Chapter 17

The high thread-count sheets felt like silk. Before opening her eyes, she stretched her arm towards Marcelo, to run her fingers through the dark, baby-fine hairs on his washboard stomach. She could feel his breath tickle her neck as he took her in his arms. The musky smell of his skin made her loins ache. His hand caressed her thigh, then tugged at her cotton panties. She arched her back, lifting her chin to kiss his beautiful soft lips...

In an instant, Jenna was awake, eyes wide. She snatched her phone from the nightstand, panicked, reading the time in a state of terror. It was seven-thirty. She'd overslept; the one thing she couldn't afford. She was supposed to go shopping with Russ at seven to get supplies.

She swept her hair up in a disorganized ponytail, pulled on sweatpants and a long-sleeve T-shirt, and raced down the stairs in her socks.

Hearing voices in the kitchen, she ran toward them.

Fred, Mindy and Russ sat at the island, drinking what smelled like coffee and eating round sandwiches wrapped in yellow paper. Some type of takeout food.

Mindy looked up. "Hey, sleepyhead. You hungry?"

"Sorry. How long have you guys been up?" Jenna yawned. "Where did you get coffee?"

Russ said, "I borrowed Mindy's car and went to Dunkin'. I got coffee and breakfast sandwiches, but they might be a little cold now." He pointed to a cup and sandwich by the stove.

"Wow, thanks Russ."

Fred said, "It was my idea, don't take all the credit there, Russ." He smiled. "I don't function well without my java. Need something to get the ol' engine running."

"Well, thanks to both of you." She looked around the kitchen. Something caught her eye. Two brand new ABC fire extinguishers on the floor next to the pantry. She pointed. "How? When?"

Russ said, "I got to the hardware store when they opened at six. Before I picked up breakfast."

Her eyes misted. In that moment, she wanted to hug Russ and never let him go. *Who was this miracle of a human being?* Surely, he was an angel beamed down from heaven. She clasped her hands to her chest. "Oh, wow, Russ, that's…you are…I can't…"

Russ smiled. "It was no problem."

Mindy crumpled up her sandwich paper. "What's the plan this morning?"

Russ said, "I'm going out for more supplies soon. What else do we need?"

Her head was too foggy to recall. She inspected the list, now a mile long, pinned to the cork board next to the pantry door. "Creamer, sugar, coffee, serving spoons, champagne, vanilla, olive oil, cooking spray, piping bags, chocolate sprinkles, a pound of fondant, toothpicks, dishwasher soap, a cake serving knife, twelve large disposable warming trays, some paper doily things, paper baking cups, Scotch Tape for the toilet paper dresses, and a cake stand." Jenna scratched her head. "Dang. That's a lot."

Russ said, "Are you still coming with? We could split up the list at the store. It would go faster."

"Yes, good idea." She picked up her cup of coffee and took a sip. It was cold as Russ had warned. She drank it anyway, in one long motion, then stuffed her sandwich into her bag for the ride in the car.

After finding her sneakers and putting on her coat, Jenna left with Russ. On the way, she checked her account balance through her phone. Yesterday was pay day. She could pay by debit if needed. Her credit card was for emergencies. But this surely felt like an emergency.

For the next hour and a half, they visited three stores. Unsure of sizes or quantities needed of some items, Jenna texted Mindy every ten minutes. Ultimately, they got everything except the piping bags.

Back at the house, Fred came out to the driveway to meet them. It was now close to ten. Three hours left to pull off the near impossible.

Jenna and Russ began unloading. She picked up the bag with the stack of warming trays and candles.

Fred said, "There was a lady looking for you."

Jenna kept walking. The bag was heavy. "Who?"

Fred followed her. "She didn't leave her name. Tall blonde, wore a suit, sexy shoes, serious expression."

It had to be Mack. *Why didn't she just call?* "Where is she now?"

"Said she'd come back later, around noon."

"Hey, help bring stuff in."

"Righto." Fred went to the car.

At the kitchen, Jenna dropped the bag on the counter.

Mindy was putting something in the oven. Looked like chicken. "Did you get everything?"

"Nearly. After we're done unloading, what can I do?"

Mindy took a bowl out of the microwave. "I need someone to roll out fondant and fill muffin tins with batter. Empty and reload the dishwasher. Fill and test the fountain. Make me another cup of coffee before I lose it. Set up a table for the warming trays in the ballroom. We have to do a buffet. It's the only goddamned way."

Jenna relayed the tasks to the guys. The team was like a swarm of ants, moving this way and that, trying not to bump into each other. Every so often, when Mindy started cursing, Fred would tell corny jokes. Russ, who thought this was a brilliant strategy, began chiming in with bad knock-knock jokes. Mindy wasn't amused and ordered them out of 'her' kitchen if they didn't shut up. That cracked the guys up even more.

A couple hours later, they heard a voice. "Hello? Where are you?"

Dread washed through Jenna. Blanche had arrived.

She realized she hadn't showered, put on clean clothes, or even combed her hair yet. Jenna looked down at her navy t-shirt covered in flour and random tomato sauce stains. She was—in two words—a stinky mess.

Blanche sashayed into the kitchen, wearing a striped black and white fur coat, long white satin skirt and sparkly white heels. "There you are. I called earlier. Why don't you ever answer? Unbelievable. I came to inspect. To see what I'm paying for." She pointed to Mindy, Fred and Russ, who instinctively backed themselves into the corner by the fridge, like Dalmatian puppies frightened by Cruella De Vil. "Are they with the caterer?"

She wondered if it would be a complete lie to say yes. "Sure."

Blanche looked them up and down. "Hmm. Not what I expected." She turned and strode to the ballroom.

Jenna raced after her. The ballroom was far from picture perfect.

Blanche shook her head. "Jenna! Half the balloons are dead." She lifted a napkin. "This is peach. I specifically asked for blush pink. How could you let this happen?"

The question was rhetorical, because Blanche kept inspecting the room. She stopped at the fountain. It was recently filled and tested, but the power was off. She inspected the bottles of champagne, open and sitting on the floor, like the remnants of some wino orgy. Jenna had meant to bring in a recycling can to cart them off, but got distracted with other tasks.

Blanche lifted a bottle and squinted at the label. Jenna sucked in air and held her breath. Earlier, at the store, she grabbed five cases of the least expensive brand they carried. At ten dollars a bottle, the total was over three hundred dollars. A fortune for someone in her position.

"What kind of crap is this?" Blanche sneered. "This is non-alcoholic."

It was? In the time crunch, she didn't bother looking at the label.

Jenna said, "I didn't realize…"

"I knew I should have taken charge. I mean, look at you." Blanche shook her head. "Unbelievable. I have to do everything myself. Fine, I'll go and get the right stuff." She gestured at the room. "You'd better have this presentable when I get back. This is the last thing I need. I have a nail appointment, then I'm picking up John's aunt, Mary Rose, and *now* I have to fix your disaster." She strode off toward the front door.

Jenna followed her to the foyer. She shouted, "I'm really trying. You don't have to be so mean."

Blanche spun around, "Mean? I wasn't the one that made poor Raven cry the other night. You need to look in the mirror, missy. Raven's been so worried about her augmentation surgery. She calls me almost every day. The last thing she needs is this party to go to the shitter."

Jenna's eyes grew three sizes. "Augmentation?"

"You didn't know? I keep reassuring her. She's so worried about healing in time for the wedding."

Did she hear this correctly? Raven *doesn't* have cancer? "A boob job?"

"Yes, that's what augmentation *means*. Honestly, don't you know anything?"

Jenna swallowed. Raven had been lying. Lying by omission. But still, it was cruel. Maybe she was a timid loser. She hung her head. "No, I guess not."

Blanche said, "First true thing you've said." She buttoned her coat and grabbed the front door knob. "I want this spotless by the time I get back." The door slammed shut.

Mindy entered the foyer, clapping slowly. [clap] [clap] [clap] "Fuck that cow. Her stupid coat looks like Pepé Le Pew." She tilted her head, examining Jenna's face. "What happened?"

Jenna stumbled backward, taking a seat on the circular staircase. "I…I can't believe it."

"What did I miss?"

"The surgery. I thought Rae was sick. All this time, I was worried about her dying during open heart surgery. Or going through rounds of chemo. Why would she lie to me like that?" She held her head, staring at the floor. A guttural cry burst forth through her clenched teeth. "Aaagh. Shit."

Mindy sat on the step next to her. "Yeah, I'd say that's supremely shitty."

"All this time, Rae wanted this party moved up so she would have time for her stupid new gigantic boobs to heal before the wedding." After a few seconds of silence, Jenna inhaled and clenched her fists. "That fucking bitch."

"Hey, I've never heard you curse before. But I like it." Mindy put an arm around Jenna's shoulders.

Jenna stood and leapt to the center of the hall, spinning in a circle. "You know what? She can't treat me like this and get away with it. This is *bullshit*."

"Good. So, what do you want to do?"

Her mind blanked. *What did she want?* And then it came to her. "Fuck this party."

Mindy smiled. "I agree. Fuck this party in the ass."

"This idiotic party must die…like Todd." She spun around again, sliding her socks on the slick floor, and grinned. "Are you with me?"

Mindy shouted, one fist in the air like Braveheart, "You can take our pastries, you can take our gift bags, but you will fucking regret this day!"

Fred and Russ came down the hall. Fred said, "What are you ladies shouting about?"

"War," Mindy said. "Fucking full-on war. Because fuck that bitch." She walked toward the kitchen. "Everyone, follow me."

They walked in procession behind her. At the kitchen island, Mindy put her forefinger in a bowl of tomato sauce. She spread a line on each of her cheeks, like war paint. Then did the same to Jenna. "There. Let's huddle. How do we sabotage this mo-fo? Ideas. Now!"

Russ said, "Is that what we're doing now?"

Jenna smiled. "Damn straight."

Russ said, "Like…what level of sabotage? Like dead insects in the cake?"

Fred chuckled. "Piss in the pretentious champagne fountain?"

Jenna frowned, "Bugs? Not a problem. Piss? Too far."

Mindy laughed. "I guess the vegan option is out."

Jenna said, "I don't want to trash the house. That wouldn't be fair to the homeowner. And nothing that would injure or cause illness. But we can be creative. Just enough to send a message to Raven that she can't fuck with me like that. First, I'm cancelling the valets. People can park their own damned cars."

The posse walked through the rooms, examining opportunities for mayhem. Russ chuckled, "I'm taking all the toilet paper out of the bathrooms. I hear ladies hate that."

Mindy looked at Jenna, scanning her clothing. "You know what the best revenge is?"

"No. What?"

"Come with me." Mindy took her hand and led her upstairs.

Jenna didn't argue.

* * *

A half-hour later, Jenna walked down the circular staircase, feeling good and ready to face the world head-on. At the bottom of the stairs, she checked her reflection in the foyer's large gilded mirror. The make-over that Mindy gave her was astonishing. Eyeliner, false eyelashes, rouge. Lipstick that matched her dress. Her now clean hair fell around her shoulders in loose waves like a movie star.

Yes, she thought, looking good *was* truly the best revenge. And she was doubly happy not to be wearing white. Maybe the best passive-aggressive middle finger of all, because it would show up in the pictures for posterity.

Mindy came down the stairs, also cleaned up, wearing a satin, army-green jumpsuit and her high-top sneakers. She stood behind Jenna, peeking over her shoulder at her reflection. "Pretty good, eh?"

"I look like a different person."

Russ came over, "Wowza."

Jenna turned away from the mirror. "Isn't it a glorious dress?"

He said, "No. You. Wow."

Jenna blushed. She needed to take attention off herself. "How is everything coming along?"

Russ said, "Good. Fred took the casserole out of the oven when the timer went off. And we straightened up the ballroom and emptied the fountain. Mindy, Fred called the valets to tell them not to come. I just got back from the pet store with the special ingredients. Oh, and Jenn, I found something." He pulled his phone from his pocket and tapped open a browser. "Is this the groom?"

A newspaper article on the phone showed a mug shot of Jack. The headline said, "Area man arrested for identity theft." The date on the article was four years ago.

"Shit. Yes." Jenna smiled. "We *have* to put that in the slideshow while the presents are being opened." She went to find her purse. The thumb drive from Raven had a slew of pictures of her and Jack's courtship. She handed it to Russ. "Take my laptop. It's in the den. Make it so."

"Aye, aye, Captain." He saluted and headed away.

Mindy said, "I hired a stripper. When you were in the shower. Amazing what you can order on-line."

"What?"

"There's an app for everything. She arrives at two. You can thank me later."

"Mindy! You didn't! One of the guests is a nun." She put her hand over her mouth. "That's awesome!"

"Do you want to help me spray paint the wishing well black and orange? We'll need some smocks."

"Absolutely. Let's go."

* * *

Jenna checked her phone. It was a 12:40. Nearly everything was in place. The florist had just dropped off the table centerpieces. But Mack was M-I-A. She wondered if the FBI operation was still a 'go'.

Russ was creating a playlist on his phone from a genre called "Japanoise". He played a sample for Mindy, who called it 'righteous'.

Without warning, Blanche came striding in, Sister Mary Rose following behind. Without saying hello or introducing the nun, Blanche walked toward the ballroom. Everything was ready and spotless. Jenna couldn't think of one thing she could complain about.

Sister Mary approached Jenna. She must have been in her late seventies, wearing a brown cotton shirt and skirt, her white hair tucked under a white kerchief. On her feet, blue Crocs with pink socks. But the sparkle in the nun's green eyes was other worldly. "Hello dear, I'm Mary Rose. Are you Jenna?" She took Jenna's hand.

"Yes, I'm Jenna. Nice to meet you."

"Thank you for inviting me today. Is this your home? It is quite a place."

"No, Sister. We're just renting the house for the party today. Can I get you anything?"

"Oh, I'm just fine." Mary scanned the kitchen. "Where should I go?"

Fred came over. "Sister, would you like a tour of the house before the party starts? How about a game of air hockey?" He offered his arm.

Mary smiled. "Why, yes. That would be delightful."

Mary Rose and Fred left arm in arm toward the foyer.

Blanche stormed back into the kitchen. She pointed to Russ. "Young man, could you take the champagne out of my car?" Without waiting for a response, she dropped the keys on the counter next to him.

Blanche turned to Jenna. "Is that what you're wearing?"

Jenna looked down at her attire. "Um. Yes?"

"Are you stupid or purposefully trying to ruin Raven's pictures?"

"No." Jenna narrowed her eyes, placing her hands on her hips.

"No to stupid or the pictures?"

"*Shut up, you fucking evil bitch.*" That's what Jenna wanted to say. Could have said. But a commotion outside caught her attention. Down the hall, through the front door's sidelight windows, she noticed two buses had arrived, parked along the road, and dozens of young women streamed out, walking up the slate path to the front door.

It was game time.

She smiled sweetly. "Blanche, why don't you find your table and help yourself to the hor d'oerves? I need to greet the guests."

Blanche scowled, shook her head, and waddled off toward the ballroom.

Jenna was wondering where Mack was when someone tapped her shoulder.

"Jenna?"

She turned. It was Mack. Dressed in a white skirt suit, her dark hair held up with a clip. She wasn't wearing makeup but looked amazing.

Jenna sighed. "Where the heck have you been? Blanche is here."

"Sorry. The guys and I had to take fire watch training at the fire house. We couldn't tell the chief who we really were, so we had to sit through a crappy hour-long training video and take a written test. But we got the permit." Mack shook her head. "Anyway, take this." She handed a walkie-talkie to her. It was so small it looked like a toy. "Keep me posted on the schedule. And keep tabs on Blanche."

Jenna didn't have any pockets. "Um, I don't know where to keep this."

Mack said, "Just keep it close. You'll figure it out."

Jenna nodded. *Why didn't all dresses have pockets?*

In the foyer, a group of five women wearing flowy white dresses walked past her. One held up a tray, calling out to another group ahead of them, "We brought Jell-O shots!" Another woman cradled a large glass bottle of amber liquid.

Jenna took the walkie with her to the hall bathroom. *Where to hide this?* Her dress was tight. She tried placing the walkie down the middle of her chest. But her tiny breasts didn't provide adequate cover, revealing a boxy lump. Could she strap it to her thigh? She'd need Velcro. Ultimately, she tucked it under her dress beneath her left armpit. When she kept her arms down, it was barely noticeable.

Before she exited the bathroom, she noticed the empty toilet paper holder on the wall. Russ hadn't been kidding before.

As she opened the door to the hall, she bumped into Russ. He seemed to be waiting for her, holding two cases of champagne. "Hey, come with me," he whispered.

"What?" she whispered back. *Why were they whispering?*

"I need to put these away first. Just come."

She followed him to the ballroom. Several guests were already milling about, looking for their place cards. As part of the sabotage, Fred offered to mix them up. Knowing how long Raven and Blanche agonized over creating the right groupings, this was an excellent strategy to mind-fuck both of them.

Russ left the champagne on the floor. He bent over to whisper in her ear. "I think there's blood in that woman's trunk."

"What?" Jenna said this loudly. Perhaps too loudly, because a few women turned to stare.

Russ whispered, "Come with me. I'll show you."

Jenna didn't bother to find her coat and followed him outside. The sun was shining, with a blue sky and almost no clouds.

She recognized the vehicle immediately. Blanche had driven the same red Audi that Jack drove the first time they'd visited the mansion. It even had the miniscule smudge of spider guts on the driver's side window. But now it had Pennsylvania plates, where she could have sworn it had New Jersey plates last time. Russ opened the trunk.

"See?" He pointed inside to the far corner on the left.

It looked like a bloody bit of scalp, because strands of human hair were attached. Well, it looked human. Definitely not animal fur. "I see. Hold on." She walked to the other end of the car and while Russ was busy retrieving the last case of champagne, she fished out her radio.

She turned it on. "Mack? You there?" she whispered.

A loud squawk, then a woman's voice, "Go for Mack."

Russ said, "Who are you talking to?"

Jenna said to Russ, "Give me her car keys. Go inside. Take the bottles. But don't touch the car."

He handed her the keys and opened his mouth to say something.

"Just go." Jenna's eyes bore into his, her voice stern.

Russ shook his head, picked up the box and walked away.

Jenna waited until he was out of sight. "Mack, meet me at Blanche's car."

As she waited, an icy breeze stung her bare arms. She shivered and hugged herself. *Had she told Russ to go away too unkindly?*

Mack appeared. "What is it?"

She pointed inside the trunk. "Thought you might be interested."

Mack scanned the small fleshy blob. "Jenna, this changes everything. We've been searching for this car for days. We have to impound it to preserve evidence." She got on her phone. "Boss, we need a warrant. Call Judge Milford now. I'm sending you pictures." She turned to Jenna. "Give me the keys and keep Blanche away from any windows facing this side of the house."

"On it." She went back inside.

She entered through the kitchen's side door. Russ, Mindy and Fred were waiting there, staring at her.

Mindy whispered, "Is that tall foxy lady with the FBI? Fred told us everything."

Jenna's eyes widened. "Fred!"

"Well, Russ said there was blood in the car. And you have that concealed walkie. I figured your friends had a right to know."

"Ugh. Can't you keep a secret?"

"Apparently not." Fred put his hand on her shoulder. "Come, now. They just want to help. It'll be fine. What can we do?"

Jenna sighed. There was no time to stay mad. "Ah. Okay. Keep eyes on Blanche. Any time she leaves the ballroom, let me know. Follow her if you have to. And they're going to tow her car. Do not let her outside. Wait. Shit. Raven will arrive soon. She can't park in the driveway or she'll see." She looked at Russ. "Russ, intercept Raven. Park her car for her. Lock this side door and make sure everyone uses the front entrance. I'll tell the fire watch agents. Go!"

"Yes, Ma'am." Russ jogged to the front door.

Mindy said, "I'll start putting out food. That will keep the zombies occupied. Fred, fill that goddamned fountain. If they get plastered, we might be able to contain them."

"Good plan. Now break." Jenna locked the kitchen exit behind her, including the top dead bolt.

They scattered to their assigned tasks.

After Jenna spoke with the fire watch agents—Bob and Ron (probably not their actual names)—she went to the ballroom to monitor Blanche. As she drew closer to the large room, she heard the most annoying music over the flush-mounted ceiling speakers. It sounded like a group of wounded cats singing in, well, Japanese. Fred was in the center of the room pouring champagne into the fountain. In one corner, a group of young women already had a bottle opened on their table, their hands raised in a toast to something. Two middle-aged women by the rear French doors were dancing—vogue-ing like Madonna—to the irritating song. The attempt at musical sabotage was not going well.

Blanche was nowhere to be seen. Jenna cursed under her breath, "Shit."

A moment later, Blanche appeared. She stalked to the corner table with the pyramid of toilet paper, taking two rolls. Then she strode toward Jenna, scowling. "There was no goddamned paper in the bathroom. Jenna, what's wrong with you?"

Jenna smiled.

Blanche lumbered off.

Jenna wondered, "*Was it cruel to be enjoying this total shit-show?*"

She helped Fred finish his task, gathering the empty bottles.

No, she thought, this was going to be the best party ever.

Chapter 18

Raven arrived at 1:43. Jenna knew this because Russ came over to her and said, "She's here. Forty-three minutes late."

This left only forty-seven minutes to begin and finish the party games. There was Pin the Ring on the Jack, Mad Lib vows, wedding movie trivia, and fantasy date. They were supposed to begin a half hour ago. She would have to make cuts. Fantasy date would take the longest and was the first tossed out. Even Pin the Ring was a long shot, but she didn't cart that stupid cut-out figure across the state to admit defeat now.

If they didn't serve the cake and begin the toilet paper wedding gowns by 2:30, the entire schedule would be shot to hell.

Jenna told Russ, "Get Mindy. I need her. Now."

Raven dashed table to table, hugging and kissing all her friends and relatives. So much squealing. Blanche was eating her second helping of pasta at a table with other women close to her age and the nun. Aside from the nun, dressed in brown, Jenna was the only guest not wearing white. Mack was sitting at the far end, by the French doors, eating a salad but keeping her eyes on the room.

Jenna walked up to Raven. Rae was wearing a silk white dress, knee-length with billowy long sleeves and a deep V-neck, showing her cleavage. Jenna couldn't help but stare a little, wondering why Rae would augment herself. She was a full B cup on a small frame and looked like a Victoria's Secret model. What monstrosities could she be considering?

Jenna said, "Hey, what took you so long?"

Rae smiled. "Sorry. The place looks great. I'm so glad everyone came."

"We had to start the buffet without you. I'll get the games started in a minute."

Rae gave her a hug. "Thanks, sis. You're staying over and coming to the Walk-a-Thon, right?"

Before she could give an answer, Raven's gaze went towards some friends waving; she left to greet guests at a table near the middle of the room.

It reminded her why she never visited Rae at school after that first time.

Mindy came over, still wearing her apron. "You rang?"

"Sorry, I need to get everyone's attention to start the pin the ring game. Would you do the honors?"

A sly look crept across Mindy's face. "I have something better."

"What?"

The overhead speakers roared to life again. But this time to 50 Cent's *Candy Shop*. The lights dimmed. Jenna looked over and saw Fred was standing at the light switches. At least, it looked like Fred's silhouette. Russ was closing the drapes across the French doors to darken the space further.

A woman dressed in a patent leather cape, with matching skull cap, strode in holding a leather whip. She had bright red lipstick, black eye makeup, black polished fingernails that came to long, sharp points and most notably, fang-like teeth. The teeth looked so realistic. Not like the plastic versions Jenna won playing Skee-ball as a kid.

Mindy's voice boomed across the darkened room with the help of the microphone. "Everyone, take your seats and enjoy the sexy and sinister moves of Mistress Nightshade."

A spotlight illuminated Nightshade at the front of the room. *Where had that come from?*

The eight tables of sorority sisters near the front erupted with cheers and clapping.

And Nightshade began to dance. She threw off her cape, revealing a black rhinestone bikini, overlaid with leather straps, tattoos of serpents running the length of both arms, and a tattoo of Satan on her belly. Cracking the whip, she walked to Raven and grabbed her wrist, seating her on a chair in the middle of the dance floor. At first, the dance was coy and borderline respectable. As in, not showing too much. But then it got downright…nasty? Nightshade wrapped her whip around Raven and gave her a lap dance. The dancer pinched the back of her brassiere, taking it off with a seamless motion, leaving only satin nipple-covers with short metal spikes, connected by a gold chain.

Jenna looked toward the exit. Mindy was ejecting Fred and Russ, pushing them outside. Despite the pounding music, she heard Fred say, "I just want to stay for research purposes."

Jenna joined the trio in the kitchen.

Mindy and the boys were laughing.

Jenna said, "Mindy, I can't believe you didn't warn me first. How long is her act?"

"I told you she was coming at two. I paid for the twenty-minute version. It was all I could afford."

Jenna shook her head. "I'm afraid to ask how much. I can reimburse you."

Mindy smiled. "No way. This is all on me."

Jenna laughed. "Okay, fine. I'll need your help when we start the *real* games. I have to go back to keep an eye on Blanche."

Fred said, "I can watch Blanche."

Mindy said, "Nice try, old man."

Fred and Russ laughed.

Jenna sighed and walked back to the ballroom. She stood in the doorway. Nightshade was all over Raven, the pair surrounded by whooping and giggling sorority women. The next song was Darling Nikki by Prince. Nightshade buried her face in Raven's lap, lifting Rae's skirt, pulling her thighs apart. Raven kept smiling, grabbing Nightshade's head, pulling her closer.

Was Raven enjoying this? A chill ran through Jenna's skin.

But the dancer shifted gears. She straddled Raven and kissed her. A full-on, mouth to mouth, lipstick to lipstick, fang to teeth, possible French kiss that lasted an uncomfortably long time. Was Rae wearing her tongue-stud? She hadn't noticed before, and now the thought gave her the willies.

One of the sorority girls yelled, "Get it, Raven." Another cried, "That's our girl." The room echoed with laughter. One table of women began stomping their feet.

After the kiss, Nightshade crossed the long room, sidling up to Blanche, who was covering Sister Mary's eyes with her hand. The dancer grabbed Blanche's face and buried it in her thick bosom. Blanche screamed, tossed her chair back, and ran. The nun looked up and made a cross sign over Nightshade, but smiled.

Blanche strode at high speed toward Jenna.

"You! You did this." Blanche stuck her finger in Jenna's chest. "My poor Aunt Mary. I need to get her out of here. How dare you?"

Jenna looked across the darkened room towards Blanche's table. "Sister Mary just stuffed a dollar in Nightshade's G-string."

"What?"

"Look for yourself." She pointed.

Blanche turned and stared. Her mouth dropped open. Nightshade handed the whip to Sister Mary, teaching her how to use it. The other guests began clapping in time for Mary's attempts to crack the whip. Blanche went back in, holding her forehead, and sat back down at her table.

This again was a misfire, thought Jenna. She wanted to make Raven's guests unhappy, upset, shocked, outraged. Perhaps they had given out the champagne too early. Or maybe it was the bottles of whiskey and Jell-O shots the sorority sisters brought with them. No matter what outwardly dastardly act of sabotage they tried, the women didn't care, or worse, embraced the acts with joy.

The second half of Nightshade's act was a mix of stand-up comedy and a roast, where she asked the audience personal questions about their sex lives. Then she started in on Raven.

"Honey, I hear you're getting married. My condolences. Because after the honeymoon, you'll wear out your vibrator or take up yoga to suck your own…" Nightshade wagged her tongue, licking the air for maximum effect. "Tell me about this lucky stud. Does he make you squirt?"

Raven smiled slyly. "His name is Jack, and he does the job."

"See, she's already calling it a job. Ha! Now, Jack, no, let's call him pinkie-dick," Nightshade held up her small finger, "when was the last time he finger-banged you properly in the grocery store parking lot?" She shoved the mic in Raven's face.

The women laughed. Raven giggled. "Um, I'd rather not say. My future mother-in-law is here."

"Why? Does mommy like to watch?" Nightshade hissed like a serpent.

More laughter. The jokes and dirty banter continued. When her session was up, Nightshade shouted, "You've been a wonderful audience. I've been Mistress Nightshade. Stay sinister and sexy, y'all!"

The guests gave Nightshade a standing ovation.

Nightshade waved goodbye, gathered her cape, and cracked her whip to punctuate her exit. Two of the sorority girls jogged after her, stopping her in the kitchen, begging her to stay.

Fred said, "You must be hungry after such athletic dancing. Come, sit at the island and have something to eat." He took her hand. "Make an old man happy."

She slapped him lightly on the shoulder. "Sure, for a few minutes. My name's Nancy."

"I'm Fred. Do you need a man-slave? I'm newly on the market. Although, I got a bad hip. So don't hurt me." He grinned ear-to-ear. Jenna could tell he was teasing in his corn-ball way, but his eyes betrayed a soft devotion. Perhaps he was being half-serious.

Nancy smiled, "Thanks, hon, but I go the other way." She grabbed his cheek and wiggled it affectionately. "But I'll keep that in mind."

Jenna looked at her watch. They had time for one or two of the games. She grabbed Mindy and they went into the ballroom to start the lame ring game. Although one guest fashioned a penis shape out of some scrap paper and the contestants began using that as the 'pin'. These women were juiced up and highly creative. Mad Lib vows came after that. The answers were all dirty, except for the clean version from Sister Mary's table.

Finally, at 2:55, it was time for cake and toilet paper wedding dresses. Jenna, Fred, Russ and Mindy frantically cut the cake and served it on china plates, bringing servings around to each guest.

When that task was finished, Mindy turned to Jenna. "Russ has the slide show ready. Do you want to start that now?"

Jenna thought. "No, after the benediction, champagne toast, and group picture. While Raven is opening presents. That would be ideal."

Mindy said, "Roger Wilco. By the way, we're out of the 'good' champagne. I'm transferring the non-alcoholic stuff to the real champagne bottles."

Jenna said, "Good idea."

Raven came up to her, slurring her speech. "This cake is delicious. I love the cookie crumble layer. Did you try it?"

Jenna grinned. "No, but I'm glad you're enjoying it." She wanted to say, "That's what you get for lying to me." The cake had a secret ingredient. An awful ingredient. Mindy made the crumble layer with dead, ground-up cockroaches. Earlier that morning, Jenna left the kitchen when Russ brought the insects back from the pet store. Despite knowing they were dead, just looking at them gave her the heebie jeebies. Fred, on the other hand, had no qualms handling the bugs, pulsing them in the food processor along with some chocolate wafer cookies, manually removing the recognizable bits of roach wings from the mixture.

Raven walked away to help some women who were draping themselves in toilet paper like deranged drunken mummies.

Out of the corner of her eye, she noticed Blanche heading out the rear French doors to the patio with two other women. *Should she follow her?* Bob was on fire watch in that area and surely would keep tabs on her. But what were they doing out there? She walked over and stood by the window.

Blanche joined a cluster of five women outside smoking and chatting. But Blanche didn't smoke. She laughed at something, but it sounded more like a loud cackle. Even through the glass door, Blanche's laugh grated her nerves like fingernails on a blackboard. Jenna thought back to all her interactions with Blanche. She couldn't remember hearing her laugh before. In that moment, she considered herself lucky.

Agent Bob came over to Jenna. "Miss Mott, Ron and I have a problem. Some women are smoking in the front yard. Some here. It would be best if there was a single, designated spot so we don't have to keep moving from our posts."

Jenna nodded. "Fine, which do you prefer?"

Bob said, "This rear patio is ideal because I can see them through the windows and with the surrounding steep hills, they can't wander too far. Could you go inform the ladies at the front? Ron needs to stay at his post."

"No problem. I'm on it." *One more thing to do.* She returned to the kitchen. The first person she found was Fred.

"Fred, I need you."

He was bundling up a trash bag. One of several they had gone through this day. "Well, of course you do, but what's up?" He chuckled at his own cleverness.

"Could you round up all the stray smokers in the front yard and order them to *only* use the rear patio. Tell them it's fire regulation. Tell them anything. Use your charms." She realized she was scratching her scalp again. Inspecting her fingernails, she saw no blood…yet.

"No worries. I'll have them eating out of my palm. Wait, no, that would be gross. But don't worry. I have my ways."

"I bet you do." Jenna laughed.

Fred left the trash bag and walked to the front of the house.

Jenna checked her watch again. Only thirty more minutes until the slide show from hell. Showing Jack's mug shot to Raven and her friends would be an eye opener. That would surely entice guests to leave early, giving the opening to Mack to confront Blanche.

It was time to end this abomination of a party.

* * *

Sister Mary Rose gave a toast, although it was more like a full church-service. She blessed Raven and her upcoming union.

Jenna stood in the doorway and listened, checking her watch frequently.

Mary continued, "From Corinthians, we know love is patient and kind. It keeps no record of wrongs—"

Jenna certainly felt like she was keeping a record of wrongs. All the lies Raven and Jack told her. Jack's insults and deceit. *How could wrongs be fixed without keeping a record of them?*

The sister added, "Love does not delight in evil but rejoices with the truth."

Jenna said, "Amen, Sister."

The room looked at her. She hadn't intended to say that so loudly. "Um, sorry, Sister Mary. Go on."

Sister Mary gave her a sweet smile and readdressed the room. She talked about the need to keep God in their lives, and about the power of forgiveness and the hope for many children. It was a long speech. Jenna checked her watch. This would push back her schedule by at least fifteen minutes.

Mack came up to her. "What's next?"

"Group picture. How are you enjoying the party?" Jenna smiled.

Stone-faced, Mack said, "I'm here to do a job, nothing else." She narrowed her eyes. "I wasn't expecting Miss Nightshade. You have to tell me when you deviate from the plan."

"Sorry, Mindy's idea. Nightshade is still here, in the kitchen, having a late lunch."

Mack's face brightened. "I'm just fucking with you. Best day I've had at the agency in years." She winked. "Her lesson will improve my whip technique tremendously."

Jenna laughed. Was Mack being serious? "Well, after Sister Mary is done, we'll do the picture, then the presents and try to shove people out the door by four o'clock."

"Except for Blanche."

Jenna nodded. "Except for Blanche." She chewed her fingernail. "Um, how exactly do I keep her from leaving?"

"Tell her you need help cleaning up."

"Ha!" Jenna bent over laughing. A mistake because she felt light-headed. She straightened. "Right. Do you think Blanche ever washed a dish?"

Mack put her hands on her hips. "I don't care how you do it. The warrant is close to being signed. We have a tow truck waiting on the side of the road a half-mile down. Blanche and her car *cannot* leave."

"Fine. I'll think of something."

Mack returned to the ballroom. Sister Mary was leading the Lord's Prayer. Hopefully, this meant the end of her speech.

Russ came up, carrying a box of 'new' champagne bottles. "How are you holding up?"

"You're the first person to ask me that today."

"It'll be over soon. Did you eat anything?" He shifted the weighty box in his arms.

Jenna sighed. Breakfast had been six hours ago. She'd had a few nibbles of salad and a bite-size spinach quiche, but nothing substantial. She'd been more consumed with her sentry duties. "I guess I could use some food. Are there any more muffins?"

"Sorry. Muffins are all gone. After I drop this off, I'll make you a plate. Something without too many bugs in it, I swear." He smiled.

"Thanks, Russ."

One of the fire watch dudes, Bob, walked by, radio in hand, and then he disappeared again.

Jenna kept listening at the doorway. The benediction was finally over and everyone drank a toast. Jenna strode inside and announced, "Group picture. Everyone, line up along the wall. Tallest in back." She clapped her hands and began arranging chairs in a row. Mack met her gaze, nodding in approval.

Getting the women out of the bathroom and other rooms, getting them to put down their food and glasses, getting them to stop talking, getting them to organize in height fashion; it was truly like herding cats. Worse than herding a group of Thumpers.

Each woman handed Jenna their phone to take a picture with it; one after the other. She must have taken fifty pictures. It was at picture ten when she noticed someone, probably Mindy, had propped up 'paper Jack' in the back corner of the ensemble, with the paper penis stuck to his forehead. Raven beamed in every picture, using a different pose for each one.

Mistress Nightshade—wearing her fully covered ensemble including the cape—poked her head into the room to wave goodbye. Raven jumped up and ran toward her. "You have to join our picture. Pretty please?"

Nightshade cocked her head. "Okay, just one, sweetie." She took Raven's chair and Raven sat on her lap. Nightshade bared her fangs, pretending to bite Rae's neck. Raven made a goofy face with her eyes crossed. The guests laughed and smiled.

Jenna couldn't help laughing as well. Maybe it was delirium from lack of food. Or she saw the playfulness in Raven she had always adored. She didn't want to stay mad at Rae. Perhaps lying about a boob job wasn't the worst thing. She regretted putting bugs in the cake and all the other attempts at sabotage. Thankfully, the party was a success and Raven would never find out about the cockroach crumble.

After the pictures were completed, Raven excused herself to fix her makeup.

Jenna's watch read 3:47. There was no way to finish opening presents by four. She'd be lucky if the party broke up by five with this crowd.

Sister Mary came up to her, a gift bag hanging from her wrist. "Young lady, I wanted to say thank you for giving dear Raven such a wonderful day. God bless you, my girl." Mary took her hand and clasped it between hers.

"Um, thank you. That means a lot."

Sister Mary smiled and said, "Please take my gift bag. I don't need this fancy stuff. I'm taking a taxi back to the hotel. Tell Blanche I was a little tired."

"Thanks. Will do. Nice meeting you."

After Mary left, Jenna shook her head. What a sweet lady. How could she be related to a family of shallow thugs?

Russ came up to her. "Your food is getting cold again. Do you want me to reheat it?"

"No. I'm coming."

It was truly sweet of Russ to look after her. She followed him to the kitchen where he had laid out a plate and silverware, with a single pink carnation in a tall glass. He must have taken it from one of the centerpieces in the ballroom. "Thanks, Russ."

He pulled out the chair for her. "Can I get you something to drink? We have milk, coffee, tea, and orange juice."

Jenna stuffed her mouth full of chicken. It was a little cold, but she didn't care. "Coffee." She stabbed some cold russet potato slices and shoved them in her mouth like a ravenous hyena. Not ladylike at all. But sitting and eating after hours of worry, standing watch, and dealing with questions made her realize how weary and raw her nerves had become.

Fred came by. "Hey, there, slow down. I know the Heimlich but don't fancy using it today."

She responded with a muffled, "I'll be fine."

Fred said, "Sorry to disturb your lunch, but Mindy wants to start the presents and we don't know where Raven is."

Jenna put down her fork. She chewed and swallowed the mass, coughing. "What? Did you check the den? The basement? Shoot. What if she's outside and sees the tow truck? We've got to find her."

Mindy walked in. "Jenna, have you seen Raven?"

Russ said, "We'll split up. Mindy, take the basement. Fred, check every inch of this floor. Jenna, you check upstairs. I'll check outside. We'll meet back in three minutes."

Jenna pushed her plate away and headed to the foyer. There were seven bedrooms with seven bathrooms. It shouldn't take long to check. She stormed up the stairs, taking two at a time. The sound of fabric tearing caught her ear. She paused to check the rear hem of the dress. The back slit had ripped upward about two to three inches.

Was no article of clothing safe in her possession? She sighed, hoping the damage to the dress was easily repaired. With a grimace, she decided this was all Raven's fault. But she kept racing upward to complete her mission.

Jenna checked the first bedroom to the right. Nothing. She tried the next, the one she'd slept in the night before. Her overnight bag was on the bed where she left it, with her travel clothes laid out for after the party.

She heard noises coming from the master bedroom wing at the furthest end of the hall. Like moaning. But not like a ghost or an injured person. Moaning of a particular sort. She took a deep breath and crept toward the door. The noises grew louder. Her hand hesitated on the door knob. She didn't want to open it. But another part of her needed to know.

She gradually eased the door open, peering inside. The master bedroom was covered in ornate silver wallpaper of cherubs, winged horses and clouds, with a king-sized four-poster bed. White and black clothing crumpled on the floor. In the middle of this bed, two very naked women were kissing and pleasuring each other, unaware of Jenna's presence. Nightshade was on top, the leather whip wrapped loosely around her waist, and Raven was wearing the skull cap.

Jenna ducked her head back out and gently closed the door.

In shock, she leaned against the wall, dizzy and sick to her stomach. Her fingers picked at a seam in the wallpaper, her throat constricted, her legs unable to move. Her breath came out in short, shallow bursts. *Breathe, breathe*, she willed herself. She couldn't stay there. The only thing she wanted in that moment was to be anywhere else. Drive like the wind. Wash these images from her consciousness.

After sixty seconds of training her lungs to receive air, a fire of rage surged up her spine. The friend she loved, had sacrificed for—a person she was risking all to save—was truly an inconsiderate, selfish asshole. Jenna wanted to go home. Forget she ever met Jack and his family and never see Raven again.

She strode to her bedroom and stuffed her clothes in her bag. Stepping out of her heels, she picked each of them up and threw them across the room, hitting the opposite wall, then slipped into her blue sneakers. Heading down the stairs, bag in hand, she ran into Mindy.

"No luck in the basement. Did you find her?"

"Yeah."

Mindy squinted in confusion. "Is she coming downstairs?

"No."

"So, what do we do?"

"Tell everyone the party's over. Mindy, call the bus drivers. Tell them to be out front ASAP." Jenna took out her walkie talkie. "This is Jenna. The party is over. I'm leaving."

A man's voice answered. "Jenna? This is Agent Bob. Does Mack know?"

"Tell her for me."

Jenna tossed the radio on the marble floor. The case cracked and bits of plastic flew off. "I'm done. I'm going home."

Mindy said, "What about Blanche?"

"I don't give a damn."

Jenna strode into the kitchen with her bag.

Mack intercepted her, placing a hand on her shoulder. "Jenna, what happened?"

"I'm going home. Let go of me." She slapped Mack's hand away, stepped back and headed to the side door. She twisted the top deadbolt.

This time, Fred stopped her. "Honey, what's going on?"

Tears flooded Jenna's eyes. Tears of rage, sadness, confusion, but mostly weariness. "Just tell everyone to go home. That's what I'm doing."

Mack said, "I can't keep you here, but I'm *imploring* you to stick this out for another half hour. Please. You are better than this."

Jenna tossed her bag on the ground. "You don't know me. None of you know me. The only person who ever knew me…is a liar and a selfish asshat." She had to give Mindy props for that curse-word; one she'd used around the office more than once.

Mack said, "Jenna, let's get some air. Come." She opened the side door.

Jenna followed Mack outside to the driveway. Blanche's car had already been towed. The sun was shining and the air temperature was at least fifty. Not freezing but still cold enough to clear her head. Agent Ron walked toward them, but Mack gestured for him to back off.

"Jenna, I'm sorry for all the stress you've been under. Maybe it was too much to ask. But I'm begging you. We're so close now. Blanche needs to think nothing is wrong. If you leave now, she'll be suspicious. You need to go back in and get her to stay after everyone leaves."

"Yeah, what if I don't care anymore? This is your problem, not mine."

Mack crossed her arms and looked at the ground. "You're right."

"What?"

"You're right. Our team will just have to storm the party and drag off Mrs. Forero. If people get hurt, who cares."

"What do you mean, get hurt?"

"I didn't want to tell you this, but it's possible that Blanche has a concealed firearm."

"What?"

"Her husband bought her a small Ruger for her birthday last September. And, from her phone's GPS records, she's been to the shooting range at least three times this year."

"Double fuck."

Mack looked into her eyes. "You are stronger than you think."

Jenna wondered if that was true. Because she had a decision to make and lives were on the line. She scowled. "You know what, Mack?"

"What?"

"I expected more from you. I *specifically* asked you if Blanche was armed. Remember? You, Blanche, Jack, Raven…are all a bunch of lying…" She considered her next phrase. *What was that curse that Fred always used?* "…Clown fuckers." She made a mental note to learn better curse words. Her new words of power.

"I'm sorry. I'm here to do a job. By any means necessary. Sometimes it involves omitting information based on need to know. I'll try to make it up to you. Promise."

Jenna said, "Fine. Whatever." She stalked back toward the house, through the kitchen and directly to the ballroom.

The room buzzed with chatter and laughter, people eating cake, clattering silverware.

Jenna took a deep breath. "Ladies!" she yelled.

The din of chatter continued.

She waved her arms over her head.

No one noticed her.

Jenna grabbed a white ceramic plate from a nearby table and stood on a chair. "Ladies!" She smashed the plate on the floor. *BLAM!*

The conversation stopped. The room grew quiet as a hundred pairs of eyes trained themselves her way.

"Raven told me to thank you for all being here today. I'm sorry to say there's a gas leak in the kitchen. I need you all to collect your belongings and head to the front door. Do not go into the kitchen. Do not run. Do not stop at the bathrooms."

Women came up to her singly or in clumps asking a million questions.

Them: "Is the party over?"

"Yes. Everyone should go home."

Them: "Should we take our gift bags now?"

"Yes, take all your belongings."

Them: "What about the presents? We can't leave them."

To maintain the illusion of imminent danger, she had to come up with something. She got back up on the chair. "I need volunteers to help move the presents out. Bring them to the front walkway for now. I'll make sure

Raven gets them."

This resulted in a flurry of women dashing back into the room, converging on the gift table to find the present they brought to save it.

Jenna smacked her forehead. *Not smart.*

But the questions continued, along with the screech of chairs skidding across the floor and disgruntled conversations.

Them: "Can I take the table center-piece?"

"I don't care."

Them: "What about the pictures? Can you send me a copy? Where can I send my pictures?"

God, so many questions about pictures. This one required Jenna to get back on her chair and announce she'd mail out a photo sharing website to everyone. Another whopper of a lie. She couldn't care less about the pictures or whether they were ever seen again. She realized that all these new lies were just rolling off her tongue easily. *Too easily.* Is that how lying worked? You just kept doing it until you didn't know the difference between truth and falsehood?

Them: "Where's Raven? I want to say goodbye."

This was a difficult one, requiring a big lie. "Raven had a migraine and had to leave. But she is so grateful you could attend and will be in contact soon."

Women continued to file out. But it was painfully slow. If there had been an actual fire or emergency, all these women would have been long dead.

Bob, who had been outside convincing the smokers to put out their cigarettes and leave through the ballroom, entered the room and blew a handheld air horn. [BLEAT, BLEAT, BLEEEEAT]

The women froze and stopped talking. Some held their ears.

Bob shouted. "Ladies. This is NOT a drill. You have thirty seconds to get out NOW!" He hit the air horn a couple more times.

Jenna had forgotten that Bob and Ron had air horns as part of their fire watch apparatus and she was suddenly jealous that she didn't have one. Would it be weird to own one for casual purposes? She imagined using it on Thumper when he got out of line. But no, that would be insane and cruel.

Blanche was headed her way, pushing through the other.

Jenna, still standing on the chair, called out, "Blanche! Come see me, please."

Blanche came up to her, her fur coat and handbag in her arms. Her eyes were wild, like a rabid raccoon, but with more eye makeup. "Jenna, we need to get out. Come on."

Jenna got off the chair and whispered something in Blanche's ear.

A look of alarm washed over Blanche's face. "Oh, my God. Show me."

Jenna eyes narrowed.

Yes, she would show her all right. And enjoy every moment.

Chapter 19

Jenna led Blanche up the stairs and turned right, toward the bedroom furthest from the master.

Jenna explained, "Raven is having serious second thoughts about the wedding. She told me to ask everyone to leave so they wouldn't see her crying. Sorry for scaring you. I didn't know what else to do. She says she still loves Jack but needs to talk to you." Jenna pointed to the door. "She's in here. I'll wait downstairs."

Blanche whispered, "Thank you for getting me." She patted Jenna's hand. "You're a good friend." She opened the door and walked in. "Raven? It's me, baby. What's going on?"

Mack and agent Ron silently appeared from the bedroom across the hall. Mack walked in behind Blanche and closed the door behind her. Ron stood watch with his hand on the hilt of his gun.

Ron said, "We have this, Miss Mott. You and your friends can go now. Bob is manning the gate. He'll close it behind you."

Jenna nodded. Through the walls, she heard Blanche yell, "Who are you?".

Mack shouted, "Sit down, Mrs. Forero, FBI."

Jenna walked toward the stairs but desperately wanted to hear the conversation with Blanche. She darted around a wall and pressed her back to it, out of Ron's line of sight. The voices in the room were muffled, but she could mostly make them out.

Mack said, "…we have enough audio, video, and paper evidence to lock you, John and Jack away for at least twenty years."

Blanche said, "This is an invasion of privacy. If you've told sweet Raven any of your tawdry lies…I'll sue you into oblivion. I want the name of your supervisor. My lawyer will have some choice words for him. [something muffled] I'd like to leave now."

"Do you really want to do that? We have signed warrants for your arrest, plus your son and husband. Or, you can give me an answer now and spare your family from prison. Mr. Radcliffe and his team are ready to confiscate your dealership and all your property the second you leave here without signing the deal. I'll wait while you read it."

Jenna smiled. She'd been wondering what Ben was up to. She envisioned him swooping in with a team of IRS agents ransacking the dealership offices.

Ron peered around the corner at her. Busted. He gave her a stern look, waving at her to keep going. She nodded, embarrassed.

Jenna descended the stairs. At the foyer, the last of the women were filing out. Mindy was holding the door for them.

Jenna and Mindy stared at each other when the last woman left. Jenna closed the door and turned the lock.

"Free at last." Jenna put up her hand for a high-five.

Mindy threw her arms around Jenna. "You did good, kid."

Jenna laughed. Nothing about this day was remotely good.

Mindy took her hand, and they went back to the kitchen. Russ and Fred were doing dishes at the sink. Fred washing and Russ drying. All their coats were draped across the island.

"I think we can go now," Jenna said.

Fred said, "Good, I don't know about you, but I'm damned tuckered."

Russ put down the dish he was holding, "What about all this mess? The ballroom is a disaster."

Jenna smiled. "Not my security deposit."

Fred laughed. "Smartest thing you said today. I'm riding back with Mindy. She said I could nap in the back seat. No offense."

"None taken."

Mindy checked the fridge. "Aha. There it is." She pulled out a bottle of champagne. "I squirreled away a bottle of the expensive stuff. I think we should have a toast."

Jenna sighed. "Thanks, but I want to hit the road. I hate driving the Pennsylvania Turnpike at night."

Russ said, "How about I drive you home. Let you rest?"

That stopped her cold. *Alone with Russ? Was that a good thing? Or would it be full of awkward silence?* But the promise of sleep was more than enticing.

Mindy, still holding the champagne, tapped Fred on the shoulder. "Good plan. Let's go." They took their coats and headed to the side door. Mindy waved a 'hang ten' hand sign above her head, shouting, "Peace out."

And in a flash, they were gone.

It was a solid conspiracy. Mindy was as subtle as a sledgehammer.

Russ said, "I guess that settles it."

"What about your stuff? Isn't it in Mindy's car?"

"No problem. I know where she works."

"Um, okay."

A loud crash reverberated above them, followed by a woman's scream, a thud, the crack of a gunshot and feet pounding down the stairs.

Russ grabbed Jenna's arm, "Come on. Outside."

Too late. Blanche ran into the kitchen, holding a small pistol. She came to a halt, her eyes wide in surprise to see them. "You! I should kill you right now." Blanche pointed the gun at Jenna.

Russ froze.

Jenna called, "Mack! Mack!"

Blanche growled, "Is that tall bitch your friend? Figures. But I took care of her."

Did Blanche kill Mack? Maybe it was exhaustion. But Jenna felt something snap in her brain. The fury returned. Blanche would not get away on her watch. She'd lost too much. Fear had no purchase in that moment. She unhooked her arm from Russ's grasp and walked up to Blanche, standing squarely at the point of her gun. "Do it."

She suspected Blanche didn't have the guts, or they would already be dead. If she was wrong, she'd get a few weeks rest in the hospital. Or a forever rest. It didn't matter. Nothing mattered but the hatred she felt.

Russ said, "Jenna, stop!"

Blanche sneered. "Ha. So they can add twenty-five years to my sentence? You aren't worth it."

"Yeah? Fuck you." Jenna stomped on Blanche's foot and fumbled for the gun.

Blanche reeled back on her other foot and the weapon skittered across the wood floor toward Russ. But to Jenna, the scene unfolded in slow motion. He picked up the weapon, examining it.

Blanche's face showed alarm at first, but then she jutted her chin at Jenna. "Get out of my way."

Jenna laughed, her arms in the air, "Ha! Where are you gonna go? They impounded your car." A sly smile crossed her face. "But, fine. Be my guest." She held up both hands and backed away, stepping to the side.

Blanche strode past, reaching for the knob of the side door.

With Blanche's back turned, Jenna lunged and grabbed the collar of her fur coat with both hands. With a tug, Blanche lost her footing; the coat came off, now in Jenna's hands. Blanche toppled backwards into Jenna. They crashed to the floor like dominoes.

Russ yelled, "Jenna! Stop. What are you doing?"

Jenna, now pinned to the ground, realized Blanche had the weight advantage. An easy sixty pounds. But Jenna's pent up rage found its target. She slid out from under her foe, threw a leg across Blanche to straddle her. The perfect position to slap the squirming Blanche across the face. More fabric ripped, the slit at the back of her dress rose up to her butt, but this was worth it. Her fist barely landed as Blanche gripped Jenna's throat. Hard.

She couldn't breathe.

Russ pulled on Blanche's bicep. "Lady, stop!" Instead of loosening Blanche's arm, the pair slid across the floor, unshaken, like rag doll cats, but still brawling. He gave up, shouting, "Stop, don't make me shoot you."

Jenna clawed at Blanche's hands, pulling away one of her fingers, bending it backwards. A purple press-on nail popped off and hit Blanche in the eye. But the leverage worked; Jenna broke free of Blanche's death grip. Gulping for air, Jenna reached sideways, grabbing a dishtowel from the oven handle and stuffing it in Blanche's mouth. As Blanche gagged, Jenna extricated herself, scrambling back, standing. She looked for a weapon and snatched the colander on the counter. As Blanche sat up, spitting out the towel, Jenna smashed the metal bowl across her face.

Blanche shook her head, her lip bloodied. "Is that all you've got?" Blanche pressed herself up from the floor, like a Terminator, unfazed.

Jenna stared, her back against the stove, in shock at the battle-axe's resilience.

Russ called out again, "Lady, just get out of here! I *will* shoot."

Blanche grabbed a dirty plate off the center island, chucking it at Jenna's head. It missed and cake crumbs spewed as the ceramic shattered against the tiled backsplash. Jenna looked for something heavy to throw. But too late. Blanche threw a second plate. Jenna ducked, but it glanced off the top of her head.

She sank to the floor. In her blurred vision, she saw Blanche reach for another plate. She imagined it would hurt, but didn't know how to move.

Russ yelled, "Shit! Lady! Stop or I WILL blow your fucking head off." He pointed the gun at her, steadying it with both hands. Even in her daze, Jenna sensed his hesitation. The tone of his voice was more convincing than before, but it was clear: Russ was no killer.

Blanche must have also sensed this. She threw the plate at Russ, running past him toward the ballroom.

The plate missed Russ and landed three feet away. He aimed the gun above her head, toward the ceiling, and pulled the trigger. It clicked with no gunshot. He pulled the trigger again. No bullets.

Jenna felt the knob of the lower cabinet press into the flesh between her shoulder blades. She regarded her splayed feet, one with a sneaker, the other bare. She wiggled her free toes. They seemed silly. Her hands lay in curled balls on her lap. She thought about moving her arms but decided it was too much effort.

Russ' face came into view. He said her name once, maybe twice, and looked concerned. Even with the blur in her vision, she concluded she liked his blue eyes. They were sweet and kind. She felt blood in her mouth, with a hint of metal, like at the dentist's office.

Then everything went black.

* * *

Jenna's head throbbed. A beam of light flashed across her eyes.

"Ow. Stop."

Russ said, "Thank God. Welcome back."

A young man put away his pen light and held her wrist, taking her pulse. "Miss, do you know where you are?"

She looked from side to side. Her head throbbed. It wasn't the kitchen. The fireplace and oil painting above it seemed familiar. *The den?* She took a guess. "At the party?"

Russ nodded. "Yes."

She was resting on the sofa. "Oh, no. Where's Blanche?"

The medic released her wrist. "Can you tell me what day it is?"

Thinking, she blinked and shook her head. "Saturday. God, why can't this day be over?" She touched the part of her skull that ached.

The medic said, "Her vitals are good. Might have a bump on her head." He packed up his bag. "Miss, you can go home now if you wish."

She swung her legs to the floor and sat up. "Russ, tell me. Where's Blanche? What happened? We have to go catch her."

"Jenna, let the FBI do their job. Blanche fled through the back door and headed into the woods. Federal and local police are conducting a manhunt."

"Where's Mack? Is she dead?"

Mack walked in, a gauze bandage around her forearm. "Miss Mott, how are you feeling?"

How was she feeling? A crazed Mafia queen nearly killed her and Russ. "I'm…I'm mad as heck. I mean hell." Yes, she needed to work on her expletives.

Mack nodded. "Good."

"What happened to *you*?" She pointed to the bandage.

"I wish I had time to tell you, but Russ can fill you in later. There's someone else who wants to see you."

Raven poked her head around the wall. In a soft voice, she said, "Hey, Jenna, can I come in?"

All of her troubles were Raven's fault. The last person she wanted to talk to. "No. Not now. Not ever. Russ, take me home." She pushed up on the arm of the sofa to stand. No, too fast. Dizziness overcame her. She sat again, blinking fast to clear her vision.

Russ said, "Let me get you some water." He looked at Raven. "Could you leave her alone for a while?"

Russ said this too gently, Jenna thought. He was a good guy. Polite. She was not feeling as polite.

Raven crossed her arms. In a snippy voice, she said, "Fine. Whatever." She turned and left.

Mack said, "Jenna, we'll be using the house as a base of operations for the next few hours until we apprehend Mrs. Forero. You can rest upstairs if you'd like."

The thought of sleep was tempting. But upstairs was where she had found Raven, discovering her friend was a selfish jerk. No, she didn't want to sleep upstairs. She needed her own bed. To snuggle with Thumper and try to forget this day ever happened.

"Thanks, Mack, but I'm going home. Russ, let's go."

Russ took her forearm and helped her stand. She held onto him as they walked out of the den into the kitchen. They stopped at the sink and he filled a glass with tap water. "Here, take a sip."

In the background, Jenna heard Mack's walkie-talkie buzz and the words, "…the bloodhound found her trail."

She drank a little water. The floor was still littered with shards of ceramic. Blanche's ratty fur coat lay balled up against the pantry door like an obese Tribble. *Where could she have gone?* She yawned. What did it matter, anyway? Her new mission was to go home and sleep for a thousand years.

Jenna found her coat and Russ helped her put it on. They exited out the side door to her Miata. The sun was setting behind the forest and the temperature was dropping. She was thankful Russ offered to drive. She found the keys in her coat pocket and handed them to him.

Glancing around the parking area, there was an EMS truck, three police sedans, a white unmarked van, and a blue truck with a dog kennel in the back seat. Swirling and flashing vehicle roof lights of red, blue and yellow danced across the buildings and tree line. Police were milling about. An officer was draping police tape across the gate at the end of the driveway. *How long had she been unconscious?*

Russ said, "I'll go ask them to open the gate for us. Stay here."

She did what she was told. Gazing upward, the first star of the evening was shining in the dim purple sky. It was pretty. For an instant, she felt connected to that small, distant orb. Wanting to trade places with it, far away from the chaos surrounding her.

The slam of the kitchen door interrupted her momentary solitude.

Raven strode towards her, closing the distance fast. "Jenna, why are you running away? And why are all my presents sitting in a pile on the front yard? What's wrong with you?"

It occurred to Jenna, in that moment, Raven sounded exactly like Blanche.

Jenna put her hands in her pockets. "Do you even know what happened here tonight? Didn't you hear the gunshot?"

"Yeah, I heard. The FBI lady told me they're looking for Blanche to arrest her. But wouldn't answer my questions."

"Ha. Your fiancé Jack is a fucking criminal. His entire family. Blanche pointed a gun at me. She tried to killed me."

Raven glared at her. "Oh, come on. Jack told me about the IRS harassing his family. Said the government is just trying to scare them into confessing to stuff they didn't do. Maybe Blanche was just scared. And Jack isn't a criminal."

Russ returned. He said to Jenna. "We can go." He turned to Raven. "You don't deserve a friend like Jenna."

"Who the fuck are you?" Raven spat the words.

Jenna got in the passenger seat. Russ took the driver's side.

Raven pounded Mia's hood with her fist. "Jenna, stop being a little bitch."

Something in Raven's tone made the hair on her neck stand on end. In a night of insults and chaos, every nerve in her body was raw. She wasn't going to 'run away' until she got some choice things off her chest. Jenna turned to Russ. "Stay here."

She whipped open her car door, stomped toward Raven, shaking her finger at her face.

"YOU are the fucking BITCH!"

Raven clasped her hands to her chest. "What did I do?"

"Breast implants? I was worried for days about your health. Worried sick. I thought you might die. And you didn't care. You are a vain, selfish ASSHOLE!" Jenna waved her arms. "Oh, and what the hell? You abandon your own party? Who does that? What about your guests? I sacrificed every waking moment to deal with your party crap. I enlisted friends who gave up their weekends to work on your FUCKING idiotic party. To cater to your shallow friends and that NIGHTMARE of a human being, Blanche. And you disrespect me and everyone else by arriving late and then casually wander off to have sex with the stripper?" She gave two middle fingers to Raven. "FUCK you."

She wanted to call Raven more nasty things. But her mind blanked. No words could measure up to the hate she was feeling.

Raven's eyes widened. "You know about that?"

"I saw you. I saw EVERYTHING."

Raven smirked. "You need to grow up. You were always a little mouse. Such a prude and goody-two-shoes. Always judging everyone. I don't need you to be my mom."

Jenna stood up straight. "And I don't need a friend like you. I NEVER want to see you again. And DO NOT fucking touch my car." Jenna walked around Mia and got inside. "Russ, let's go."

Raven hammered the hood of the car again with her fist. "Fine with me," she yelled, her voice echoing off the pavement. Some police stared in their direction.

Russ backed up the car and made a k-turn before heading to the open gate.

Jenna concentrated on breathing. Her heart was pounding in her chest. Her face felt hot. Was this a heart attack? A panic attack? Did she need a hospital? Dying now would really piss her off. She lowered her window, tilting her head so the breeze cooled her face. She inhaled for a two-count, exhaled for a two-count, repeating the sequence over and over.

"Are you okay?"

"Yes. I'm sorry, Russ. I just need to breathe for a couple minutes."

They drove in silence until they came to the first stop light. Russ turned to her and said, "I'm proud of you."

"What for? For having an asshole friend? I must be the worst judge of character on the entire planet." Her heart rate felt better. Maybe she wasn't dying. She closed her window.

"Hey, I'm your friend, right?"

Jenna winced. "Present company excluded."

Russ reached over and extended his open hand across the center console. It wasn't a romantic gesture, and she was a little unsure what it meant, but it would have been more awkward to refuse. She sighed and placed her hand on his.

He looked at her. "You know what she said was bullshit, right? You're one of the best people I know."

The light changed and he removed his hand from hers, placing both on the steering wheel and focusing on the road in front of him.

She felt far from a 'best' person. An average person, perhaps. On a good day. She looked out the side window. "Mindy says I'm too nice. Everyone keeps calling me a loser."

"Well, I don't think so. And Mindy and Fred. Listen, my best friend growing up? The one who gave me the Scooby mug? We were like brothers. But people change. After high school, he began doing heroin and nearly died. He's in jail now for armed robbery. Sometimes people disappoint you. It has nothing to do with you."

She looked at him. "Sorry about your friend."

"Yeah. Me, too." He kept his gaze on the road.

She turned to look out the side window again and whispered. "I should have stayed on the boat."

"What's that?"

"Nothing. It was something Raven and I would say when something terrible happened. It's a line from a monster movie we watched when we were kids. Komodo Vs Cobra. Have you ever seen it?"

"Hmm. Don't think so."

"We used to watch it every year on my birthday until we both left for college. Raven and I could recite every line. We'd make popcorn, camp out in the living room. Sometimes made it a double feature. I just don't know what happened." Jenna sighed. The contrast of recent events with those simpler times made her heart feel heavy. "Maybe she's right. I need to grow up."

Russ said, "It hurts right now. But it gets better. I promise."

She turned to face him. "I hope so."

He took his eyes off the road for a second and looked her in the eyes. "Don't grow up too much." He smiled. "Grownups are boring. I still have my Ninja Turtle action figures."

"Ha. Nice. I'll keep that in mind." She sank down in her seat.

"Why don't you take a nap. I'll wake you when we cross into Jersey."

"Thanks, Russ. I'm glad you came with us." She nestled her head in the corner between the headrest and the window. Part of her wanted to cry deep cleansing tears. Cry until she had no more feeling left in her bones. The other part didn't want to waste another neuron of thought on Raven and their destroyed friendship.

She closed her eyes.

Russ whispered. "Hey, Jenna?"

"Yes?" She kept her eyes closed.

"In all the commotion this morning, I forgot to tell you. I left a present for Raven."

She opened her eyes. "What?"

"A tarantula. Got it at the pet store earlier when I picked up Mindy's cockroaches. A Rose-Hair breed, to be specific. They aren't dangerous; just scary looking. It was an impulse purchase, because I figured it would have been bad manners not to get her a present for her bridal shower. I was going to put it at the bottom of the wishing well, but instead I slipped it in her backseat when I parked her car. More personal that way I figured."

"Really?"

"Yup."

"Ha. Good one, Russ. I wish I'd thought of that."

She closed her eyes again and began picturing Raven's reaction. A vat full of tarantulas would have been better. Or some snakes and leeches. She envisioned a whole monster movie script of evils to inflict on Raven. Chiggers were the worst. Difficult to see and painful for weeks. Yes, her fictional movie would include them.

Mindy had mentioned that next week, at the Y, the kids would be putting on a puppet show. In her sleepy brain, she created a mental script about a monster that learns who his real friends are. There could be all kinds of fun side characters, like snakes and puppies and panda bears. Maybe they could make them from felt and cardboard.

The tension eased in her shoulders. The lump on her head seemed to ache less.

She drifted into a blissful sleep.

Chapter 20

Jenna woke to Russ softly calling her name. "Jenna, we're crossing the river. Do you want to sleep for another fifteen minutes?"

She looked around. They had just passed the toll for the Benjamin Franklin Bridge.

"No, I'm up." She yawned and stretched her legs.

"Your car could use some gas. I was thinking of stopping. Maybe get a small snack. Are you hungry?"

"Starving."

Jenna checked her phone. A text from Raven saying she was sorry. Part of her wanted to send a snarky text back asking her if she found the Rose-Hair. Instead, she hit delete. She scrolled through her phone's menu, looking to remove Raven's contact. Was she ready to close the door on their relationship? They both said and did things they couldn't take back. And she had new friends now. Friends that cared and helped and didn't lie. But she was tired. Not the best state to decide anything.

It was close to ten. She wondered if they had caught Blanche yet. Finding a woman wearing a long white satin skirt in the woods couldn't be so difficult, right? She was glad Blanche didn't have her stupid skunk coat.

A few minutes later, Russ pulled into a 24-hour diner off Route 70. A local landmark. Jenna used to waitress there summers in high school.

"Do you mind?" he said, "They have the best pie."

It was a most excellent idea.

They each had pie and decaf coffee. Russ gave her the details of the altercation between Blanche, Mack, and Ron. It seemed unbelievable. She had to ask more than once if he was kidding. Then they talked about her work project. He had some ideas on how to present it and invited her to come over the next afternoon to work on it. Eager for feedback, she accepted his offer. Jenna told him some of her waitressing stories. When the waitress came back to check on them, Jenna asked for a side of bacon to-go. She explained to Russ it was for her and Thumper's breakfast later. Actually, a peace offering to Thumper for being away two nights.

Russ asked, "You know, I'm never sure how to order my bacon crispy enough. I always say 'well done' but it's never quite right. Always underdone or burnt."

"Just say 'deep-fried black'. It's the best."

"I'll remember that. So, I hope you don't take this the wrong way, but with all your experience at the diner, you never learned to cook?"

"Nope. If you saw what happens in the back, you wouldn't want to cook either."

"No, don't tell me." He pointed to his pie plate, now filled with mostly crumbs. "This was delicious and I won't have you take that away from me."

She laughed. "I think the pie is fine. Just don't be a pain and keep returning your food. The kitchen staff don't play around."

"Well, we could take a cooking class together sometime. I'd like to learn." He chuckled, "I hear Mindy has a good recipe for slugs."

"Ick." She recoiled in disgust.

The waitress dropped off her to-go bag.

Jenna yawned. Her phone rang. *Candy Morris's number.* In a fit of giggles, she hit decline, removed the contact, and blocked her number. "On that note, I think it's time to go home."

At the car, they changed places, with Jenna driving the five minutes to Russ's place. He pointed out each turn. He lived remarkably close to her, but in a more residential section.

She turned onto a wide street lined with mature trees, with older but well-kept homes. She pulled up to his small cottage-style house. Even in the dark, in the middle of winter, it looked like a dream, with an eyebrow window, a porch-swing and a winding brick walk-way up to the craftsman style door. Russ had excellent taste in houses.

He got out of the passenger side and walked around to her side.

She rolled down the window and said, "Thanks for driving. See you tomorrow."

With outstretched arms, he said, "Nope. At my house, we hug it out."

She yawned. Just a quick hug and she'd be off. She opened the door, the car still running, and stood in front of him. The neighborhood was dark and still, Mia's headlights and a distant streetlight the only illumination. He leaned over, wrapping his long arms around her, their thick coats meshing together. It felt like falling into a warm cloud. Maybe it was the exhaustion, but in that moment, she couldn't feel the ground beneath her.

He smelled nice. Like the scent of her favorite cotton t-shirt when it comes out of the dryer. And his breath had a hint of the peach pie. When his five o'clock shadow brushed her cheek, she instinctively wanted to run her hand along his chin. But she caught herself in time. The close call jolted her brain; she backed away and said goodbye.

The drive home was a study in mental gymnastics and emotional confusion. Russ was a considerate, happy person. Easy to be around. And just like Fred, he had a way of making her feel normal. She could enjoy getting used to that.

Was she falling for Russ?

Probably.

And maybe it wasn't the end of the world.

* * *

Sunday morning, Jenna woke up wondering if the whole of yesterday was just a bad dream. At least, the party seemed like a bad dream. The last part of the drive home with Russ wasn't bad. Actually, it made her feel bubbly inside. She remembered they made plans for her to come over at noon to work on her white paper together. That was before the hug and the shocking wave of romantic feelings it invoked. At least on her part.

Now, after some sleep and reflection, she wanted to go to his house for non-work reasons. But the rational side of her brain said to take things slow. He was a coworker. Anything other than friendship could get complicated. She needed life to be simple for now, after the last two weeks of constant drama.

At six, Thumper made his desires known. Groggily, Jenna fed him his regular food. But, for good measure, she took a piece of bacon out of the fridge and dropped it on his dish. Normally, she would have broken it down into smaller bites for him, but she didn't have the energy and he could figure it out on his own. He had sharp fangs…ironically, like Mistress Nightshade. Her dazed brain wondered if Nightshade's teeth were functional. *Were there such things as tooth extensions?* She imagined trying to explain that to a dentist. Jenna shrugged, took two pieces of bacon for herself, and crawled back into bed.

At nine, Mindy called. She answered, still in bed.

"Jenn, I talked to Russ. He told me about last night. Damn. Are you all right?"

"I'm fine."

"I can't believe Blanche had a razor hidden in her shoe. Jesus. That's like John Wick level stuff. Satan's mommy came prepared. If she wasn't a criminal, I'd be fucking impressed."

"Yeah, thankfully the gash on Mack's arm wasn't deeper. Honestly, when Russ told me, I thought he was making up funny stories again. I can never tell when he's being serious. I mean, how does someone like Blanche have the reflexes to tase two federal agents and escape a bullet at the same time?"

"She's a tough broad. I can't believe you tackled that cow. Do you have a death wish or something?"

Did she? An excellent question. Hopefully not any more. "Could be. Honestly, everything seems like a blur now."

"Well, did you see the news this morning?"

Jenna yawned. "No, what?"

"They caught her. Blanche was spotted hitchhiking. All the news channels are running body cam footage. You need to see it. They put her in the back of the police car, and she spits on one of the officers. The cam goes dark after. Probably beating the shit out of her."

Jenna sat up, her mind racing. *What did it mean?*

Blanche obviously wasn't interested in taking the FBI's cooperation deal. If Blanche got word to the mob...

"Shoot. I mean, that's good. Hey, Mindy? I can't talk right now. See you tomorrow. Bye."

She needed to talk to Mack or Ben. Assess the danger, if any. She called Ben. After the tenth ring, he said, "Good morning, Miss Mott."

"Ben? I need to know; is the mob coming for me? What do I do?" She racked her brain. Did she put the chain on the door last night? Should she go check? She bit her lower lip, nervously twisting her ring.

Ben said, "Mack is here. I'll put her on."

Mack came on the line. "Jenna, how are you feeling today?"

She clutched the edge of her comforter. "For the last time, I'm fine. But am I safe? Tell me."

Mack cleared her throat. "You don't have to worry. It's official. The

Forero's took the deal. That's all I can say. And you are completely safe."

"All of them? None of them are going to prison?"

"I can't divulge details. But they are going somewhere. No one will bother you."

"You aren't lying to me again, right?"

"No, Jenna. You are one hundred percent safe. No one in the mob will ever know of your involvement."

She exhaled. "Good to know." She sank back onto her pillow.

Mack said, "Thank you for all your efforts. You did a noble thing. I'm going to look into ways the Bureau can repay you."

Mack's words did not bring comfort. Yes, it was good she didn't need to buy Kevlar underwear, but the shit-show yesterday couldn't be made right by a few platitudes. Not knowing what to say, she settled on, "Thanks, Mack."

"Goodbye, Miss Mott."

"Bye." Jenna hung up.

She went through her mental checklist. No more party. No more concern over Raven's health. In fact, concern about Raven was gone…*for the rest of time*? No more Forero's. No FBI or mob worries. She had a reliable car and good friends at work.

Plus, Fred seemed better. He hadn't seemed blue at all over the weekend. Not that he was necessarily happy. But perhaps he was handling Ava's passing well enough.

The only thing left to concentrate on was the white paper for Grant. The one that had been nagging at her for the last two weeks. She needed to do a good job. Preferably, an outstanding job. The white paper had to be stellar, with citations and data to back up her premise. And it had to look snazzy and make her points crystal clear.

Jenna's brain had felt far from crystal clear the last few days. Every time she tried to write the narrative of the paper, her words seemed jumbled or sloppy, with redundancy and second grade words. Now was her time to change all that. To put on her big girl pants and show Grant her worth.

She got out of bed and sat at her kitchen table. She constructed a new outline, using her index cards. Thumper jumped from a chair to the table and began swishing his tail across her cards, shooting them onto the floor.

After a few minutes of 'fetch', she locked Thumper in her bedroom. For a moment she had silence. Then the scratching at the door began and meowing at 85 decibels. It was hard to concentrate.

She opened the browser on her phone, looking for footage of Blanche's arrest. After searching several keywords, she finally found a video from CBS Channel 10 News. A young female reporter stood in front of a truck stop, interviewing a bearded trucker wearing flannel.

Reporter: "The small Town of Altoona had some excitement overnight, as an FBI fugitive escaped into the State Forest. The name of the fugitive is being withheld at this time, but after hours of searching by local and federal law enforcement, they received a tip from Mr. Bret Conway, a local trucker."

The reporter turned to the trucker, "Mr. Conway, when did you encounter the woman and how did you know to contact law enforcement?"

The trucker rocked on his heels and straightened his ball cap, looking directly to camera. "Well, this lady, she runs onto the road. Mind you, it's dark outside, before dawn. But I see her cause she's wearing this white skirt, um, except for all the mud. And she didn't look so good. No shoes; her feet are all wrapped in burlap. Scratches all over her face, briar sticks in her hair. And I say to myself, this person needs help."

Reporter: "At this point, you didn't suspect she was a fugitive from justice?"

"Well, no, but she was wearin' this canvas coat with the logo for Thomas Farms, and I know Mr. Thomas, and this ain't adding up. Like she must have been trespassin' on his place and stolen it."

Reporter: "What did she say to you?"

"She said she got lost hiking. Kept asking to use my phone. Said her husband would give me a huge reward if I drove her back all the ways to New Jersey."

Reporter: "But you called the police instead?"

"Well, I was heading to Pittsburgh, so I told her nicely I couldn't take her to Jersey, but I could drop her off at a bus stop or something, and she got enraged. Told me to go…well, I can't say this on the air. But a bad thing. And she starts walking down the road again, her thumb out. So now I know she's crazy. A lu-lu bird. And I get back in my truck and call the cops so they can make sure she gets somewhere safe."

Reporter: "Did they tell you she was a wanted person?"

"Yeah, they asked for her description and when I told them, they said to go along and drive her to Jersey, but, really, the feds would pull us over a few miles down the road on the turnpike."

Reporter: "Were you scared when they asked you to transport a violent perpetrator?"

"Well, she seemed kind of tired, like she hadn't slept, so I figured it wouldn't be a big deal. And sure enough, she got into the cab and fell asleep. That's pretty much it."

The reporter to camera: "The Town of Altoona is safer tonight for your brave actions. Back to the news desk."

Jenna closed the video. Blanche did, in fact, look like a crazy lu-lu bird. She wondered if Raven saw the video yet. She resisted every urge to forward it to Raven. Instead, she sent a link to Fred.

It was time to focus on her white paper. Thumper was slamming his body against the bedroom door now.

A change of scenery might help her concentrate. She called Russ. It was ten. Two hours before their pre-arranged meeting time.

"Russ? Is it all right if I come over early?"

He said, "Sure. I'm not doing much. Just watching that Komodo movie you recommended."

Her favorite movie? Tingles radiated up her spine. "Isn't is wonderfully cheesy? Did you get to part with the giant leeches?" She grinned from ear to ear, imagining Blanch covered with toaster-size leeches. *If only.*

"No," Russ laughed. "No spoilers. Come on over whenever you want. I'll be here."

"Great, see you soon."

In that moment, all she wanted was to watch the movie with him. Hold his hand. And perhaps he would kiss her…

No. She needed to keep her head in the game. Work on her project. Besides, he was a coworker. Too messy.

She took a quick shower and checked Thumper's food dish. After gathering all her notecards, folders, and markers, she headed out the door. The sun was shining, and the air was warm. Some purple crocuses were blooming in the neglected flower beds by the parking lot, stretching toward the sunlight. An early sign of Spring.

On the drive over to Russ's house, she sang along with the radio with full force, delirious with anticipation to discuss the all the best worst lines of her favorite movie with him. Especially the parts where a character would shoot a hundred rounds from a single handgun at the monster without reloading. *Always hilarious.*

Just one more challenge left.

But after the last twenty-four hours, her white paper seemed like a piece of pie.

Chapter 21

On Tuesday morning, Grant briefed her white paper at the managers meeting. She had attended, waiting in the back of the room to field questions. When management had no more questions for her, they dismissed her and the meeting continued.

Now, she waited at her desk, chewing her fingernails, trying to stay busy, but wondering what the reaction would be. After an hour, Grant returned and invited her into his office.

She sat across from Grant. "What happened?"

Grant sat with his arms folded, leaning back in his chair. "Your findings intrigued them."

"Is that good?"

"It was nearly unanimous. We're reassigning you."

She studied his face. He didn't seem angry. "We? Assigning me…where?"

"You'll be leading a project team to review the design of the next home printer model. Plus, implement the changes to existing product lines. A tiger team of four. Do you know who you'd like to join you? Think about it and give me three names by the end of the week."

"Wow. Really?"

"Really. I'll send you some details. You'll be moving to the next building over."

"What about my customer hotline and tech manual work?"

Grant chortled. "Consider yourself 'graduated'. Ha. You know, back in the day when I was a new hire, I worked the hotline for three years. At the pace you're going, I need to watch my back." He seemed to be kidding by his expression. But there was a slight tremble in his voice that showed a smidgeon of concern.

This all seemed too good to be true. Leading a project team entailed much more responsibility. A task suited for someone above her pay grade. Then she thought about Mack. Mack was her new spirit animal. How would she have handled this news?

Jenna cleared her throat. "I'm really honored and excited by this. But I think given this new role…"

"Yes?"

"I'd like you to consider moving up my next raise."

Grant stroked his chin. He held up a hand and then rifled through his desk drawer. He pulled out a file and began leafing through it. "You've been here eight months." He closed the folder. "I can't think of a reason we couldn't move your first year raise up four months."

Jenna's insides bubbled. That was easier than she imagined. "Thanks, Grant. It will really help. I have this accelerated plan to pay off my student loans…"

Grant put the file back in the drawer and slammed it shut. "That's nice. Jenna, I have a call in ten minutes." He pointed to the door.

Another cue to leave. She got up and said, "Thanks, Grant." Heading back to her desk, she wanted to skip the whole way, but instead, added a small bounce in her step.

A few minutes later, Mindy poked her head around Jenna's partition. "Hey, count me in."

Jenna was on a call with a customer. She said into her headset, "Ma'am, can you hold a minute?" She hit the mute button. "Mindy, I'm busy. What's going on?"

"Count me in. For your new tiger team."

"You heard about that already?"

"Girl, everyone's talking about it. I overheard one of the managers in the break room. He said he was thinking about cashing out some company stock, but now he wants to hold on to it. Way to go, sister."

Jenna looked down at the blinking light on her phone. She didn't have time to celebrate. "I have to come up with three names for Grant by the end of the week, but you'll be my number one. Promise. I've got to get back." She gestured to her headset. "See you later?"

Mindy gave her a thumbs up sign and bounced out of view.

An hour later, Russ came by Jenna's cube.

"Hey, congrats," he said.

She was still on hotline duty, but the customer was occupied re-booting her laptop. *Two minutes free.* She hit the phone's mute button. Russ looked a little different today, but she couldn't quite place it.

"Thanks, but I couldn't have done it without your help."

Russ asked, "Do you know who you want on your team?"

Jenna laughed. "Mindy already cried dibs. Why? Are you interested?"

"I could be. I didn't want to say anything before, but I'm interviewing with another company next week. Don't tell Grant."

And it came to her. Russ was wearing a shirt without wrinkles and his hair was newly cut. He looked, well, presentable. Was he trying to impress her? Or was his new look in anticipation of his upcoming interview? She nodded. "I won't say a word."

As he walked away, Jenna wondered if she could handle another person leaving. Even if it was just a coworker. Although, Russ was feeling less like a co-worker and more like a potential boyfriend. And what if her success on the project had more to do with Russ's contacts and Power-point prowess? Not her own ideas? She let out a deep sigh. These thoughts were counterproductive. A form of self-sabotage.

New Jenna needed to stop that shit.

During some of her downtime between customers, she'd googled cooking classes at the local community college. Had Russ been serious about taking classes? She found one on Saturday mornings starting next month. She copied the link into an email, held her breath, and sent it to Russ.

Before leaving for the day, Jenna walked to the next building to check out her future work space. The room was brighter and cleaner that her current area. The ceilings were tall with clerestory windows, modern office furniture, and sleek ergonomic office chairs manufactured in the current century. Compared to her current depressing and bland office space, this new one was like the Land of Oz, but without flying monkeys.

On her drive home, she stopped at the hardware store and bought two gallons of bright white latex paint, a roller and brushes. With all the recent changes in her life, she wanted to give her apartment a much-needed blank slate. The awful wavy stripes on the living room wall had to go.

She arrived home and began moving her furniture away from the walls. Thumper acted miffed at being dislodged from the couch, but became curious and played with the plastic sheeting on the floor. She was cutting in around the ceiling when someone knocked on the door.

Could it be mom returning her dinner knife? Everything was going so well right now. The last person she wanted to see was mom.

She opened the door. It was Ben. Ben from the IRS. He wore a brown tweed suit and a yellow tie, his briefcase in one hand.

"Hey, Ben, I'd shake your hand, but…" She held up her palms. Her hands were covered in splotches of white paint.

"Jenna, how are you doing? I should have said this before, but I'm so sorry. You could have been seriously injured or worse."

"Do you want to come in?" The question seemed ludicrous, because with her furniture crammed into the center of the room, there was no place to sit.

"Um," he peered past her, examining the room. "I just came to give you this." He handed her an envelope. "Courtesy of the task force. To show our appreciation." He backed away and waved, "Have a good life, Miss Mott."

She waved goodbye.

Ben trotted down the stairs and disappeared from sight.

The envelope in her hand was plain and white, except for her name in typewritten capital letters.

Was it some kind of hush money? She closed the door and walked to the kitchen. She held the envelope up to the ceiling light. *Why was she scared to open it?* Bracing herself, she slid a kitchen knife under the flap.

Inside was a certificate with an ornate blue border and official State of New Jersey watermark across the body. It was a vehicle title. The title to her Miata. She found another piece of paper; a letter from her bank. Her car loan was paid in full. *Could it be?*

In the corner of the letter was a sticker. Like one of those small bright stickers little kids collect. It was a bowl of spaghetti and two large meatballs with smiling faces. Next to the sticker, scrawled handwriting, '*Thanks for everything -Mack and Ben*'.

Jenna jumped and screamed. Mia was *hers*! Free and clear.

She sealed her paint can and wrapped her brush in plastic wrap. Within five minutes she was out of her painting clothes and back into her work outfit. She grabbed her coat, dashed down the steps, and rang Fred's doorbell.

When he opened the door, she sang out, "Fred! We need to celebrate!"

He stood there wearing a white undershirt and pajama bottoms, beads of sweat glistened on Fred's forehead. "Hey, kiddo."

Something was wrong, different. The floor behind him was littered with corrugated cardboard boxes and black plastic garbage bags filled to the brim.

"Fred, what are you doing?"

He arched his back and stretched his arms over his head. "I was gonna tell you. I'm packing. Come on in."

She stepped inside, scanning the room. All his kitchenware sat piled on the counter, a bucket of cleaning supplies on the floor next to his armchair.

"The FBI paid off my car. I came to see if you wanted to go out for dinner. Why are you packing?"

"I'm moving to Minnesota. Just gonna donate most everything and drive up next weekend."

"Just like that? I mean…"

"Decided this morning. Look, I've been doing some soul searching. I want to live near my grandson. Try to fix the relationship. I can't do that from here."

She grew silent, wanting to be supportive, but her heart had a dagger in it. "I don't know what to say. I get it. But I wish you could stay forever."

He placed his hands in his pockets. "Oh, don't look at me like that. You can come visit anytime. But leave your blasted cat home." He chuckled. "Hey, I'm making good progress here. Can I take you up on dinner tomorrow?"

She threw her arms around him and hugged him. He tensed, but she didn't let go.

Fred patted her on the back. "Now, now, enough of that. Let this codger get some work done."

Jenna released him. "Right." She opened the door. "Tomorrow. Seven. Wear something snazzy. We're going somewhere fancy."

He saluted her goodbye.

Back at her apartment, she changed again into her painting clothes and began cutting in along the baseboards. The thought of losing Fred made her insides raw. *Would she ever see him again?*

Her phone rang. It was dad.

Anger seethed inside her core. He had a lot of nerve calling her after not answering her calls over the last few months. Her first impulse was to hit 'decline'. The second was to call him a jerk and hang up. The third was to satisfy her curiosity. She went with that one. She mustered her mental fortitude and hit accept. "Hi."

"Jenn, I've been trying to reach you."

She'd seen his number come up twice during the day at work, but declined both times. He hadn't left a message. "What?" She didn't hide the hostility in her voice.

"Honey, look, I understand if you don't want to talk to me. I just wanted to let you know your mom's in a rehab facility near Reading. She can't have visitors for a month. But when she can, I think we should see her together."

Mom was in rehab? That was a first. She had so many questions.

Was dad finally taking his responsibilities seriously?

Did she have the strength to give a shit? "Um, I'm glad she's getting help."

"I'm retiring next week."

Jenna put down her paintbrush and rested her butt on the arm of the couch. "Wait. What?"

"I won't be on the road anymore. Your mom needs me. I'm going to try harder."

Jenna's chest felt tight. Was this finally happening? Could her family be repaired? But no, it wouldn't be that simple. The problems were too deep. Her anger was too deep. "Like I said, I'm glad."

"Jenna, can I take you out to dinner this weekend? I miss you."

She missed him, too. But not current dad. The dad that gave a crap. The dad that loved her before their lives were destroyed. "I...I'll think about it. Give me a couple days."

"That's fair. Take your time. Call me when you're ready. I love you."

"Bye, dad." She hung up. Was the universe taking away Fred and replacing him with dad? That would be ironic, perhaps cruel. But after all the mess with Raven, maybe she needed to consider forgiveness over vengeance.

What did Sister Mary Rose say?

Love keeps no record of wrongs.

It sounded nice, like something on a Hallmark card. But life wasn't like that. Trust had to be earned.

She picked up her paint brush and contemplated what she would say to her dad on the weekend. But there was nothing really to say. She needed solid proof of his efforts and significant progress by mom before she could consider forgiving them. It would take years, not days or weeks.

During the intervening time, she'd focus on her own happiness. Create the life she wanted for herself. Start over, just like the fresh white wall in front of her.

After a few minutes of painting, her phone in her back pocket buzzed. It was a text from Russ.

"Want to see the Mothra marathon tonight? My place 8 pm?
I'll get Chinese."

He'd added several emoji: a fortune cookie, chopsticks, and a smiley face. After that, he texted an animated Godzilla gif shooting blue flame from his mouth. Adorable.

A jumble of thoughts crossed her mind. Like, how did she not know the marathon was on tonight? What should she wear? Did she need to clean her paint brush first or would it be fine in plastic until tomorrow?

She texted back a gif of Velma saying, "Jinkies" and wrote, "Yes. Be there soon."

At the bedroom mirror, she checked her appearance. Paint on her face, hands, and forearms. Her hair had an unflattering kink from her ponytail holder. She thought about the makeover Mindy had given her. *Where was Mindy when you needed her?*

A voice in her head told her she needed to kiss Russ tonight. Or let him kiss her. Or not worry about rushing into things. Either way, the voice said the new Jenna needed to be unafraid, confident, perhaps a smidge sexy.

She put on a silky navy button-down shirt, but instead of keeping only the top button undone—as she did most of the time—she undid *two*. Not the top three like Mack. Baby steps, she told herself.

In her dresser, she dug out her tightest jeans; the ones Marcelo used to like. The ones that made her backside look not so flat. She scrubbed off the paint, straightened her hair to get rid of the weird creases, and added a tinge of blush to her cheeks. Brushing her teeth, she inspected her tongue in the mirror and clumsily knocked her toothbrush stand into the sink.

And she saw it. Marcelo's blue toothbrush. It had been in the stand next to hers and it hadn't registered before. It had only been thirteen days since their breakup. Not a long time in a cosmic sense, but long enough.

Thumper wandered into the bathroom and bounded onto the toilet seat, looking at her expectantly. She picked up Marcelo's toothbrush and tossed it outside toward the living room. Thumper clamored after it. She smiled, knowing before too long, the plastic toothbrush would inevitably end up under the entertainment center with the dust bunnies and other cat toys. A fitting resting place.

On the drive to Russ's place, she stopped at a light. She used the opportunity to pick more white paint off her fingers, but her eyes locked onto the faceted blue stone on her left hand.

Twisting the ring off her finger, she wondered if she should sell it to a pawn shop. Get a hundred bucks for it and buy herself something nice. Like a new area rug with substantially less cat vomit.

The sun was setting off to her right. The sky glowed orange with a crisp shade of cyan above. Despite the dense traffic and the jumbled business signs lining the road, the glorious sunset vanquished the urban blight and transported her soul. A sense of peace washed over her.

No, she thought, the night held too much promise.

The *new* Jenna frowned. She recalled Marcelo's last text.

In a whisper, she said, "I can't either."

She powered down her window and dropped the ring onto the pavement. And didn't look back.

ABOUT THE AUTHOR

 DS Whitaker is an environmental engineer who began writing fiction later in life. She and her husband live just outside Washington DC. When she isn't writing, she enjoys running, hiking and attempting Cracking the Cryptic Sudoku puzzles.

Her debut novel, Antigenesis, was a finalist in the 2020 National Indie Excellence Awards.

Shower of Lies is her third novel, inspired by a former coworker's story about planning a last-minute bridal shower for her best friend.

Other novels by DS Whitaker:
Antigenesis
Planet of the Creeps
Johnnie Finds a Dead Body
Johnnie the Pirate King

Follow her on Twitter at @ds_whitaker and visit her website at dswhitaker.com.

Dear Reader! While I have your attention, please consider leaving a book review on Amazon or Goodreads!
Thank You!